HOODS LANDING

LAURA VINCENT

Pushkin Press

Pushkin Press
Somerset House, Strand
London WC2R 1LA

Hoods Landing was first published by Āporo Press in Aotearoa New Zealand, 2025

First published by Pushkin Press in 2026

ISBN 13: 978-1-80533-843-7

A CIP catalogue record for this title is available from the British Library

The authorised representative in the EEA is eucomply OÜ,
Pärnu mnt. 139b-14, 11317, Tallinn, Estonia,
hello@eucompliancepartner.com, +33757590241

Offset by Tetragon, London
Printed and bound in the United Kingdom by Clays Ltd, Elcograf S.p.A.

FSC www.fsc.org MIX Paper | Supporting responsible forestry FSC® C018072

www.pushkinpress.com

1 3 5 7 9 8 6 4 2

Pushkin Press

HOODS LANDING

'Vincent has the rare gift of making every member of her richly drawn cast feel indispensable. Funny, moving and alive with family lore, *Hoods Landing* is a novel to savour'

Catherine Chidgey, author of *The Book of Guilt*

'This is a deeply affecting book . . . Vincent seamlessly and skilfully weaves the aesthetics of film, musical, opera, food and the occult to create a work about love and death like no other I can remember' **Pip Adam, author of *Audition***

'Quirky and playful, with a gently self-deprecating Kiwi humour and a dash of romantic sizzle. A delightful comfort read that's full of heart' **Scorpio Books**

'A darkly funny and profoundly domestic exploration of the ways in which families operate . . . Vincent's eye for the sharp detail lifts it sensuously off the page' ***Takahē Magazine***

'*Hoods Landing* examines what is lost and what remains in the face of collective tragedy . . . A raw, raucous and riveting slice of social realism' **Dominic Amarena, author of *I Want Everything***

'One of the most intricately crafted debut novels I've read recently . . . Vincent has made the Gordons feel not just real but full of heart and soul, using the tools of a writer deeply skilled in the craft of fiction' ***The Spinoff***

© Julian Vincent

LAURA VINCENT (Ngāti Māhanga, Ngāpuhi) is an author from Waiuku, New Zealand. She has written her food blog, *Hungry and Frozen*, since 2007 and published a cookbook of the same name with Penguin in 2013. She spent five years as the Wellington café reviewer for the *Sunday Star-Times*, and has also written lifestyle and travel features, as well as publishing poetry internationally. Her work has appeared in *Tenderly* magazine, *The Toast*, *Vice* and an anthology from The Muswell Press. Laura's debut novel, *Hoods Landing*, was first published in New Zealand by Āporo Press and shortlisted for the Ockham New Zealand Book Awards.

For Zelda, Pourewa, and all who walk with us

☾ The Gordon

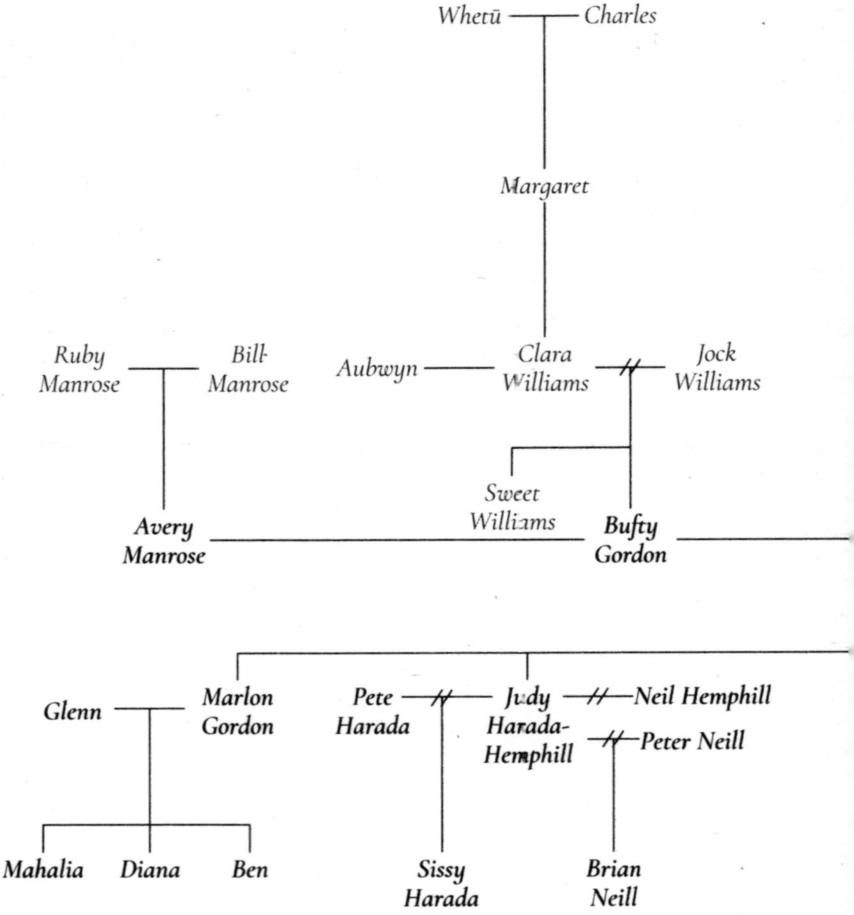
Whetū
Charles
Margaret
Ruby Manrose
Bill Manrose
Aubwyn
Clara Williams
Jock Williams
Sweet Williams
Avery Manrose
Bufty Gordon
Glenn
Marlon Gordon
Pete Harada
Judy Harada-Hemphill
Neil Hemphill
Peter Neill
Mahalia
Diana
Ben
Sissy Harada
Brian Neill

Family Tree »

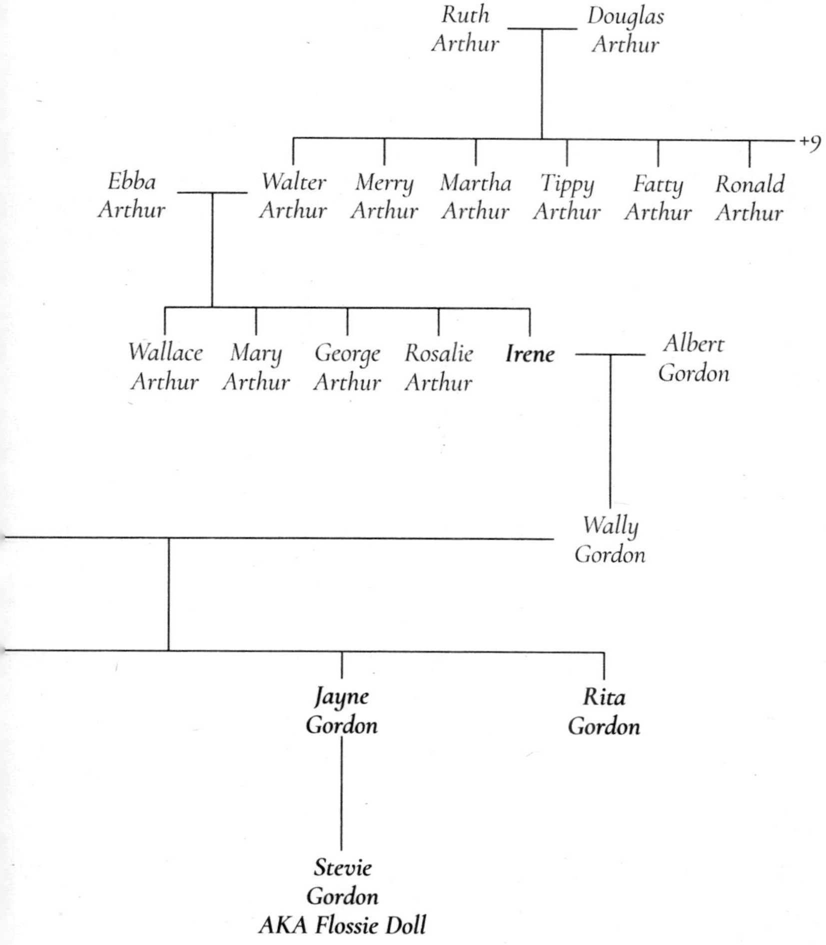

Ruth Arthur
Douglas Arthur
+9
Ebba Arthur
Walter Arthur
Merry Arthur
Martha Arthur
Tippy Arthur
Fatty Arthur
Ronald Arthur
Wallace Arthur
Mary Arthur
George Arthur
Rosalie Arthur
Irene
Albert Gordon
Wally Gordon
Jayne Gordon
Rita Gordon
Stevie Gordon
AKA Flossie Doll

Chapter One

Rita counted the dead.

She showed up early for her appointment. Not on purpose. Didn't treat a trip to Auckland like an international passenger ship voyage the way her mum did. It just happened that way. And now Rita waited. They had said it'd be a few months till they could book her in. Treatment came after that. She'd be able to drive home after round one. For round two, she'd need a whānau member. A partner. A close friend. They don't get free parking.

"So we'll both be suffering," Rita had said. The GP didn't laugh. Fair dues. It wasn't really a joke.

The Americano burnt her mouth. Two blinks of a tungsten cathode later it turned lukewarm. Rita prised off the plastic lid and dipped her blistered tongue into the cooling liquid. It stung. She made herself drink the lot while flicking through a women's mag, its pages tenderised by the sweat of nervous hands. The coffee had cost $5 at the hospital cafe. She might need a full bladder.

Rita pointed at pictures in her magazine. *Bags that chocolate cake. Looks almost as good as Mum's. Bags that car.* Had one of her older sisters joined her on these stiff orange chairs, she might've raced them to claim these goodies. Marlon would say she doesn't need anything, hypothetical or otherwise. Judy would target the dresses and makeup that Rita didn't give a stuff about, slapping the page. If Jayne were there, Rita would point to the most preposterous celebrity she could find and say, "That's your boyfriend." Jayne would laugh like a goose with laryngitis. Rita picked up another tattered magazine. *Bags that credit card. Bags that dog. Bags that plane ticket.*

Hard to describe to outsiders how insignificant the place was where she grew up. The decaying village she'd returned to. Maybe for the last time. Maybe five square miles. An empty school. Two or three dozen pupils when she started in 1967. A church. The bowling club. Grass overgrown. The abandoned aerosol factory. No shops. No footpaths. Walk down the white painted lines at noon or midnight and you'll only meet a sparrow's pulpy carcass ground into the tar-seal. Sometimes trucks smashed past. Industrial. Abrupt. Timber, cattle, milk. Or developers scurried through to divide and conquer the beach where her grandmother lived.

A real all-or-nothing place. Mostly nothing. The back of beyond, they called it. "No one's in a hurry round here but the ants chasing jam," her mother would say.

Cancer had killed at least ten women from the village in Rita's lifetime. Maybe a normal quantity of women to die. It got her dad too. His lungs first. Metastasised to his liver. Then his bones. And then—him. Could've added Caretaker Ned to the tally but cirrhosis ended the old inebriate first.

Rita knew things. More than her sisters.

She knew you couldn't expect to hear secrets in broad daylight. They came out later. After the crowds had gone home. After the dishes had been dried and put away. After the lights dimmed and Avery boiled the kettle. You might have to sit still through an episode of a TV show. Fighting to stay awake. Only then, if you didn't draw attention to yourself, would you learn things. You might even tell people things.

What did she know about the deaths? No more than she did the day each person died. She hadn't thought about the women like that before. As a grisly mass. It made her feel a bit guilty. Only relevant now that their stories lined up with hers.

Rita considered the dead. Shut her eyes. Rolled their names around her brain. Stacked each person in order like folded laundry, warm and crisp from the sun.

She wondered how her name would sound amongst them.

Chapter Two

Mrs Pauline Barley
Breast cancer
27 January 1995

The last day of the summer holidays comes like hot breath leaching from a deflated balloon.

Rube Barley didn't have much to offer a woman visually. But a few hectares and a good tractor go a long way, and everyone agreed he'd hit the jackpot with Pauline. Mrs Pauline Barley was what you'd call a treasure, and it was hard to remember the village before her arrival or that Rube had sat on the shelf for so long. The eldest Barley boy came up with Marlon's twins, the younger born in the same week as her boy Ben, snivelling on the outskirts of their monthly baby group meetings, clinging to Pauline's slacks. With the heir and the spare accounted for, the tireless Mrs Barley turned her attention to committees, inescapable as she manned the sausage sizzle, pushed the clicking metre wheel to mark out tracks for athletics day or festooned the hall with decorations for the end-of-year recital. After wrangling the kids' homework and lights-out, you'd half expect her to leap from the wardrobe gripping a whistle and stopwatch to time your exhausted attempts at lovemaking.

The Barley boys were absent the first day back at school that year. And the second.

Their mother's death slingshotted the brothers to notoriety. Upon their return, the schoolchildren, with macabre fascination they could feel but not name, forced Cameo Cremes and blackcurrant Roll-Ups into the brothers' hands, let them run to home base in tiggy, insisted they serve first in handball.

Long after the brothers returned to rightful obscurity, a schoolchild calculating seven plus six using their fingers would look at a Barley boy, really see them, a whole kid the same age as them without a mum, and that humongous loss would be unbearable, and they'd start blubbering in the middle of the basic facts test. The twins, Mahalia and Diana, only stared, volunteering neither platitudes nor emotion, but their little brother Ben felt his heart jackknife into his throat when the younger Barley tackled him in bullrush, and Ben pressed his face into the grass and sniffed to halt his tears. Later on in bed he proper cried, leaving wet patches all over the Power Rangers pillowcase that his mum and dad got him for Christmas.

Rube Barley thought his wife could've made a decent monarch—not that they set a high bar for decency lately. Whether filling lunchboxes, overseeing the books for the farm or appointing names for the phone tree, service and duty enriched her days. Nothing went wrong for Pauline Barley. The first girl she met on her first day of school became her best friend. She sailed through exams without being labelled a swot and captained the netball team. She married young but not too young. Her pregnancies were easy and welcomed, and her sons, though dull, were kind, with teeth that grew straight and limbs that evaded greenstick fractures during schoolyard roughhousing. No one ran over her cats. Rube never raised his hand or eyed another woman's rear.

She could duraseal a stack of schoolbooks without a wrinkle. And she always took the mutton roast, wrapped in its plastic bread bag, out of the garage chest freezer in time to defrost for dinner.

And in June she felt a lump, and everything went bad, worse than she knew it could be, very quickly.

The school flag was lowered to half mast for a week, and a cup was arranged in Mrs Barley's honour for prizegiving. Neither Barley boy ever won it.

Chapter Three

December 2018

"Well, I just don't think they should raise the minimum wage. Businesses will have to up their prices to cope with the increase, and that'll hit us all in the pocket. And you're not *supposed* to make millions of dollars flipping burgers. Otherwise, everyone would do it. Anyway, it's a kid's job, and kids don't need to earn a so-called living wage. I'm all for hard work and earning a bit of dosh in the holidays, but the parents should support them. Where are the parents?"

The afternoon was rising to a boil. Three sleeping wasps dotted the wall above the red satin brocade curtains, like a recurring pattern someone gave up on.

"Well, that's a reasonable point of view, isn't it? I'd argue raising the minimum wage adds fat to the fire. It'll force small businesses to cut staff with all the extra payouts."

Sunshine oozed through the windows onto carpet the colour of bubbling porridge daubed with brown sugar. It had been many years since a paper doll underwent repeated near-drownings in those threaded umber rivers, but if you traced the river's path you could—valuing theatrics over ecclesiastical logic—still almost see Aurora, Queen of the Fairies, gliding down from Heaven in the nick of time to rescue the misbegotten dolls.

On the TV, a gardening show played on mute. Flies hovered in woozy circles, curious and uninhibited, landing on the Christmas tree, or warming their onyx bellies on the windowpane. The only surface where they couldn't get a stable footing was the *Merry from Lena* record spinning on Bufty's turntable.

"That's spot on, isn't it? I have to agree with you there, I don't mind telling you. Small businesses are the victims here."

Outside, the stately peach tree's arms shielded the lawn and verandah, dispersing heat through featherlike leaves, a dappled canopy under which grew tomatoes, cucumbers, runner beans, spring onions, spinach, kale—not all at once, but each year one took its turn to flourish while the others waited, like young women at a country dance hoping to be chosen for the Gay Gordons or Maxina. This year the tomatoes ran riot. The cucumbers were coming along fine, though—not a glut for bread-and-butter pickles, but the table didn't go wanting.

"Right you are. But if they're on minimum wage, they're not milking the benefit—"

"God, Nana! Do we have to listen to these idiots?" Sissy swivelled to face Bufty and Marlon in the kitchen. "It does my head in. What's wrong with the classical station?"

"Patience, bub." Bufty shuffled a paper crown over her forehead. It promptly slid back up again, mushrooming her silver hair out the top."It's my birthday."

It was Bufty's birthday. Eighty-three years old, with her family gathered for a meal. *Bring a little stay-the-night bag*, read her message on the family group chat. *I need all my girls under one roof on my birthday*. You could often find one daughter or another napping in the study, bothering their youngest sister Rita in the sleep-out or snoring on the couch. But she'd told them to stay. Not I-was-just-wondering, not making it seem like it was your idea or bribing you with treats. *Let's face it*, Judy sent to Marlon in a separate message. *There's only so many reasons an elderly woman would summons you like this, and it's probably not to tell you she won the lottery*.

Sissy shifted one cushion over as her mother Judy settled on the mustard-coloured couch and ran her hand over its velvety fleur-de-lis pattern, flattened here and there by the occupancy of many buttocks. Its texture still evoked opulence long after Judy learned it took more than a bit of synthetic velvet to make you rich.

Rita formed a knot on the La-Z-Boy, the Christmas tree lights raining colour onto her face. She hadn't turned a page of her Carson McCullers novel all afternoon, focussing on the sleeping wasps in a silent showdown. They looked calm enough. But they'd appeared out of nowhere. They could attack out of nowhere, too.

Glenn and Ben, Marlon's husband and son, knitted on folding chairs by the bay window: Glenn an intricate blanket, Ben a ribbed beanie, both to go under the tree at the upcoming Christmas church service. Contained by a sunbeam on the carpet, a grey tabby named Widgeon extended her paws like a Swan Lake ballerina in her spotlight.

"I only wanted to hear the weather, Sissy, to see if there's any rain coming in." Bufty turned the 8 Transistor's dial, admiring her pink, glittery fingernails. "Thank goodness Wally put in the second tank, that's all I can say. And we can't pick up an ant's hiccup on this radio, except for the blasted talkback, which you could probably hear in the middle of Antarctica with a piece of wet string. You're right though, bub, that's enough of that." Bufty tugged the paper crown again. "And we *can* get the Concert channel on TV. Or I can stream it on my laptop. But there's something trustworthy about hearing it on the radio, isn't there?"

Marlon removed handfuls of cutlery from the top drawer, running her thumb over the rows of dots at the end of each stainless-steel knife and fork. "There is that one Concert announcer," she said, "he talks—like—*this*, sends me into a bit of a trance. Can you imagine him at the A1 asking for a tarakihi and two scoops?"

Bufty hooted. Common as muck, her father had called their family. Her mother had clung to the notion that they'd fallen from wealth down the line. Not right about much, her father had hit the nail on the head with his assessment. That was no noblewoman's laugh.

"Can I just say, these flies are a curse." Judy swiped at the air. "Where's your fly spray, Mother?"

"Is the birthday cake vegan?" asked Sissy.

"No . . ."

"Hmm, thought not."

"I made a vegan caramel pecan slice," said Marlon. "It's in the fridge."

"You did? Thank you." Sissy did not backtrack her expression of discontent. "Don't use spray, Mum, it's full of chemicals."

"We can't all live up high in an apartment in Auckland, Sissy," said Judy, "some of us have to deal with winged livestock in summer. I'm going through a can of fly spray a week, no word of a lie."

"Remember those awful flypapers the Hearns had dangling everywhere?" said Marlon. "They looked like a Chelsea bun's insides after a while. Rather off-putting, hanging right above the dinner table and everything." She mimed eating with a knife and fork in revulsion.

"Mrs Hearn," said Judy, "was the sort of woman who was gagging to talk to you about van Gogh to seem high-brow, and too scared to in case she pronounced his name wrong."

Rita had only visited the Hearns once, with Bufty. She refused to go play with Mary Hearn, instead hiding behind the couch in the lounge—though Mrs Hearn called it a settee—watching the flies straining against the glue. Were they aware of their doom? Were their tiny brains weighing up the merits of tearing off their legs to be free?

"Put on the oil diffuser," said Bufty. "Flies don't like peppermint or lemongrass, that's what the essential oil company says."

"The heat pump is right there, Nana," said Sissy, "and we can turn it on cool, and—"

"And the green grass grew all around. That's a fine idea, Sissy, why don't you do that, then put on another little record? How about Robert Goulet? Oh, I *love* Robert Goulet."

Judy jiggled the window, freeing it from the frame's swollen, wooden grip. "It's far too nice a day to have everything all shut up," she said.

"I know, I know," said Bufty. "You'll change your tune when it slows down the flies, though. Folks go on about heat pumps too much, but the cold air is a lifesaver." The morality of *a bit of fresh air*, and the thrill of artificially altering the temperature without an adult telling you to put on or take off a jumper still pushed and pulled within Bufty, even though she'd been the adult in the room for longer than she ever got to be a child.

Sissy threw the heat-pump remote to Judy and lifted the stilled needle off Lena Horne, replacing the record with *This Christmas I Spend With You*. Regarding the faded cardboard sleeve, she shook her head.

"It's not Christmas without Robert Goulet, I'll say that much for him."

"Dad looked like Robert Goulet, didn't he?" said Judy.

"To me, Dad had a Don Ameche thing going on." Marlon hoisted a roast chicken in a black speckled enamel pan from the oven to the bench and wiped her fogged glasses on her tunic hem. "I need to see a photo, one of us must be right."

"Where is Avery, Mama? Shouldn't she be back by now?" It amused Judy to pronounce "mama" and "mother" in a drawn-out way, throwing in a "mater" when in high spirits. Hardly the pinnacle of comedy, but her sisters echoed her phrasing, to Judy's delight.

Bufty, stacking plates from the pantry, glanced over her shoulder. "The Papakura rev got crook at a christening from a ham on the turn, so Avery filled in at another christening this afternoon, and then she had to call in on Rev Jev for ministerial administration, or *administeration*, as they call it, and it's a bit of a drive—and then she's picking up Irene. But she should be here soon. She won't be late, not on my birthday."

Marlon pushed aside her potato dish on the long kitchen table and laid plates, clinking bundles of cutlery, and fabric serviettes. Whole worlds within universes were born on those four table legs, and as children they marvelled at it shrinking as they grew. Jayne said mischievous goblins shaved off pieces while they slept. Judy said a wicked witch put a spell on Jayne to grow taller and taller and bust through the roof and die, but if she fetched the firewood for the rest of the year Judy would have a quiet word with the witch about undoing her spell. Marlon found Jayne under the bed and made Judy apologise.

"And the twins will get here as soon as they can. Saturday's their busy day. It's a real hot spot."

"Not much competition though, is there," said Sissy.

"You're just mad they don't do mate's rates," said Ben, not looking up from his knitting.

"To be fair," said Glenn, "there's so many of us, the business would go under if the girls gave us all free drinks."

A commotion of beeps skipped around the room, from couch to mantle to kitchen. In an open-plan living area those message alerts could be as much of a hindrance as the flies. Rita's phone was hidden in her underwear drawer since she gave it to Bufty to sort out her messages, which kept pinging without showing her anything. After half an hour she took the phone back and turned it off. Bugger it, she said to Bufty, everyone's here all the time. I'll find things out when I'm meant to.

"Ah, speak of the devil, as it were, Avery's got Irene and they'll be here in two shakes." Bufty put her phone on the bench and rustled in the second drawer down for serving spoons.

Everything Bufty touched told her a story, bore other people's handprints. The chopping board, a neat, bevelled hexagon, sawn and sanded by fourteen-year-old Wally. The teacups, wedding presents from the girls at the factory. One chipped, from the time Jayne dropped it from the peach tree during a lofty teddy bears' picnic. Bufty still had the embossed card her friends signed under the legend, *A set from "The Set"*. Her mother's teapot. Tilting it sent forth a volley of drips, yet no other could dethrone it. For a moment, distorted in the convex teapot, her mother's face reflected where her own should be.

Sissy sniffed the lemongrass oil and sprinkled it into the diffuser on the hutch dresser, wedged between poetry volumes; springy piles of rubber bands; a mug with Princess Diana's face printed on it filled with a lucky dip of working and dried-up biros; The Good Dinner Set, its grey plates with the icy spray of flowers and the larger serving dish propped on a stand with curling feet; and framed pictures of the grandchildren and family pets.

The dogs' ears pricked up, hearing the compressed crunch of car tyres meeting the asphalt driveway before everyone else did.

"Oh! It's Avery and Irene," Bufty flapped her hands at her granddaughter, still standing by the dresser. "Sissy, with your youthful legs, go see if they need a little hand."

"We cannot have spiritual growth without pain and suffering, as St Irenaeus once said," boomed Avery from the front door. "Hell, I've said it a few times myself." She walked in with Irene, parcels and bags held to her chest. "But Murphy tests the limits of my diplomacy. He's spraying the paddocks again. Can someone call the dogs inside?"

"Roger! Jimmy Jimmy Jimmy!" called Sissy, propping open the window behind the couch. "Move over, Mum."

Avery followed Irene to the kitchen, lowered her parcels onto the bench and rested her palm on the nape of Bufty's neck. "Sorry I took so long, birthday queen. How can I be of use? Irene, would you like a cuppa? Goodness, it's cool in here compared to the hellfires out there!"

An opaque cloud climbed over the fence lining the property. Roger and Jimmy Stewart leapt through the window onto the cushions below, Roger making an unwelcome bee-line for Judy's lap, Jimmy Stewart following the scent of roast chicken to the table. Though the deck gave him a leg-up, it was an agile feat for Roger, a portly German shepherd.

Roger was thirteen years old. A good age. Along with his advanced years, Roger carried an air of immortality, for there had always been a dog named Roger in the Gordon house. Whenever one Roger shuffled off this mortal coil, the family renamed the remaining dog in honour of those who went before. The younger dog, called Jimmy Stewart until his transition into the next Roger, was an ebullient mutt who urinated on strangers' shoes. Everyone reckoned Rita trained him to do it. No one could prove she did. No one could prove she didn't. Fortunately, strangers were infrequent round these parts.

Irene tucked her wooden stick under one arm. She gripped her daughter-in-law's shoulders, her tapering fingernails the colour of blood oxidising in an open wound. They kissed each other's cheeks.

"Happy birthday, my girl. May you have many more. And you will. I always knew you'd live a long life."

"Thank you so much, Irene, it's lovely of you to say. Now, how about a little cup of tea? Or we can fix you a glass of punch. And would you like us to help you to your chair? Dinner's nearly ready." Bufty found it easier to digest Irene's portentous statements after a square meal, or at least a cup of something.

Irene forged a three-legged path to her favoured straight-backed chair. To the outsider, a shameful tableau: young whippersnappers lounging on the comfy chairs with their matriarch austere as a monk at the table. The family, however, knew Irene sat exactly where she intended to; had she the impulse to eat dinner on the roof, they would've relocated their party up there without question.

Irene was 102 years old. A very good age. Having buried her husband and son, she called longevity a greedy master that took with both hands the more it gave you.

No living soul remembered the eleven months where Irene answered to Mrs Gordon. She discarded the surname after her husband's death and later officialised it by deed poll so her driver's licence—achieved in her sixties, thanks to Rita's lessons, and only recently relinquished—stated *Irene*. She put food on the table for baby Wally by pulling tarot cards, reading palms and selling herbal remedies. The mononym stoked her public image as the local mystic. Now slowed but not incapacitated, her days lacked for nothing, and she declined Bufty's offers to move her into their house. The family visited, rotating grocery drop-off duty, or, if one had time and emotional fortitude, drove her to the fruit and vegetable shop—she refused to patronise the New World—and followed as she scrutinised each apple and onion. She still received the occasional customer, meditated, wrote numbers and sought meaning in their sum, held crystals to the moon; or sat on the verandah, motionless as her wooden chair, the eternal west coast tides below.

"Don't mind me—it was a long day on my feet." Avery dropped to the carpet in front of the piano and pulled her knees towards her chest. "Leading a service is murder on the lumbar" was Reverend Avery Manrose's most consistent opinion about religion.

Judy lowered the creaky sash window to block the dust

cloud skulking beyond the glass, like a child spying on a party they weren't invited to.

"Bloody Murphy." Bufty's eyes narrowed. "Spraying again. He does it to vex me, I'm sure. And on my birthday. We got through thalidomide, asbestos, smoking while pregnant and lead paint, but we can't escape Murphy's spray."

"Yeah," said Judy, in the precise, defensive tone always followed by, "It was the 70s," or "That's what we did back then," or "You knew if you fell off, you'd die, so you were careful." Today, she chose the second option.

"He doesn't do it to vex you," said Marlon, pouring more ginger ale into the punchbowl. "He does it because—well, I'm not a farmer, I don't know why, but I'm sure he has his reasons to do it every year. What a word though, Mama. *Vex*."

"Did you hear they took Bayer Roundup to the Supreme Court in the US, and they claimed it was safer than dishwashing liquid?" said Judy, sniffing in disdain at the acumen of the appointed nine. "Meanwhile, everyone's dropping like flies with cancer, and two plus two equals five . . . don't get me wrong, but do they think we came down with the last shower? *Silkwood* was basically a documentary, you know?" She slid a slate laptop from a satchel by her feet. She didn't see Rita's lips part, her fingers dig into her book, the colour blanch from her face, before continuing to pretend to be engrossed in her reading.

"While we're waiting for everyone to arrive, let me show you the new connections I found on the ancestry site." Judy plugged a corded mouse into the side of her laptop and rolled it on her thigh like a wind-up toy car. "Now, someone else has listed Margaret, I mean, *Margaret*-Margaret—Whetū's daughter—as a shared ancestor, and they live down the line—"

"Someone's here," interrupted Sissy.

"It's Jayne!" called Bufty, clapping.

"Sorry I'm late, whew, what a fug out there." Jayne leaned her guitar against the hutch dresser and placed a gladwrapped plate on the bench. "Hullo Mama, happy birthday, love that pink dress on you. I've got pigs in blankets. I just couldn't decide what to make, but I think they'll be really neat."

Judy and Sissy met each other's eyes. Judy's rice salad wasn't any more or less upmarket, chic or even relevant to the current decade than pigs in blankets, but there was something bereft and sad about her younger sister's confident offering. Her confidence made it sadder. Judy knew it. Sissy knew it. Maybe everyone did. Everyone except Jayne.

"Pigs in blankets sounds lovely, Jayne," said Bufty, "and you're right on time for dinner. Oh! All my daughters together again. Lovely!" Jayne embraced her mother.

"How is we all? Hullo Sissy, hullo Ben. Is that a new shirt, Rita? It looks fabbo on you."

"No," said Rita, which raised a laugh from the room. "What, it's true."

Jayne kissed Irene and sat cross-legged at her feet.

"Looking fabbo yourself, Jayne," said Marlon. "How's the shop? Did you have the day off? Was it a long trip up?"

"Good as gold, thank you, I should show you my photos of the gorgeous new wedding dresses we got in, if you like. My boss let me do a half-day today, and the car flew up here! It's a much easier drive than it used to be, isn't it?"

"Where's that daughter of yours?" Irene squeezed Jayne's hand. "Where's Flossie Doll?"

"Stevie's not here, Irene. She hasn't been here for a long time, remember?" Jayne smiled too brightly. A 102-year-old being absent-minded shouldn't be surprising, but . . .

"She's back in the country, isn't she?"

"Oh, I get you! Yeah, last week just gone. But you know Stevie, she's a real busy bee."

"I think she's coming here. I can feel it."

Jayne patted Irene's hand without condescension. "Thanks, Irene. We all want to see her again."

"Is she still saying *haitch* instead of *aitch*?"

"I'm not sure, Judy, we didn't recite the alphabet when she phoned me."

Alas for Judy, who thought she detected feistiness, Jayne spoke in earnest.

"Must be challenging for her coming back to little old New Zealand after swanning about in London." Judy had only ever travelled as far as Brisbane, on her second honeymoon, and couldn't help carrying the air of only having travelled as far as Brisbane in all meditations on travel.

"Will she be home for Christmas?" asked Marlon. "Imagine a white Christmas, though. With Harrods all lit up, like in *Mr Bean*."

"What about the twins? What are they up to?"

"They're working tonight, probably till the wee smalls, being a weekend and the silly season." Marlon mimed shaking a cocktail over her shoulder.

Irene turned her laser beam towards the La-Z-Boy. "And what about you, Rita?"

"I mean, I'm here," said Rita, pinching two pages from her book and rubbing them against each other. "Last time I checked." She tucked the book into the side pocket of her chair to stop fidgeting with it.

Irene knew she had a secret. Rita knew Irene knew. Those bloody eyes, like two tunnels boring through you. Made it feel like you didn't even have eyes of your own. Like she was the only one who ever saw anything.

Two doors and a car boot slammed shut. "Coo-ee!"

"Door's unlocked!" yelled Judy.

"That sounds like Pete and Peter to me," said Bufty, sitting up in her chair.

In strode two men, one holding a bouquet of pink gerberas, the other lugging a blue insulated chilly bag.

"Dad!" Sissy jumped up to hug the man with the bag.

"Jee-hosaphat, it's horrible out there," said Peter. "Bloody Murphy, at it again I see. Happy birthday, mother." He stepped across the lounge to kiss Bufty. "You look ravishing. Love the tree. Did you chop it down, Avery? No flies on you, hey?

Gidday Rita, Ms Judy, yes. Hallo, Irene! How are the stars and moon treating you?"

"Hello, sorry we're late," said Pete, dodging Jimmy Stewart. "Same old story, caught behind a combine harvester on the old Smith Road. I've made a vegetable curry with—somewhere under here—coconut sambal and coconut rice. Not too spicy, don't you worry."

"Let's face it, you've got to take the Breem Road," said Judy, "and turn onto Smith at the crossing." Of course, this tardiness never would've occurred if her ex-husbands still had her at the wheel.

"This rice can't sit," said Pete, "so if we're not eating right away it'll need to go in the microwave. Mel and I did a cooking class on our last anniversary, it was so much fun, and we have this all the time at home. Hello, Avery. Can we find room for this on the table?"

"If you go the back way, you don't have to take the loop road," said Avery, lurching out of her yoga pose. "Here we go, put the curry on the potholder by the tabbouleh. Now, the back way has the Hastings shoulder where you can't see cars coming from your left—but, as Alain de Lille said, all roads lead to Rome."

She batted the hardy flies not curbed by the air conditioning away from the table. Anyone could've told you with eyes shut what food they'd eat: Marlon's potato dish; a roast chicken and Bufty's bread, its cosy scent reaching out to greet you; Judy's rice salad; Rita's tabbouleh, flecked with mint and parsley from the garden; splintered wedges of Sissy's spinach and mushroom filo pie; minted new potatoes; sliced cucumbers in white vinegar; tomato wedges, red as the approaching sunset. On the kitchen bench, a scalloped glass bowl of punch made from cold black tea, ginger ale and pineapple juice, draped in a vast doily to prevent dive-bombing insects.

"Don't I know it," said Peter. "Hallo Jayne, how was the drive? Isn't that new highway fan-bloody-tastic? You used to need a map and a cut lunch and now the car belts along it in half the time. Unlike the old Smith Road, I might add—"

"Alright, alright," said Bufty. Her family could sustain this line of conversation for a remarkably long time, despite how few paths led to the village. "If we don't eat dinner soon, we'll have to plant another candle in my cake. Your vege curry smells scrumptious, Pete."

Six weeks after her nineteenth birthday, Judy married Peter Neill, a man as tall and handsome as her late father. They had a son, Brian, who now lived with his dreary English wife and their son in Huddersfield. Next, Judy married Pete Harada, who looked nothing like her father, but that didn't work either. Sissy's arrival meant their congress wasn't entirely for naught, however. Neil Hemphill took up the mantle third, and like those who fell before him the union ended in divorce, and Judy often forgot what he looked like altogether when he wasn't standing in front of her. All three men attended Gordon family functions, established a friendship through their shared escapades and remained Judy's husbands despite their respective legal dissolutions. She didn't reciprocate attendance at any of Pete, Peter or Neil's family gatherings, nor, truth be told, would their relatives have rolled out the red carpet for her. Both Judy and her ex-husbands' families reckoned they'd got the better deal out of the situation. With Judy's exacting standards, three men on call for odd jobs and moral support without having to put up with toenail clippings or picky appetites suited her fine.

"Potatoes for you, Irene?" said Bufty. "Now, has everyone had potatoes?"

"You're first in line, Mater," said Judy. "We're all waiting for you to feed Irene, aren't we?"

"Oh! So I am. Turning eighty-three, so it begins, you'll be fixing me a plate soon . . ."

"This rice salad, phenomenal as per. Is there no way we can wangle the recipe off you?" Glenn heaped several spoonfuls onto his paper plate.

"Not on your life, Glenn," said Judy, "but bless you for trying."

"Don't look at us," said Peter. "You'd think being married to her for eight years would afford me secret information, but this rice salad is more highly protected than the Kremlin." He loaded salad onto his plate. "In fact, it's the only reason I keep showing up to these events. Isn't that right, Pete?"

"Hey now, don't implicate me here."

"What's that interesting taste in your little pastries, Jayne?" asked Judy.

"Mayonnaise," beamed Jayne.

"You don't say."

"You'll be chuffed to not be doing all the cooking for once, won't you, Rita!" said Glenn. "But tell me, is your chocolate mousse . . ."

"In the fridge."

Marlon's fork clattered to the floor. "Taxi! Can't take me anywhere." She bent forward to scoop it up. "Oof, my back. Might join you for yoga, Avery."

"Fork on the floor, a visitor walks in the door." Irene banged her stick for emphasis. "Someone's coming."

"You've got a little saying for everything, don't you Irene?"

"That's right, Judy, the Bible doesn't have the monopoly on proverbs."

"Are these your tomatoes, Bufty?"

"They are, Pete, and all organic, apart from the glyphosate, but I've washed them thoroughly, you're quite safe, no thanks to sadist Murphy. It was 1965—"

"Here we go," mumbled Rita through a mouthful of roast chicken leg. She ran her finger across her plate, picking up a slick of chicken grease and oven-sizzled rosemary needles, and licked it clean.

"It was 1965, and he killed all my tomatoes—that garden was mine and Wally's pride and joy, not to mention you lot wouldn't have got fed otherwise. That year was the best crop I'd ever had, and our tomatoes died overnight. Not a word of a lie. Shrivelled and blackened! It's the best spot to grow tomatoes, too! And Spencer Tracy, the little cat who liked to eat the tomatoes—he died a week later."

"He got run over though, didn't he," said Judy, back at the table serving herself seconds of rice salad.

"Yes he did, Judy, and it was Murphy's bloody wife Bev behind the wheel."

"That's right. What a po-faced woman. And we had a funeral for Spencer. Do you remember—all the other cats lined up at the grave? Like they knew."

"They knew," said Irene, dabbing her mouth with a pink cloth napkin.

"Nana, how many cats did you have?" asked Ben, though he knew the answer.

"I'm glad you asked, Ben, there was little Spencer Tracy, and then Carole invited herself in, and Darelle and Jonty's little cat had kittens, so we got Mrs Bennet from her. And Gloria, our first cat." Bufty gestured at the stout black cat with a white bib in a framed photo on the hutch dresser. "She showed up when Wally and I first got married, as if she knew we needed her."

"Don't forget Roger," said Jayne. The ur-Roger was a tranquil German shepherd, with a second mate named Lana, an idiotic mutt acquired from a litter at Old Bunratty's farm.

"The best dog in the world," said Bufty. "A living angel. Her and Lana looked like they could kill you, but neither would hurt a fly. The cats walked all over them. Of course, I wanted them to be guard dogs, with your father's shift work, but they were pets. No, not pets—they were *family*. Roger was like—oh, who was she like, Baby Ree?"

"Aunt Bee from *The Andy Griffith Show*." Rita wrapped her arms around her legs and rested her chin on her knees. Bufty was at her best in front of a crowd. Especially the usual crowd.

"Yes! And Lana was more of a—"

"Shelly Tambo," finished Judy. "*Northern Exposure*."

"It must be cake time," said Avery. She shut the dishwasher and leaned against it in a deep lunge.

Ben completed his row of knitting and put the half-done beanie into a cloth tote bag. "Do you want to come to the table, Nana? Or should I bring the cake to you?"

Marlon and Glenn hung their tea towels over the oven rail to dry in its residual heat. The upturned punch bowl dripped sudsily into the sink. Rita put away the last orange-stained Tupperware container in the fridge. Jayne guided Irene back from the bathroom, one hand at her elbow.

"Bring it to me, I think. Seems these days, once I'm sitting, I'm sitting. Do you want us to shuffle your chair closer, Irene?"

"I'm fine over here."

"And it's not too cold for you, with the air blowing?"

"I'm fine, girl."

Marlon had baked her chocolate cake—hers in the sense that if you cook a recipe from a book enough times, your family will attribute its origins to you—in a square tin and plastered it with pink raspberry-flavoured icing, with hundreds and thousands sprinkles sinking into the soft, sweet surface and four candles stabbed into it like flags upon claimed ground. Ben, carrying the cake across the room, narrowly avoided tripping over Roger bounding towards the front door with Jimmy Stewart capering behind.

"Oop—who can that be pulling in?" said Bufty, tapping her pink fingernails. "Taihoa everyone. Hold your horses, Ben."

Two identical women appeared in the hallway doorframe, each clad in black mesh and ripped denim, each with a fist wrapped around the neck of a Lindauer bottle.

"Oh! Hullo, twins! We didn't expect you so soon!"

"We shut up early," said Diana. "And we brought champagne."

"It's Lindauer," added Mahalia. "But the price is right."

It entertained Diana to refer to Lindauer as champagne and gravely offended Mahalia. Though not much use in practical application, this was the one discernible difference separating the twins.

"Ooh, how fancy," said Jayne, who would've given the same response whether you'd presented her with apple juice or the finest aged Côtes du Rhône.

"We put a sign on the door saying 'Nana's birthday, back tomorrow'," said Mahalia. "Stuff the lot of them. You got birthday wishes though. Old Tom. The Sneaths."

"Oh yes, Smyrna Sneath posted a lovely message on my Facebook this morning. I'm tickled pink to see you both, what a treat." Bufty beckoned her granddaughters over.

Mahalia placed her bottle on the kitchen table and kissed Bufty. She turned to Ben, waiting with the cake, and punched his shoulder.

"Need one of these?" She took a lighter from her jeans pocket. "It's for the candles at work, Mum. Settle down."

"Did you take those bottles from behind the bar, girls?"

"I wrote the stocktake. Di counts the stock."

"And we might sell them for $25," said Diana, "but we buy them for much less."

Marlon laughed. "Is $25 a good price for a bottle of plonk?"

"You'd be lucky to get one cocktail for $25 in Wellington," said Diana.

"Ker-rist," said Judy. "In my day $7 covered your night out, with a mixed grill afterwards at Vinnie's, with fried oysters, two planks of bacon, pork sausages and—sorry Siss—a steak, as thick as a King James Bible. Mind you," she fluttered her eyelashes, "a lady never had to pay for her own drinks. You crossed your legs like so to show off your ankles, and a fellow bought your drinks for you. Let me put it to you this way, I'd be mortified to know what drinks cost. I'd be losing my touch. *Those* were the days."

"So do you want bubbles?"

"Oh god, yes. I suppose there's no accounting for city folk, as I tell Sissy. Do you sell many Brandy Alexanders at your bar, girls? Now, there's a drink."

Not much, according to Judy, worth preserving in this world had occurred after 11:59PM on New Year's Eve 1979.

Sissy feigned a yawn at Mahalia: *you know what's coming.*

"And tell me," continued Judy, "did you pay for your jeans to be that ripped? Or was it an occupational hazard?" Mahalia handed her aunt a glass of bubbles, an effective distraction.

"Hallo, twins!" Peter waved from his folding chair by Glenn and Ben. "I'll have a splash if you're offering. And how many candles is it this year, Mother? Thirty-five?"

"Oh, Peter, you rapscallion!" Bufty tossed her hair over her shoulders, sending the paper crown down the back of the chair. "Such applesauce! But I don't look it, do I?"

"You're right, I shouldn't lie to you on your birthday. You don't look a day over twenty-one. Here, let me retrieve the crown for you, m'lady."

Peter knew which way the wind blew, but his flattery came weighted in sincerity. Just as the centenarian Irene kept startling mental and physical dexterity, Bufty enjoyed a youthful visage for a woman of eighty-three. Short, round and pink, when Bufty stood next to statuesque Avery they called to mind a nobly weathered German shepherd guarding a hothouse-ripened peach.

"Are we blowing out these candles or what?" said Ben. "My arms are shaking here!"

"Quit your job and come work for us at The Chariot," said Diana to her brother. "Get you replacing kegs and lifting stock, you'll be He-Man in no time." To the twins, running a bar was decidedly more arduous than Ben's plumbing work. Depending on the day, they weren't wrong.

"*Ha-aaappy,*" began Jayne, resonant and silvery. Bufty, jubilant at all the attention, pretended to conduct as her family sang.

"Hip hip—" called Peter.

"Hooray!"

Bufty burst into a hacking cough.

"Mum!" admonished Judy.

"Nana!" cried Sissy.

"I'll eat it," said Pete. "Wouldn't miss out on Marlon's handiwork—am I right, Marlon, this is one of yours?"

"That's Marlon's alright," said Glenn.

Bufty blew out the two remaining candles not yet extinguished by her coughing.

"*Why was she born so beautiful, why was she born at all,*" sang Judy.

"I'll cut into it," said Bufty. "I *have* to make a little wish—but can one of you nimble-fingered twins please take over the slicing for me?" She cleared her throat with a noise you might expect to hear after a magician unsuccessfully whips a tablecloth out from an abundantly laden dinner table. "What's a few germs between whānau?"

"Can't be worse than thalidomide," said Judy, hands outstretched for cake.

"Or whatever Murphy's spraying out there," said Rita. The last sliver of sunlight stained the sky scarlet. Like a heat rash crawling across bare skin. Too dark to see the dust.

"Now, the jug's boiled—who's a starter for tea, or caffeine?" Avery held up the coffee plunger. "No Gregg's instant on Bufty's birthday!"

"I think I'll have a little coffee," said Bufty. "That way I can stay up and not miss a minute of my birthday."

"These scones don't even taste vegan!" Judy took another from the plate. "What was it, bub—coconut cream? I'd say you could only taste coconut if you thought about it. But it's definitely there. You could give this to anyone, and you wouldn't have to tell them it's vegan. But you *can* taste the coconut, can't you?"

"Bloody coconut cream detective," said Sissy, licking caramel off her fingers. "This slice is delicious though, Marlon. You'll have to post the recipe in the chat."

"I'm so lucky to have all the girls here," said Bufty, "and my grandchildren, it's the best present of all. But it's not my real present, is it? Shall we do presents? Oh yes let's, shall we?"

If Baby Rita were Irene's age and not over half that, Bufty would still refer to her daughters as The Girls, and the villagers considered it a serviceable collective noun. To be fair, the Gordon girls had given the villagers enough raw material for discourse over the years, so a shorthand term paid for itself.

Thirty-five years ago, Rita shocked her family and the wider village by running off to Venice with Sidhal, an Italian chef she met in Auckland. A postcard every Christmas let them know she was alive. Which was fairly verbose for Rita.

Bufty missed her baby but welcomed the spectacle Rita's departure stirred up. She would dip her head, devout as Jackie Kennedy shadowing JFK's casket, when fellow congregants included wayward Rita in their prayers during Avery's services. Those who prophesied that no good could come of letting your child move away to Auckland had their suspicions gratifyingly confirmed, and many hands kneaded and re-shaped Rita's narrative. Some reckoned she was busking in St Mark's Square covered in tattoos, some got halfway through their suppositions before realising they were recounting the plot to *The Italian Job*.

On a numbing, squally August day in 1985, Rita showed up on the doorstep of the Gordon homestead with as little warning as when she left, and locked herself in the bedroom.

No sooner had Rita arrived than Hetty Loomis rang.

"Did I see that Rita coming up the road just now dressed in black," said Hetty, not troubling herself with opening salutations. "She looked awfully peaky."

"Yes," said Bufty, stunned into clarity. "I guess she's back."

You couldn't get a peep out of Rita about the Italian chef. Speculation abounded, mostly from Judy's direction, that she'd killed Sidhal. A small faction said there was no Italian in the first place, a rumour disproven by the unwieldy pasta machine Rita lugged back in her suitcase. It took all afternoon to crank the dough through its irritable, squeaky rollers, causing everyone involved to bicker and threaten to throw the lot to the dogs, but the pasta it produced? Out of this world. There's no way she would've found out about pasta around here. Rita repeated this pattern, moving out and coming back, never settling. Bufty suspected the more questions she asked Rita, the less likely she was to stay. But finally, at Christmas 2018, the prodigal son was home for good, Bufty knew it.

Wally Gordon died in 1974, when Marlon was twenty. Saddled with four lively girls and a flighty wife, and no son to carry on the name or provide, Wally always got sympathy from the other factory workers and their wives, who asked "How does he manage, I couldn't do it". They called him a quiet man. It was more that his family was very loud.

But his mild geniality gave Bufty and the girls space to bloom, in the way waterlilies could not open their showy petals without a pond beneath holding them up. And in his way, within his abilities, Wally was as happy as he could be. The lung cancer was no surprise in hindsight, when a cigarette hung from his lips in every grainy photo of him piggybacking the girls or sawing into bits of two-by-four. But that's what you did back then. He held on for one final Christmas, one last round of birthdays. Wally's funeral fell on the hottest day of the year, with the family sweating through their scratchy best clothes. The flowers on Bufty's hat wilted before they finished singing 'Immortal, Invisible, God Only Wise'.

Reverend Avery Manrose moved in not long after.

Well-fed on *Anne of the Island* and *Good News* where dashing young gels wore school colours and developed fervent sorority friendships, teenage Bufty had been crestfallen to discover higher education in New Zealand would be a more sombre affair. Four male boffins studied in the academic stream at her school, while Bufty was directed towards the commercial stream for Pitman shorthand, bookkeeping and typing with a musty khaki bib stretched over the keys until she could hammer out fifty words a minute. The switchboard at the new aerosol factory needed girls with secretarial common sense, not book smarts, so that was that. Without the luxury of displeasure, Bufty enjoyed answering the phones with the other "Hello girls". It kept the wolves from the door, and there she met the steadfast Wally Gordon.

The factory brought in families, a store and Boone's car repair. The bowling green memberships swelled, the old church's pews filled, and the dances at the hall carried on till the sun lumbered over the hills at 4AM and the farmers had to leave to milk their cows, yawning, heel bones aching, ears ringing.

As the Gordon family grew, the village shrunk into dormancy, the bowling green disused, the store concealed by two privet trees spitting sticky buds onto its broken windows. Boone's closed up a few years back, the last place you could spend money without getting in your car. A grubby freezer by the front desk housed lemonade Popsicles, Topsys and Jelly Tips. Those brave enough could rap the bell, and a grumpy giant named Boone would reluctantly snatch your fistful of coins and chuck your ice creams into a greasy paper bag. No one knew why Boone kept the freezer there if he hated selling ice creams so much. The school closed in 2009, the government's promise to replace its lead pipes and asbestos ceilings fading from memory with each year.

Most people forgot solemn Avery after she entered St Swithin's Theological College. After she took over from Murray Morgan, the retiring reverend, as Local Anglican for Hire, the Gordons absorbed her, Bufty's dearest school chum. In photo albums, there was Avery. On the one family trip to stay in a buckling chartreuse and orange panelled canvas tent, Avery hammered pegs into the grass, and Wally stayed at home.

In the end, when he knew his number was up, Wally asked Avery to lead his funeral, in her church, her way.

Of course, Avery and Bufty's deviant union plunged the Gordons into the snapping turtle-infested waters of gossip and disrepute. But between the fear of Irene turning you into a frog, and the intermittent need for a reverend to pour water on babies' heads and read the Lord's Prayer at funerals, and Bufty's aptitude for acting as though everything was fine, and Rita's aptitude for landing a punch without being suspected of the deed—well, people got on with it. And the accepted definition of normal moved with the years. Still not what you'd expect to see round here, mind you.

☾

The family had clubbed together to give Bufty a hardback book about *The Wizard of Oz*.

"Oh!" she inhaled, trailing her fingers over the pages. "These pictures are stunning! And look at how thick the paper is! Poor Judy Garland. The tragedy. There was no one like her. They put plugs in her nostrils to change their shape, you know. Now, is this what you'd call a coffee-table book? I'll certainly put it on display where we can all see it."

"Here's my present," said Avery.

"Oooh, is this a bottle I can feel?"

"No, it's a puppy," said Rita.

"Homemade passionfruit liqueur," said Avery. "I made it at Rev Jev's back in April when their vine shot off like a horse on roller skates. I picked it up today, that's why I was so late."

"Oh!" Bufty unscrewed the lid on the bottle of butter-yellow liquid. "This smells heavenly! I'm tempted to dab it behind my ears."

"I admit, I've had several taste tests while it's been in their custody," said Avery.

"Purely quality control, hey?" Marlon mimed taking a long swig from a liquor bottle.

"That's the one."

Bufty peeled the tape from the second package and stuck it on her wrist, setting the paper aside for future use. She could still see, still *feel* the ball of string made from smaller pieces of string her mother tended to during the war.

"Oh! Oh, it's—oh!"

"What is it, Nana?" asked Ben, using his teeth to split a length of yarn in two.

A creamy string of pearls swayed from her fingertips.

"Nana Margaret's. I'd know them from a mile off. Don't ruin your teeth, Ben, there's scissors in the second drawer down."

"I had the pearls cleaned and restrung," said Avery, "and the clasp fixed. I was so nervous you'd notice the necklace was gone."

"This is all I've got of hers," said Bufty, "and it's been in dire need of a clean-up. Isn't that perfect? What a perfect birthday."

Avery kissed the top of her head. Bufty pulled at her crown.

Irene planted her stick into the carpet. "Where did my bag go? I've got something in there for you."

The great-grandchildren leapt to their feet to be first to help her. Diana found the bag by the door.

Bufty removed a clinking box from the bag. "Oh! *Irene*. It's your mother's set, isn't it?" She inspected a bone-handled knife, reflecting the lights in its blade. "This is so special. You know I've had my eye on them, don't you! We'll have to use them at Christmas. Every Christmas."

"That's right, girl," said Irene, "I wanted you to have it. She wanted you to have it, I know. And if you look again in my bag—"

"Not your tarot cards! It's too much, I can't accept them." Why was Irene unloading her possessions like this?

"You won't," said Irene. "I'm not giving them to you. But I can do your birthday tarot reading."

"Of course, silly me, I was all overwhelmed by the silver—everything looks like a present on your birthday. Shall we do the reading now? What about more cake first?"

☾

All told, a fine birthday.

But the question lingered: why did everyone have to stay tonight?

"We'll press on and leave you to it," said Peter. You didn't need Irene's psychic powers to know when you'd outstayed your usefulness.

"We'd better rattle our dags too, Ben," said Glenn. He motioned over to Irene, her head bobbing sideways. "I think someone's ready for bed. We can run her home."

Irene's head shot up. "I'm just resting my eyes. I can hear you. Let's have a song."

Peter, Pete and Glenn sat back in their folding chairs. You didn't need Irene's psychic powers to know when to obey an order, either.

"Yes, let's have a little sing-song," said Bufty. "Jayne—can you—"

"No pressure to open the birthday liqueur," said Avery, "but can I get anyone a green ginger wine to encourage our singing? A port? I'll put the kettle on, too."

With the jug boiling, and Jayne tuning her guitar, and Avery calling for drinks, only Rita heard the gravel crunch, only she saw the striking silhouette in the doorframe: trousers over coltish legs, a black waistcoat speaking of bespoke tailoring, a liquorice-dark leather jacket that appeared cool to the touch despite the evening's heat. The silhouette stepped into the light, cropped bleached hair flung back from a high forehead, eyes obscured by round sunglasses, a bouquet of red roses in one hand and a condensation-beaded magnum of champagne under her arm, and you could sense, if not see, the riding boots she'd left by the front door; at this point, a top hat wouldn't be out of the question.

"Holy shit," said Rita. "Sorry, Irene."

Irene turned to face the person at the door.

"That's right. I knew you'd come. Hello, Flossie Doll."

Their voices dropped away, leaving only the kettle's whistle and the reverberation of Jayne's strumming.

Stevie pulled the sunglasses off her face.

"As a girl in a blue plaid dress once said, there's no place like home. Isn't that right, Nana."

"Oh! Oh! It is you! It's really you!" Bufty launched towards Stevie with a pillowy hug. "It's been so long." She pinched Stevie's cheek. "Did they not feed you in London? You're fading away! Are you hungry? We can fix you a plate, there's plenty to eat."

"What they don't tell you about London," said Stevie, "is nothing there compares to Aunty Judy's rice salad, and if you lot have eaten it all, I'm hopping on the next flight back across the equator."

Jayne approached her daughter, levering Bufty's limpet grip from her arms.

"*Mum.*"

Jayne ignored how Stevie's hair smelled of cigarette smoke. Worth it, for the hug. "Gosh, this feels like a dream, I should touch one of those thorns to make sure I'm awake."

"Thank you, Floss," said Bufty, "red roses truly speak to my soul. Let's put them in the crystal vase—the one that belonged to—"

"That's not all, Nana." Stevie fetched a framed painting the size of a broadsheet from the hallway. "A little gifty-gift, as is customary, a token of my affection . . ."

"We're still doing the British accent, I see," murmured Judy to Sissy.

"*Haitch,*" Sissy whispered back.

"This, Nana, is the church in Mangōnui where Whetū and Charles were married. I painted it for you. A making-up-for-lost-time type thingy."

"Oh—now, how on *earth* did you—I'm going to cry—" Bufty drew Stevie towards her again.

"Giz a look?" said Rita.

Bufty rotated the painting.

"Isn't it the most glorious work of art you've ever laid eyes on? Where should we hang it, I wonder?"

Rita whistled. Assertive brushstrokes. Graceful composition. Objectively good.

"Absolutely incredible, Stevie," said Marlon.

"Cogent work," said Avery. "Reminiscent of Doris Lusk."

"Bugger me days." It couldn't be *that* hard to paint a square with a triangle on top for a roof, but astonishment shaded Judy's face. "The old art course wasn't a waste then. When the hell did you have time to paint this?"

Stevie tapped the side of her nose. "A diplomat never tells. Hello, Irene, I've missed you most of all."

"At last, Floss. I knew you'd be here. Didn't I say. And aren't you clever with your painting. You're staying for a while now?"

"I daresay I will. Can I doss in here for a bit, Nana? I won't take up any space, the High Commission has me house-trained. Then I'll drive to yours, Mum, if that's fine with you, and we can come back here for Christmas." Stevie kissed Marlon and Judy, hugged Sissy, shook hands with Avery and the twins, raised two fingers to her forehead in a salute to Rita. Jayne, too overcome, couldn't speak. She nodded vigorously, eyes shining.

"Who wants champers? First glass to the birthday girl, yes?"

"Is that *real* champagne?"

"Real as the face on your nose, dear Judy."

From the floor Jayne could regard Stevie all at once, as she poured champagne into flutes—see her head to foot, not cut off by a phone's screen—so classy, she really looked like someone who'd been to London. Not just been—*sent by the government.*

Roger, startled by all the excitement, nestled in Jayne's lap. Jimmy Stewart slept under the Christmas tree, oblivious. Widgeon had long since fled the melee for Bufty and Avery's bed, sleeping beside a patchy ginger named Smoo.

Stevie raised her champagne bottle. "Stay positive, test negative. Happy birthday, Nana, and here's to you."

"Let's have that song," said Irene. "C'mon, Jayne."

"Oh yes, marvellous." Jayne picked up her guitar, battered from years of inebriated party-goer collisions, being pitched into car backseats and the time Stu O'Bannion ran over it with his motorcycle.

"Now I'm really back home," said Stevie, forking Judy's rice salad into her mouth.

They fell back on their songs with easy muscle memory. 'Bound for the Rio Grande', 'River of No Return', 'Down by the Riverside'—the "river suite", as Marlon called it. 'The Carnival Is Over', 'Pō Atarau', 'Give My Love to Rose', 'The Wayward Wind'. Irene loved 'Could We Start Again, Please?' from *Jesus Christ Superstar*, an eccentric addition for a family singalong, indeed, for the God-sneering Irene, but Yvonne Elliman was so moving as Mary Magdalene and there is no more powerful tide than repetition which becomes tradition. Sometimes they sang Jayne's late-entry favourite, 'A Kiss At the End of the Rainbow'—"It's corny", said Rita when Jayne first played it for her, "but at least it's not more goddamn Fleetwood Mac". Bufty loved 'Hine E Hine' and 'Buttons and Bows', and you could count on 'Goodnight, Irene'. In Jayne's absence, Marlon gamely strummed anything you like so long as it's three chords, and sometimes Bufty lifted the old pianny lid for 'Greensleeves' or 'Come Rain or Come Shine' or 'Somewhere Over the Rainbow', another favourite, the singularity of that word never having made an impression on Bufty.

The songs stayed the same, the food stayed the same, the plates and bowls and cups were the same, the same conversations, the same tensions papered over in the same ways, and this could comfort or suffocate, cause onlookers wild jealousy or stultifying boredom, and it would always be the same, and by the time it had changed, it would be impossible to work out when this change occurred or to which part of the whole.

The memory of their mother singing 'Hine E Hine' to Bufty and her sister was so worn from revisiting that she couldn't be sure it even happened, and there was no one left to verify it. Sissy's and Judy's stubborn faces softened as they sang, both convinced they could swing the high notes, Avery boomed the low notes from the floor, legs aloft. Rita got into the alto part in spite of herself. The twins, at the table, sang with indistinguishable voices. Pete and Peter contributed to the volume without overshadowing the real stars. Glenn knitted as he sang; Ben, less dextrous, had to pause. Jayne and Stevie flanked Irene, Stevie with her head on Irene's lap, Jayne behind her guitar radiating euphoria, singing pure and crystalline against Marlon's workmanlike warbling. Irene kept time with her stick, a wail at the margins of her words, like a bird calling to its lost mate over storm-crashed breakers.

The girls' features aptly reflected their temperaments: Marlon with her open, placid phiz, Judy and Rita with their square jaws and black brows, Jayne with her wide eyes on the brink of tears. But if Jayne were Judy, those eyes would burn with Judy's tenacity; if Rita were Marlon, she might smile more. Bufty didn't want to blink in case a frame of it vanished. Rita couldn't hide her secret forever. For now, singing, they were safe. Bufty could even pretend she didn't know it herself.

☾

"What an evening, Bufty, many happy returns."

"Thanks, Pete. You'll have to send us that little vege curry recipe, won't he Sissy."

"C'mon Ben—bags not driving. Are you coming with us, Irene?"

"Hmm. I am tired. But something's going on, I can feel it. I'll find out soon enough."

"We forgot my tarot reading," lamented Bufty.

"Come over tomorrow and I'll do it then," said Irene, accepting Glenn's hand. "You too, Flossie. You can do my hair."

Irene's scent—lavender, fresh-picked mint, orange peel, uncharted salt air—hit Stevie's sinuses with the same jolt as her dreams when she fell and hit the ground but landed awake in her bed, like she'd never stepped foot out of the country, the village, this room. "Of course I can," she said, the back of her eyes prickling. "Barely need to touch it though, you're looking grand."

"You come see me too, Rita. Sooner rather than later."

"I will." She knows. *She knows.*

The girls, and their girls, turned to Bufty. Diana eased the cork from the second bottle of Lindauer with a muted pop.

"Let's do a quiz," said Rita.

Buy a little time.

"Lovely!" Bufty understood.

The quiz emanated from a bulky 1984 edition of Trivial Pursuit, which they'd taken to answering a round or two from each night after dinner. Sharpens the mind, reckoned Avery, and Bufty, who roved Wikipedia for fun, adored it. Not one for parlour games, Rita tolerated the activity, but tonight exalted Avery for buying the book at the combined church bazaar in October.

The book's red dust jacket was tucked into last night's pages.

"Right. In 1987 and 1990, British Summer Time will start a week earlier to prevent it beginning on which day?" Avery read the questions with the same oratorical authority as she did the homily on Sundays.

"Oh, come *on*." Judy folded her arms over her chest.

"I was only crawling in 1987," said Sissy.

"You walked before any other baby in your year, mind you, Siss. Now, do you know, Stevie?" Judy turned to her niece. "You were just in England, weren't you?"

"Yes, but not in bloody 1987."

"It'll be Good Friday," said Bufty.

"I don't get it," said Sissy, "it's not summer in April in the Northern Hemisphere. Right, Stevie?"

"You should be a detective, Sissy."

"It's what they call Daylight Saving, bub," said Bufty.

"I give up," said Sissy.

Bufty, bellowing answers. The sisters finishing each other's sentences. Rita's mouth grew chalky, like she'd baked Irene's biscuits with too heavy a hand on the baking soda. The air pulsed against her head and throat in tandem with the Christmas lights. She couldn't remember the last time she'd blinked. Her family's voices faded into a blanketing silence around her.

Christ. All she had to do was tell her family she had cancer. This was no time to be sentimental.

"I've got this one," continued Avery. "Brigham Young. Strange man altogether. Next question: Who won Wimbledon's men's singles in 1939?"

"Who could possibly know that," snapped Judy. "Any more bubbles in that bottle, Di?"

"I'm going to say it was Peregrine Swift," said Marlon, twirling an imaginary moustache.

"Hughie McDiffle," Judy didn't miss a beat.

"Bertram Tallyrand," said Stevie. "This is astonishing, you've named both my High Commish superiors. Cracking chap, McDiffle. Can't say the same for the Mrs, though."

Bufty clapped her hands. "Daffyd Skunkington. Of Wales."

"I *caaaan't*. Go on, Rita," Jayne pierced Rita's thin-walled trance.

Shaking her head, brain landing back in the room like one of the flies, Rita rose to the occasion: "Clarence Beauregard-Beauregard."

"Now then, which 1935 film made Errol Flynn famous?"

"Oh! Oh! I know!" Bufty raised her hand. "It was *Captain Blood*."

"Has a nice ring to it, doesn't it," mused Jayne. "Captain Blood. Cap-tain-blood."

She smacked her knees with the words.

"Captain Blood! Captain Blood!" chanted Bufty and Marlon, clapping along.

Even the bewildered Rita joined in. Soon the whole room was chanting, "Captain Blood! Captain Blood!" and only stopped when Roger began howling. Jayne pulled him onto her lap and hugged him.

"Okay Rog, settle." Avery made use of her well-straught hamstrings as she bent forward to scritch the dog's head. "Question nine: where is the river Orinoco?"

"*Sail away, sail away, sail away,*" sang Marlon. "Sorry, I don't know. Trinidad? Argentina? Oh god, I've got the hiccups."

"What's question ten, Avery?" asked Stevie. "This is all quite diverting."

"That's it, there's nine questions," said Avery. "We usually do several rounds, but I thought a truncated version might be more amenable to the audience. Ready for the answers?"

"If someone in your line of business doesn't have all the answers," said Stevie, "I really don't know who could."

Good Friday. Ernest Borgnine. Ethel Merman. Bufty warbling 'There's No Business Like Show Business'. Alfred Schneider. Lenny Bruce.

Avery pointed at Jayne.

"Captain Blood! Captain Blood! Captain Blood!"

"Oh Christ," muttered Rita.

Roger scuttled down the hall. Jayne clambered to her feet and jogged in the same direction, returning with the dog in her arms.

"He's not used to such excitement." Rita leaned over to pat Roger's velvety ears. "We're usually much more sedate."

"Good rally." Avery snapped the book shut, and Rita's heart thumped with it.

Tempting to propose round two. But Avery was back on the carpet with her legs in the air.

At midnight, with the wine bottles hollowed, after Avery made a pot of tea, and Bufty spread Super Wine biscuits with butter, and everyone suddenly wanted Super Wine biscuits spread with butter more than anything in the world, after they let Roger and Jimmy Stewart out to relieve themselves and sorted their sleeping arrangements with a tumult of pillowcase-applying and unfolding of blankets, and after they turned up the volume to catch the end of *The Chase* rerun, only then, lit by the Christmas tree and the standing lamp behind Bufty's chair, the mermaid lamp on the piano, and the candles on the side table caving in, which Jayne couldn't stop poking to see how long she could bear to hold her fingertip in the searing wax, only then did Rita speak up.

"I won't beat around the bush."

"I thought Mum wanted to talk to us," said Judy. "Isn't that why we're all here?"

"Of course we'd be here anyway, Mum," added Marlon.

"That's right, Marlon," said Bufty, touching her paper crown, intact but split by hands oily with cake and chicken.

"What is it, Baby Ree?" said Jayne.

"If you'll let me finish."

Rita sat on her hands. Her family blurred in front of her into one enormous beast. You know what the hardest part is, said Avery to Rita that morning. The second hardest part is telling everyone. She had not ventured any further advice. Nor did she need to.

"Okay. I've got cancer."

"Oh my god," shrieked Bufty.

"Mum. I've already told you."

"Yes my love, but hearing it like that—it's like I'm hearing it for the first time."

A memory foamed in Marlon's mouth: that day she pilfered a teaspoon of sugar from a clay pot on the bench, but the white powder turned out to be salt.

"Is it bad?" Jayne looked instinctively to Irene's empty chair for guidance.

"It's cancer, Jayne."

Judy asked "How? What did you do?", Marlon listed off casseroles she could cook to fill the freezer, Jayne emitted unintelligible squeaks, Stevie swore and Bufty tried to reply to everyone at once.

"Oi!" Rita clapped twice. "It's my ovaries. I've got surgery as a first port of call. Less invasive than it sounds. If the surgery doesn't take, they can zap it away. Try to."

Marlon excused herself for the bathroom as the voices rose again. She opened the cabinet drawers. Toothbrushes in a brown mug from Stevie's pottery phase, potpourri in a terracotta bowl, fragrance long gone, a bottle of Buckley's Canadiol Expectorant and the memory of almost blacking out from suppressing a cough to avoid that caustic, horseradishy tonic. A pile of facecloths, Yardley lavender talc in a rusting tin, a tub of Nutrimetics apricot moisturiser—Judy was a star sales rep in the 1980s and still got discounts—and in the bottom drawer, a bulging and apologetic package of Tena lady pads. The fallibility of bladders, the fallibility of her family, was too much for Marlon. The gulp of a sob overtook her breath. *Come on now. Keep calm and carry on.* Marlon mopped her face with her tunic sleeve. In the sink, by the wet lip of the plughole, a waterlogged fly lay on its back, legs in the air. Like Avery doing her yoga. It probably didn't take much to drown a fly. Marlon ran the tap, flushing the little corpse down the drain. Everyone deserved a bit of dignity.

The hallway was the family gallery—the living on one side, the dead on the other, although too much overlap arose between the realms for them to stay separated. On one wall: photos of the girls and their children, orange-hued images in multi-picture frames, peeking out from oval windows with gold curlicue borders. Aunty Sweet with baby Judy on her hip; Wally and Bufty on their wedding day, squinting on Irene's verandah; Bufty and Avery's wedding on the lawn in 2013; Irene with her four grandchildren at Christmas 1965, paper crowns on every head; Jayne on her stomach caning it down a polythene sheet on the front lawn, Wally spraying it with the garden hose; Avery and Bufty at the Hero Parade with a bucket of condoms, Christmas tinsel draped across their shoulders like feather boas; the girls lined up for the first day of the school year, sweltering in the morning sun; the girls with their father in 1972, clinking brown beer bottles—even baby Rita—at the roof shout after he'd completed the sleep-out, his final project. Marlon examined herself in the photo, wearing a floral sarong tied between her legs to form loose trousers, a white t-shirt and rubber jandals with wide straps—*was my body ever so young?*

Photos of the ancestors lined the facing wall: Bufty's parents, their wedding day in sepia; young Wally in the sand shading his eyes from the sun; Irene with Wally's father, Albert; Irene's grandmother, Ruth; Avery's mother and father; a big framed photo of Whetū, Bufty's great-grandmother, in a starched middy blouse and long skirt, eyes searching far beyond the camera, holding a hunting knife as casually as a handbag. "She was a Māori princess," Bufty would say, with only her mother Clara's conviction on the subject as proof. They knew little about her, but Judy's family tree research indicated this honorific was wishful thinking. Next to Whetū hung an equal-sized photo of Princess Diana in a white bead-studded bolero. The two women complemented each other on the wall: both beautiful in a limpid, comprehensible way, both regal by public regard more than birth, both revered by Bufty. There was no talking her out of hanging Diana's picture in with the family. The way Bufty spoke about Princess Diana, she *was* family. Marlon was her mother's chief co-conspirator here—they both wore black for a month after her death in 1997—and she touched the frame on her way back to the lounge. What *would* Princess Diana do?

Back in the lounge, Jayne plucked her guitar, humming. Avery boiled the jug again, though no one needed a drink. Stevie straddled Rita's chair, imitating a colleague, stroking her chin to suggest a beard. It could've been another scene from another family party, with no bad news. The twins pored over an old photo album from the hutch dresser.

Judy looked miffed. Bufty hooted with laughter at Stevie, pressing her legs together. Rita has cancer: there's nothing to gain from indulging in melodramatics. Marlon hugged her youngest sister tight. Stevie layered herself on top, wrapping her arms around the pair.

"That painting of yours should go in the hall, Floss," said Marlon. "With the ancestors."

"For real?" Stevie retreated from the hug. "On the same wall as Princess Di?"

"Well, it is important."

"I might push off to Bedfordshire," said Avery, "since I'm on the clock soon, but you all carry on as long as you like, I don't mind the noise one bit."

"Oh god, is that the time." Marlon rubbed her eyes. "I will be stonkered tomorrow."

"Don't do that." Judy grabbed Marlon's wrist. "You'll get wrinkles."

"They won't be lonely up there," said Marlon.

"I guess that's that," said Bufty, downcast. She screwed her paper crown into a ball.

"There's leftover birthday cake you can have for breakfast," said Jayne, kissing her mother's cheek. "As long as there's cake, it's still your birthday."

☾

"Don't get me wrong, but why didn't you tell us sooner?"

Rita rolled over, dragging the duvet with her. The door to the sleep-out bathroom barely muffled Judy scouring her teeth.

"What difference would it make, crosspatch."

"Yeah, but." Judy spat out her toothpaste. "When did you tell Mum?"

"Two weeks ago. The day I found out."

"Hmm. How'd she take it?"

"Couldn't be happier. You're going to snore, aren't you."

Judy placed her phone on the side table next to a vase of flowers with dust on each faded petal. Whether the flowers were dead or dried intentionally wasn't clear. Dead, knowing Rita.

"Got it in one, Baby Ree. Might want to locate earplugs."

Rita clamped a pillow over her head.

The sliding door skidded open. Marlon's face peeked in.

"Knock-knock—only me—just wanted to say goodnight, John Boy."

"And I followed her, didn't I!" Jayne's face appeared above Marlon's.

"Fine." Rita emerged from under the pillow and lifted her chin to beckon them. "Make it snappy, don't stand there letting all the moths in."

Judy smoothed the duvet, crunching the goose down beneath its floral cover. Marlon climbed in beside Rita and ran her fingertips through her dark, bobbed hair. A jazzy cut for the unwhimsical Rita, though on her it was functional, its severe edges unsoftened by mimsy feathering.

Jayne flopped on her stomach in front of Judy.

"Are you scared?" she looked up at Rita with her big Bambi eyes, those eyes that in her youth made old ladies say, "Bless your heart, dear", and butchers hand her free chipolatas over their glass cabinets, those eyes that now sold pedestrian toothpaste-coloured wedding dresses from Shelley's Bridal to trusting brides-to-be.

Am I scared? Yes? No?

"I'm annoyed. There's so much admin." Rita tried to sound less robotic. "So much to think about. I don't want this to be all I think about."

"Susannah Hearn had cancer, hers was ovarian too, and she's all good now," said Marlon.

"Mind you . . ." Judy counted on her fingers. "There was Sharon Fuffer, she's been gone how many years? Then Tarns in 2001, and Mrs Taft."

"And Erana," said Rita. "Anyway."

"D'you remember back in the day," said Marlon, "Susannah's birthday party, when we all swung from the rope in their barn, landing in the hay bales?"

Jayne rested her chin in her hands. "I was so envious of you two for getting to play in the Hearn hay shed, it sounded straight out of Enid Blyton."

"Remember Anne finding that beer bottle and pretending to drink it, and it was full of cigarette butts and water and tipped all over her dress?" said Judy. "She was *furious*. And Irene, telling us about the barn burning down near her house when she was a kid, with all the children inside it."

"Oh, she haunted me with that one," said Jayne. "The worst was the one where the man's arm got chopped off in a combine harvester."

"What about the one with the entire family sucked into the sea? Or was it a woman riding a horse?" said Marlon.

"Both," said Rita. "That one was true, I think. Would've believed Irene if she'd told me left was right, but."

"I used to love that hay shed," said Judy. "Today's children wouldn't know how to occupy themselves on the farm like we did, what with their smartphones and Facebook and YouTubes." Most of the grandchildren eschewed Facebook long ago, while Judy slack-facedly scrolled the site every evening, sharing jokes too passé for a bathroom floor *Reader's Digest* and commenting a proliferation of emojis on pictures of her friends' grandchildren, accounts with cumbersome names like "TomAndJennySmithies" or "Susan Fenwick (née Binch)". And Bufty spent more time on the internet than all her grandchildren put together.

"Isn't it awesome having Stevie home? Mum's beside herself." Marlon dropped a foot to the ground. "Oof, my hips. Not what they used to be. Will she be around for a while, Jayne?"

"I sure hope so." Jayne shut her eyes and pressed her palms

in prayer. "I don't think this place is exciting enough for her, though. Not after London."

"How about her British accent though," said Judy. "Let's face it, it's like she's doing a bloody Hugh Grant impression."

"It must be two years since she was last home," said Marlon.

"Three, in January."

"That can't be right!"

"You're telling me."

Their voices marbled into one, Rita with her throaty drawl hinting at a meniscus of laughter which rarely overflowed; Jayne, with her cartoon voice like a door hinge in sore need of WD-40. Judy and Marlon's closest acquaintances couldn't differentiate them over the phone, and their voices in turn most resembled Bufty's, as though the inheritance had a finite value, all used up on her first two children. In laughter, too, they favoured their mother, raucous and piercing. Jayne would give a strangulated "a-*haaaa*" and fall into silent giggles. And Rita's laugh—should you ever get it—was about as captivating as it's possible for a laugh to be: low, resonant, implying great wit present in her as well as the person causing it.

Marlon's hands shook as she played with Rita's hair. This was different to their usual back-in-the-day talk. They needed to be with Rita, with each other. Did talking about old memories count as making new ones? It would do for now, a shared sentiment passed from sister to sister by osmosis.

In the study, Sissy snored on the double bed under the window bearing the same curtains as the lounge, brick-red, heavy as a dead body, and patterned with white fretwork. The twins lay on mattresses, the room so dark it made no difference if you opened or shut your eyes.

"Remember when we used to lie in here," said Mahalia, "and we'd think they were finally piping down for the night. And then one of them would start singing again."

"Remember when we played spotlight, and Ben hid out

on the road, and we couldn't find him for ages. We thought they'd kill us, and no one even noticed we were gone," said Diana.

"Mum wasn't much older than us," said Mahalia.

In the main bedroom, Bufty read her new *Wizard of Oz* book. Avery reread the Mary Oliver collection Bufty got her last Christmas.

Bufty placed her streaky reading glasses on the side table and stacked her book on top of Avery's *Introduction to Confucius* and *After Confucius*, a pairing that amused Bufty. She burrowed into Avery's lap. The sleeves of her long white nylon robe flowed onto the bedspread, like moonlight reflecting in the dogs' water bowls.

"That was a lovely birthday. Aren't I lucky, all of you so good to me. And how about Irene, giving me the cutlery set? It's funny isn't it, they all assumed I'd say something outrageous tonight, and it turned out to be Rita . . . it should be me though, shouldn't it, it's all out of order, it's not right. Irene's son dying before her, and now me with Rita . . . how is she so strong about it all? How do you learn that? How do you *bear* it?"

Avery ran her knuckles over Bufty's ear, bringing her palm to rest on her hair.

"I feel a bit jealous of Irene," continued Bufty, "not knowing yet. Although she probably does in her way. I wish we could all go back to the other day before Rita told us, don't you? It's not that it didn't exist then, but . . . if you don't know . . . then there's the girls, it's such a dreadful thing to lose a sister, I can't bear the thought of my babies going through that. Oh, why couldn't it have been me?"

Avery read from her book, low, steady.

"How can this be, but it is. 'Every day has something in it whose name is Forever'."

Over Avery's reciting, Bufty heard doors opening and shutting, floorboards yielding under footsteps, a honk of laughter from Jayne.

And in the lounge, the Christmas lights threw pops of colour like dancing stars, and on the couch, Stevie stared at the sleeping wasps, only just visible in that room drenched with shadows.

Chapter Four

Sharon Fuffer
Breast cancer
25 October 1986

"Mind you, doesn't everyone walk into a room full of strangers expecting one of them to ask you out?" Judy spooned more mustard sauce onto her potatoes. "Me and Sharon do, of course."

"No," said Marlon and Rita.

"Of course," said Bufty, squeezing Wally's hand. He'd only eaten a mouthful of corned beef and would go back to the memorial hospital tomorrow, but having the family together around the table was what mattered.

"Well, you're just a baby, Baby Ree. You'll understand when you get to high school. Sharon and I have a notebook where we've written all our little sayings because you have to be prepared: magnanimous rejections, how to accept without looking fast, sizing up who your best option is . . . you know what I mean? You could meet your next boyfriend anywhere, at school, even in an elevator. Especially an elevator."

"Where would you find an elevator round here?" asked Rita.

Jayne, breastfeeding baby Stevie, shut her eyes and swayed from side to side.

Judy Gordon was the prettiest girl in her year. The nurse had told a spent, panting Bufty that this was the bonniest baby she'd seen in her long career—"Why, she could sell Pears soap, no word of a lie!" Bufty had to admit it reassured her to be told this, after nine-pound Marlon with her square head she still hadn't grown into yet, and Hetty Loomis remarking "Isn't Marlon the living spit of you," *three times* when she dropped in for an unwanted visit. No one could tell Bufty her children weren't the most sublime expressions of the earth's possibilities, but Marlon's head really was comically large on arrival, until the rest of her caught up, like the last grains of corn popping in the bottom of the pan, in time for her first day of school in October 1959.

Everyone was privy to Judy being the prettiest in her year, as she trotted out this information in the way other people might offer party trivia about how high fleas can jump, or how three of America's founding fathers all died on the fourth of July, and everyone tolerated Judy's arrogance, treating it as an inevitability. From this vantage point, she acknowledged Sharon Fuffer's respectable good looks and pursued a friendship as if it were an act of altruism. While shared beauty isn't enough for most people to build an alliance, Judy had a keen sense of the pecking order. She knew, in her finely cut bones, she and Sharon had to be friends or the planet would roll clean off its axis.

And friends they stayed, through dances and school recitals, then later parties and afternoon concerts at Western Springs where you'd drive up, eight, nine, ten of you packed into the Triumph Herald, then weddings and babies with rotund bellies wriggling side by side on a picnic blanket.

☾

Marlon rotated her glass tumbler, using her jersey sleeve to absorb the condensation trail it left behind. On the other side of the table, Judy bounced baby Ben on her lap and smushed her nose against his head. He followed the movement of her stacked bangles in alert fascination.

"God, don't babies smell *divine*? It makes me want another one so badly. And then I think of Sissy and—zip—no way, José. She's pretty, thank goodness, bright as a button, but—I'm just going to say it—she's a real piece of work already, Marlon, not at all like her brother. Or, God forbid, I could end up with another you-know-who on my hands like Jayne . . . you are lucky with the twins, Marlon, they're ever so good. And now look at this little sausage, not saying boo. Why did you get all the luck?" Again, Judy pressed her face against Ben's.

The twins behaved because Marlon gave in to them. Ben's nappy had exploded into his car seat twice this month. It was all relative.

"Careful though, your eyeshadow—"

Judy licked her thumb and rubbed the navy-blue patch from Ben's head. "Never mind him. Am I smudged?"

"You're fine. No, wait—it's streaked a bit on your eyebrow—here." Marlon pulled her sleeve over her thumb and wiped her sister's face.

Judy stared into her empty glass.

"Oh, god! Sharon."

"Yes, of course, Sharon. Thank goodness the twins look after each other. What was left of my brain after I had them has been shot to billy-o since this little potato entered the world." Marlon rounded her arms and puffed out her cheeks. "If we're doing a toast, we'd better get another round. Don't worry, my shout, you go get it though, Jim pours more in the glass when you order. There's money in my purse." She reached over across the table and clapped. "Pass Baby here."

"Bacardi and lemonade?"

"Bacardi and lemonade," said Marlon, sniffing Ben's little head. It hadn't felt so little during the eight-hour labour. "Gosh, he does smell delicious—it's baby witchcraft, to keep us breeding."

Judy returned with two more glasses, and Marlon's purse tucked under her arm.

"Jim's shout, isn't he sweet?" Judy waved delicately at Jim behind the bar, waggling her third and fourth fingers. "Mind you, we must be getting on when a funeral is the social event of the season. I've got my royal-blue dress to wear. The taffeta one. And my slingbacks. I wonder if Rowan Clackhearst will be there. Remember him? He was so in love with me." She shuffled her bra underwire upwards, as if in anticipation. "Poor Mish, he is absolutely gone, he doted on Sharon. She got all her good looks from him, didn't she? Now *there's* a man who'll die with his boots on, believe me."

"Poor old Mrs Fuffer too," replied Marlon, bouncing Ben on her left knee. "You're right, Sharon does—did—favour Mish. Now look . . ." Marlon pursed her lips and crossed her eyes at Ben. "No one's denying it's a knockout dress, but your blue taffeta's a bit low-cut, don't you think? The funeral's at 11AM, not 11PM."

"Sharon couldn't wear that shade of blue. She was a spring, you know, darker colours drained her. Let's face it, I suit the whole rainbow. The lady at the Amway party was so kerflummoxed, she said she could pick anyone's colours, but she'd met her match with me. 'I'm a woman for all seasons,' I told her . . ." A description Judy herself found plenty of opportunity to use. "Anyway, you can't trust an Amway lady, I said to Sharon, it's Nutrimetics all the way for me . . ."

With her free hand, Marlon picked up the glass.

"Here's to Sharon Fuffer, a good woman, and a battler to the end."

Judy tapped her glass against Marlon's.

"*Amen*. And now there's no one as pretty as her left in our year, besides me of course. Did you know, when we were in the primmers, Mrs Bletch used to call us Snow White and Rose Red? I always liked that."

"How darling." Marlon knew this. She kissed Ben's head, leaving a film of Lobster Bisque lipstick matting his angora hair.

"Poor Ben," she said, patting away the lipstick. "He's ended up wearing more makeup than anyone. Honestly, I think I'm just too cack-handed for lipstick. But I'll definitely keep buying that apricot moisturiser off you."

"Looks like the Gordon dark hair is coming in already," said Judy. "You know, Sharon had beautiful golden hair . . . I always told her, Sharon, one day some man will marry you for that hair, and I was right . . ."

Judy hunched forward, chin meeting her chest. Three tears splatted onto the table. Marlon moved to sit beside her. Cradling Ben's head in one arm, she pulled a handkerchief from her bag and blotted her sister's face.

"It's such a fucking waste," said Judy. "Sorry for swearing in front of Baby."

"It's fine."

"We're too young, aren't we? This isn't supposed to happen until we're old and grey. The last time I saw Sharon she said she'd been frantic for a good night's sleep after Janine was born, and if she could do it over, she wouldn't have slept a wink so she could spend a few more hours with her daughter. This morning when I saw Sissy in her cot, it was as if Sharon were standing right behind me saying it. And I . . ." Judy flicked her hands away from her face. "Whoosh. Deluge."

Marlon shifted Ben, so she could hold him and put her arm around Judy at the same time.

"You're right, bub. It's too young, it's not fair, and that's about all there is to it."

"God, my eyeshadow really will be a mess. Fuck's sake. Sorry Ben, sorry, sorry, sorry."

"It's okay. He's a baby. He's got no idea." Marlon rumpled Judy's hair and lowered her voice. "He doesn't know *fuck all*, and he won't remember any of this, I promise."

"Marlon! I'm telling everyone at the funeral you swore, and in front of an innocent babe at that."

"Ah, got you to smile though, see?"

"I'm ringing the newspaper," Jim called over. "Marlon Gordon said a cuss word."

Marlon raised her half-empty glass and smiled at him. "Go fff—" she suddenly felt as though Irene might be standing behind her "—fly a kite, Jim."

"That's it," Jim pretended to faint. "Your next round's on me, too."

Chapter Five

Six kilometres of narrow, slanting road connected the village and its nearest town, severing drab ochre paddocks interspersed with browbeaten macrocarpas and placid, ruminating livestock yet to receive the memo about their severance. The line on the map, like an absent-minded trail of cigarette ash, was scant as the crow flies, though back when you had to drive over gravel and the entire world lived and died between the start and the end of your road, the trip north presented more of an undertaking. Wind knocked the macrocarpas this way and that till they froze, stooping or bent backwards as if struck hard in the back of the knees. Every spindly branch pointing elsewhere, warning you—begging you—to get the hell out.

Irene's Beach, as the girls had christened it in their logical youth, fringed the south edge of the village at a walkable distance. Between collective indifference and the deadly west coast tide motivated only by its next drowning, no one thought to label the area a beachy holiday destination, and little would suggest that such a magnificent natural feature lay moments away from this relative dump.

The nearby town earned a paragraph on Wikipedia noting that no fewer than three men rode in to claim and rename it, with authority, prosperity and glory surely to follow, and no fewer than three men were drummed out by the local iwi, who stood their ground and had little use for the settlers and their bagatelles. Then came World War I, the Spanish flu, depleted resources and parcels of land confiscated by the government, and the town was finally taken.

Lining its streets were: a poky supermarket; two hairdressers; three liquor shops; a church op shop; a couple of bland sandwich bars, rooted far enough in the past to be outdated, but not far enough to be quaint; the fruit and vege store; and a few corner dairies. There were three shops named A1 Takeaways to elbow their way to the top of the phone books, which most people nowadays used for fire starters, but you could tell which A1 people were referring to by the cadence of their utterance. You used to be able to buy appliances, fabric, fishing supplies, anything at all, but those shops went under, uniqueness fell from favour, and locals set their sights on the suburbs with their big box retail outlets all laid out the same. Why stump up for an expensive microwave from Pruitt's Electrical when you could compare dozens of microwaves, lulled into an extratemporal stupor by unchanging fluorescent lighting?

The busiest establishment in town was the Lans' Mostly Two Dollar Shop. Where else could you buy tin openers, those dinky leatherette phone cases with a slot for your bank cards, and colouring pencils for the grandkids, all in one place and for a tidy price? Older Pākehā locals, happy to disparage a 'Made in China' label while still doing their Christmas shopping within the narrow aisles of The Mostly Two Dollar Shop, spoke of the Lans in such a supportive way it veered round towards racism again: *these* two Chinese people were acceptable, but the rest had a long way to go and many hurdles to surmount, and would be found wanting. When the Lans moved to town, Bufty, suspecting their path into the area might not be straightforward, welcomed them by showing up at the shop on its opening day with a pasta bake, and when she found out that Tulip was expecting, she knitted her a baby blanket.

If in justifiable need of an intoxicant, you had two options. First, the dingy Cossie Club behind the rest home, though this institution's relevance took a nosedive as young people left for the cities, drink-driving laws grew more punitive and the internet taught local women to subject their wider families to great expense and upheaval by holding their nuptials at some distant waterfall or winery.

The more promising choice of establishment, and second-busiest place in town after The Mostly Two Dollar Shop, was Mahalia and Diana's bar, The Chariot. After ten years of pouring top-shelf clear spirits down the gullets of Wellington public servants, and weary from rising rent prices, the twins chucked it all in and returned home, pooling their KiwiSaver funds to purchase The Thirsty Steer and its upstairs flat. The previous owner, desperate to offload his perishing pub, sold the property for a song and threw in the keg lines and deep fryer to boot.

The name didn't sit right with the twins, who had little tolerance for mawkish pastoral motifs. Unable to reach a conclusion, they paid a visit to Irene for a tarot reading.

"No matter what card you pick, that's what we'll name the bar," said Diana. "Even if it's the Nine of Shit."

"There is no Nine of Shit card, Diana."

"That's why I'm so confident, Irene."

Irene pulled The Chariot. Determination, bringing goals to fruition, forward motion and—Irene pointed at the two sphinxes—the power of duality.

"Bloody meant to be," said Mahalia.

And so, The Chariot jockeyed to success, to the surprise of everyone but the twins themselves.

“This town sucks, Mum,” explained Diana, “but people still deserve—you know—”

“A decent pint,” finished Mahalia. “The Cossie Club carpet has stains older than us. And where else can you hang out? Not Twisted Peppa cafe. That linoleum belongs in a public toilet. Their sign’s written in *Papyrus*. Even Comic Sans would be better. And the name. Twisted Peppa. C’mon. Where’s the integrity.”

“C’mon, Mum,” echoed Diana. “Cringe. Where’s the honour.”

“They make a good hot coffee,” reasoned Marlon. “I don’t like it when my coffee isn’t hot enough.”

“That’s a low bar, Mum.”

“Low Bar—now, that would be a good name for your pub!”

The perspicacious twins gave their customers what they didn’t realise they’d been missing, without scaring them off by being too townie. Lagers, ales, no pretentious green bottles tasting only of enforced masculinity and sporting sponsorship, no over-hopped $14 IPAs flavoured with mustard. A reliable speed rack for your spirit-and-mixer crowd, an unthreatening but substantial top shelf. They served three food options: mini pies, sourced from the hot bread shop two doors down, who were pleased to have this steady income on their books; mini samosas with Bufty’s tomato relish; and curly fries, left in the oil three minutes too long to render them extra crispy. The twins had to buy a second freezer for the curly fries. People came from the next town over to order them. And no wonder.

“The Cossie Club chips are medium rare at best,” sneered Mahalia. Marlon couldn’t disagree, let alone suggest an unnecessary positive spin.

Spurning the prevailing wisdom that every watering hole should have a TV playing the sports channel on mute, the twins spent hours building music playlists, and on quiet weeknights they’d pull up a projector and run old films: *Casablanca* or *His Girl Friday*. *Mrs. Miniver* or *The*

Thin Man. Bufty came out for those, even when the wind whipped the rain into your face like an insult, and even when she had the films on her terabyte hard drive—often as not she was the one supplying the files to the twins. The town was too slight for Uber, so the twins sorted a shuttle service to ferry carousers home. The pair shouldered most of the work, paying local youths a living wage to wash dishes and help close up. Mahalia's duty manager's certificate expired before she left Wellington, but she pretended to be Diana if it came up, and the local coppers showed little curiosity. Nor did they notice how, with the click of a blue button on the cash register labelled 'piggy tax', the twins charged them a dollar more for their beers. In the bar's first week, Marlon came out every night with Glenn for a small sav and a plate of curly fries to support her girls, and to make it look as though they had customers. She needn't have: The Chariot thrived.

There was something weird about the twins. Something *off*. Staring at you like you'd run over their cat. No husbands in 'Beach BBQ Boats' t-shirts, no noisy spawn. So eerily synchronised, you never knew which one you were talking to. And why did they dress in black all the time?

Diana and Mahalia were, however, blessed with a quality that could overcome all small-town misgivings: those girls worked hard. Twin noses to the grindstone.

Had any of the locals looked beyond the layers of black ripped denim and taken a spatula to the smeared recesses of their memories, they might recall why they were correct about the twins. They *were* kind of weird.

Marlon gave birth to two girls on the fourth day of April. But Diana and Mahalia weren't twins. Precisely one year separated them.

Wrenching the devoted pair apart for school caused such misery that Marlon surrendered and sent them off together, one aged five, one aged four. Kids born before May got bumped up or held back. This decision solidified it. No longer a family in-joke, they were twins now, and if not for one or two photo albums and a Plunket book, its pages bound with pink thread, even Marlon struggled to remember which sister appeared first.

☾

Mahalia and Diana's eyes opened at the same time on the morning after Bufty's birthday.

In the kitchen, Rita opened the fridge and removed a plastic bread bag. She pulled two pieces from it, dropping them into the toaster. She handed the bag to Jayne, who also took two pieces of bread, ripping them into shreds over a shallow, white porcelain bowl with a forest-green rim, an action so decisive it should've made the sound of tearing paper. While Rita waited for her toast to pop, she hooked her finger into the flat metal pantry handle and took out the rose-patterned butter dish, the sugar jar and a shaker of cinnamon. Jayne poured milk into a 250ml Pyrex, faded red lines circumnavigating the glass like veins threading a wrist, and placed it in the microwave. She pressed start, sending the jug on a circuit of the enclosed space.

The microwave beeped. The toast popped. Rita buttered each slice, thick and yellow as marzipan hugging a fruitcake. Jayne upended three spoons of sugar over the torn-up bread pieces and slid the crock of sugar towards Rita. It made an amiable, fricative noise as it moved across the bench. Rita grabbed a fistful of sugar, containing it for less than a second before the grains fell through the cracks in her fingers. She unclenched her hand over the buttered toast, raining down sugar. Jayne poured the hot milk over her torn bread. Rita shook cinnamon over her toast, patting the jar on its glassy rump. Using her butter knife, she sliced each piece of toast into triangles, licked the flat blade, and dropped it in the sink. The sisters walked in silence to the kitchen table: Rita with her plate, Jayne with her bowl, sugar dissolving grittily into butter, sugar dissolving wetly into milk. They sat next to each other, and they ate their breakfast.

As they ate, Bufty appeared like a plump, chatty ghost in her white nylon dressing gown; followed by the twins, yawning and requesting coffee, complaining under their breath about Sissy's snoring; Judy, swathed in a green robe; and Marlon, dressed already.

Stevie, face down on the couch, rolled over and fanned herself with a dribble-stained pillow. Jayne, now wandering around in her bunny slippers strumming her guitar, lifted Stevie's feet and sat beneath them.

"How is this heat so soupy already? Take me back to winter in London."

"It's only just begun, Floss," said Bufty.

"*We've only just begun . . .*" sang Jayne and Marlon. Jayne took Stevie's pillow and bopped Marlon's legs.

"And how anyone is awake right now is beyond me," said Stevie, covering her eyes with her forearm. "Let alone singing."

"It's 9AM!" Marlon pulled the pillow from Jayne and whumped Stevie with it. "The day's half over."

"I wish the other half would get a move on too, so I could go back to bed."

"Is it jet lag, babe?" asked Jayne. "I've heard it's real harsh when you're coming from so far away."

Stevie pointed at her mother. "Yes, I think I still have a touch of the old 'lag, please forgive me being out of sorts."

Sissy drove back up to Auckland. The whirlwind of household industry sucked Judy and Marlon away into its vortex: "it's sheet-washing day", "another blasted mouse got into the pantry", "the lettuces need a good watering". Avery left for her Sunday church orbit, and the twins went back to The Chariot. Stevie drove Jayne and Bufty to Irene's for Bufty's birthday tarot reading.

Rita sat cross-legged in the window seat with her novel while Jimmy Stewart slept in the crevice of her lap. The flies droned like descending aircraft. Neighbourhood dogs postured for kingpin. Sheep let out guttural noises like laughing old drunks. The fridge hummed. The floorboards creaked as though her mother's bare feet still approached, those footsteps like a length of masking tape peeling off Formica. Nothing in this house could leave her alone. Not even the nothingness. Rita opened her book to the same place she'd propped it open on yesterday. She didn't turn the page.

☾

Barely three minutes' drive from the Gordon homestead, the gaunt road to Irene's slipped away into steep chasms on the passenger side, but rewarded you with a peep at Heaven itself, an endless horizon waiting for the sun to lower like a dowager countess sinking into a divan; miles of sand to your left and right, and those waves—chomping at the fudgy sand, luring you with their siren call. Irene terrorised the girls with stories of lost souls—"that tide could swallow a man in an instant, like losing a sock up the vacuum cleaner"—and Wally was raised in the shadow of these stories of children carried from the rip tide up to the house to be laid by the fire, covered in blankets and given a little brandy while Irene galloped on Robber Baron to fetch a doctor. Irene knew the family whose parents' bodies never washed up, knew the name of the horse that bucked Eileen Tenneman and disappeared under the foam. She did not need to embellish her stories much at all to instil fear in her grandchildren.

Her house, battered by exposure, looked as though it belonged more than the rapacious properties increasingly occupying the same area code. Out-of-towners and investors—and allegedly, one ex-All Black, though a name had never been settled on—purchased these houses when they left it too late to land a Coromandel property and visited them once or twice a year, a hint at Auckland's creeping spread into its most humble and far-flung regions. Judy still talked about the summer of 2015 when she saw a woman with *botox* in the local New World, buying herbed low-carb crackers, smoked salmon and prosecco—not Lindauer!

If you stood on the beach near the Seussical tufts of sand tussock, you could see Irene's verandah. The girls—and later their children—engraved uneven words into the sand with sticks: *hello Irene*; *happy birthday, Irene*; *we love you, Irene*. From this verandah Irene watched the sun rise and fall, holier in the presence of those waves and the sky than she ever felt in a church.

"Hulloooo," called Bufty, slipping off her shoes at the unlocked door.

Irene stood on the verandah, her thin shoulders enshrouded like a seed pod in a knitted shawl the same bloodshot shade as her nails.

Bufty, Stevie and Jayne walked through the hall and into the main quarters—an open-plan kitchen with a Kelvinator stove, a wooden floor laid with a woven mat, a rust-coloured couch draped in blankets next to the fireplace and four plain wooden chairs around a kitchen table in the corner.

"You're here. I'll make a tea, and then we'll get cracking. There's biscuits in the container in the cupboard."

"I've missed this," said Stevie, gripping the verandah railings and leaning forwards, inhaling the salty air. "*Now* I'm home."

"Don't you worry, Irene, we've brought fruitcake," said Bufty. "But the more the merrier. What's the brew today?" She found the tall, sage-green container with its round fluted lid and passed it to Stevie and Jayne. Irene made a point of keeping more biscuits than she ate.

"Fennel, with orange peel," said Irene. "They'll help a crook stomach, if anyone's worse for wear after the hoolie. I've never been hungover once in my life, but I won't assume you lot inherited my constitution."

"You always saw the hangover as a moral failing, didn't

you?" said Stevie. "I believe my mother, for one, is morally failing as we speak."

"That's right, girl."

Every last tarot card in Irene's deck was made with her two hands, and this labour and care and time lent them an air of inviolability, on top of the meaning each picture symbolically carried. After Wally's father died, Irene saved scraps of butcher paper and newsprint, whatever she could find or solicit, ripping every piece into shreds, soaking the shreds in rainwater, pressing the gruel flat and drying it out on her verandah, ballasted by rocks to stop the parched sheets flying away, before slicing them into rectangles and using the offcuts to begin again, the whole melted down and made whole again several times over, and in this process, she became whole again herself. She collected paint samples and discontinued stock, pinned a note to the bulletin board outside Reynold's shop, asked friendly looking men if they had anything she could barter for. She painted each card referencing the Rider–Waite book she'd written away for: The Tower, Six of Cups, King of Wands, The Sun, and once complete she held a blessing ceremony under the full moon. Those cards were the cornerstone of her success in the village. It was one thing to have your palms read, or to buy a herb sachet to help the baby sleep or fix your husband's bald patch, but to see those exalted cards, so evident of the dedication Irene gave her practice, felt sacred even to the pious. Like your future was not only known, but about to begin.

"Birthday girl first, shall we?"

"That's right," said Bufty, hands wrapped around a dove-grey teacup. "My birthday isn't over till I say so. And I say it'll be over at the stroke of midnight before my next birthday. Now, let me get the cards for you, Irene, you stay put."

"No, I'll get them for *you*, Mama, you should sit too," said Jayne.

"Is this my cue to offer to get them for you, Mum?" asked Stevie. "And then you can pass them up the line to Irene?

You're not getting younger, but neither am I. Is there some nearby urchin who I can enlist to duly fetch the cards for me? Let it not be said that I forced my own mother to walk across the room while I've breath in my lungs!" Stevie made a show of passing the cards to Jayne, who solemnly raised them over her head and lowered them into Bufty's hands. Bufty, giggling, handed the cards to Irene with her head dipped.

Irene unfolded the cards from their indigo silk scarf onto the kitchen table.

"Now, then. Do you want to cut the pack, or shall I shuffle them for you?"

"Let's have a little shuffle." Bufty shifted in her chair with a groan so faint it was difficult to discern whether it emanated from her or the wood below. "I want time to get my energy *perfect*, so I get the perfect card for my birthday. If we rush it, I might get the cards all in a muddle."

"Fair dues."

"Hmm . . ." Bufty squeezed her eyes shut and hovered her hands over the cards as Irene moved them from the bottom of the pack to the top. "Not yet—ooh, maybe this one—no wait, keep shuffling, it was the breeze coming through the window, oh, I don't know, maybe my energy is a bit dicky—wait! Stop! That one."

Irene, who had seen Bufty react this way to the cards every year since they first met, remained unstartled.

"Queen of Pentacles."

"Ohh, isn't that lovely? The Queen! I knew the cards wouldn't disappoint, not on my birthday! Wait, is this a good one? I've never had it before. Oh, please say it's good, Irene, make it up if it's not."

"It's good," said Irene.

"Ahh, didn't I say? Go on Irene, give me a profuse rundown please, I love this part."

"The Queen of Pentacles," said Irene, "is conscientious and generous. Her home is welcoming to guests; she is practical but loves her luxuries and makes everyone feel welcome."

Bufty clapped her hands.

"She's at home in the countryside, amongst nature and animals. A caregiver and nurturer. She has put in a lot of work to get where she is, and—see how she's sitting—she can reflect on her achievements. She represents security and safety, for herself and those in her life."

"My goodness, this is too much." Bufty patted under her eyes with a handkerchief from her handbag. "I couldn't have picked a better card if I'd had them all laid out face up."

"But see the pentacle in her lap—" Irene traced her finger over the card. "It represents riches and possessions. All nice to have, but beware superficiality and immaturity. And see how her head is bowed, and everything is behind her? She's got secrets tucked away in the back of her mind and should be mindful not to let them get the better of her."

"Oh no!"

"Calm down, girl. It's a good card. You've done fine. Look at how happy the queen is—all those roses around her, the green grass. She's a kind and magnanimous leader and taking her rightful place as matriarch of her family."

"You're the rightful matriarch, silly!"

"I've only been silly once, in 1922," said Irene, impassive as a two-by-four. "Sat backwards on Aunty Merry's horse and pretended I was in the circus. It wasn't for me. The card says what it says."

"But what lovely words," faltered Bufty. She kissed Irene's cheek. "Roses, luxuries, a queen . . . that was perfect, I'll fair float home."

"Jayne?" asked Irene.

"Not me, I'm here for the ride, to spend time with you all. Besides, I'm still dining out on my last birthday reading. That was a doozy and a half, wasn't it, Irene?"

"That's right. Floss?"

"How can I follow up a performance like Nana's? Can't I defer it till after Christmas? I left my energy somewhere over the equator, to paraphrase Dorothy."

Irene beckoned her to the table.

"Okay, okay, you're gonna make me an offer I can't refuse, I get it." Stevie rose from the couch and pulled a wooden chair around to face Irene. "Let's shuffle, gives me time to gather my wits about me . . . such as they are . . ." Stevie held her hands over Irene's.

"Sorry lads," said Stevie, after a minute of Irene shuffling, "I zoned out . . . was thinking about that fruitcake of yours, Nana, if I'm honest . . . keep going, Irene, I'll focus up, I promise."

"I do make a fine fruitcake, don't I?" said Bufty.

"Alright Irene, that will do. What's on the board, Miss Ford? Death, decay, destruction or worse, one of those funny little guys holding sticks?"

Irene turned the card over. "Three of Wands."

"There you go. A funny little guy holding sticks."

"Ooh, I've had him before," said Jayne.

"*Très* auspicious," said Bufty. "What does it mean, Irene?"

"It's terrible, isn't it," said Stevie. "Just my luck. My crops will wither, all my scones will taste like rocks, every dog on the street will snap at my heels, I'll be struck down with the clap—"

"When you're ready, Floss." Irene pointed at the figure depicted on the card. "See, he's standing on a precipice, over the water. A bit like my verandah, there. No other card has a person with their back turned like this. He's looking towards the future—but what is he hiding? Those boats on the water represent his prospects, the world past the horizon, the world he needs to embrace."

"Sounds like menial labour," said Stevie, "trust me to get a bad card."

"There's no such thing as a bad card, girl. It's what you make of it. The Three of Wands is about confidence—about making a decision and sticking to it. Fortune favours the brave, as the saying goes. If you don't like your life, change it. There, you see?"

Jayne leaned forward in her seat. "Wow, babe."

Stevie rubbed the back of her neck. "Hell's bells, Irene. When you're on, you're on."

"How so, Floss?"

"Oh, much to think about, as always! Now, shall I wash your hair for you? But first, where's Nana's fruitcake, my energy is seeking it, I foresee a small slice of it in my near future—"

They were piling into Stevie's car to head home, when Bufty said she'd forgotten her glasses.

"Hullo, Irene? I've come back for my specs, I'd forget my head if it wasn't screwed on."

Irene stood on the verandah again, her long hair rising like shapeshifting clouds.

"They're on top of your head," she said, without turning around.

"So they are, silly me. I guess I'll leave you to it . . ."

Irene rested her hand on Bufty's, her slender fingers like twigs against Bufty's cushiony paw. Their nails, garnet and fuchsia, glowed in the high noon sun.

"Life is a gift, but it's also a bloody curse when people you love die. And the more people die, the more it feels they're the lucky ones and you're the fool left alone. You have to keep going, and you will keep going. Because that's what they'd do if they could. And as long as you've got their memory, you'll never be alone. Everyone who has gone before you is here with you and they want you to live. So, you keep going. That's about all there is to it." Irene continued looking straight ahead into the glittering water as she spoke. "Matriarchs don't last forever, you know. The card wanted to find you."

Bufty blinked hard and touched the glasses on her head. "They really were here all along, weren't they?"

"I know, girl."

Chapter Six

Rhonda Taft
Bone cancer
19 April 1993

Mrs Rhonda Taft was briskly urinating in the shower on the night before her thirty-fifth anniversary as school secretary when she died five different ways.

The coroner's report relayed a narrative any potboiler author would be proud to sign their name to. Rhonda was already dehydrated when she turned the taps righty-tighty to save tank water while she shaved her legs in her mildewy bathroom. The gush of scalding water when she turned the shower back on shocked her blood pressure into plummeting, and Rhonda fainted, slamming her head against the rim of the tub. Which might have been what killed her. The fall's impact caused Rhonda to scrape her pink BIC Lady razor across her upper thigh, and its hair-matted blades sliced into her femoral artery, releasing enthusiastic red sheets of blood. Which might have been what killed her. The toxic, ammonia-scented purple leave-in conditioner intended to give a pearly bloom to Rhonda's yellowing hair seeped into her unlatched mouth as she lay sprawled in the bathtub.

Which might have been what killed her. Rhonda's left heel slotted into the plughole—*shump*—and the falling water rose around her naked, clean-shaven body, filling her sinuses and throat. Which definitely didn't help.

Had Sherlock Holmes attended this calamitous scene, he might hypothesise that Rhonda could have prevented her many simultaneous deaths by simply drinking a glass of water earlier that day. And Sherlock Holmes would be, to his satisfaction but not surprise, correct. For another week or two, at least.

The coroner's report revealed one further killer in the bathroom. Rhonda Taft was riddled with bone cancer.

Fatigue plagued Rhonda in her final months. Her joints ached, but didn't everyone's back droop and ache at her age? But Rhonda Taft's generation was mercilessly stoic. Had she been born a few decades later as a child of helicopter parents, she might've investigated the symptoms. But it never occurred to anyone, certainly not Rhonda Taft, that the frame of her body was withering away underneath her skin.

Though she started the job two weeks after her twenty-eighth birthday, Mrs Taft seemed ancient when the girls were at the primary school. It's possible that beneath the stubbly cardigans, cat's eye spectacles and bleached hair sculpted into a coil not unlike a jam roly-poly, there was a young woman to behold. The girls couldn't see it, and they shivered in fear at this spectre of their futures as humdrum grown-ups.

Her daughter Sue asked Avery to lead the funeral service.

"Daft Old Taft never liked me," said Avery to Bufty, hanging up the phone. "As for Sue Taft, if ever someone looked like they were walking around with their underwear on backwards! She insisted on calling you my *friend* in the snidest tone . . ."

"No, she didn't like you," said Bufty. "In fact, she really hated you. But they are Anglicans, and it's better than having a townie do the service."

In honour of Mrs Taft's service to the school, a small ficus was planted by the maypole, with a plaque. The coroner presumed the body evacuating accounted for the urine in the bathwater at her death, so at least some aspects of Rhonda's last moments remained between her and God.

Chapter Seven

"That was Irene on the phone just now," said Bufty to Rita, who was reading cross-legged in the La-Z-Boy. Rita sat there so often Bufty half expected the sun to have bleached the outlined silhouette of her body into the fabric. "She's summonsed you for a little visit. She knows there's funny business afoot, but she needs you to tell her, and woe betide you, Molly Whuppie, if you try to pull the wool over her eyes. Best to get it over with, don't you think? Did you have any plans today . . . ?"

Rita draped *The Heart Is a Lonely Hunter* over her face. They both knew the answer.

"Fine." She folded the corner of her page over and closed the book. "Guess I'm going for a drive."

The Heart Is a Lonely Hunter. What a title. Urgently beautiful. Made her want to write the words in different sizes and colours like a schoolgirl scrawling her crush's name. A heart perched on the *i*. Not that Rita dealt in such fancies. And she could count on one hand the number of hearts she'd drawn in her fifty-odd years. But the words looped like an incantation.

Avery flicked the kettle switch. "Cuppa before you vamoose, Rita?"

"No. Ta."

Avery called up the hallway to Stevie, who emerged from the bedroom swinging her open laptop by its base, as though it didn't matter if it hit the wall or fell to the ground.

"Just the ticket, Avery. Read my mind. You'll put Irene out of business with those skills. But I suppose you've got the advantage of God whispering in your ear."

"They're keeping you busy," said Bufty. "I could hear you typing from out in the garden. *Tacker-tacker-tacker*."

"I do have a heavy hand, it's true, Nana. It's this High Commish, they can't get enough of me. I won't go into details because it's classified stuff, but more crucially, it's monumentally mind-numbing . . ."

☾

Though no devotee of the given stereotypes of her sex, after Judy was born, Irene repainted Wally's old bedroom walls dusky pink and, with meticulous care, painted blue forget-me-nots overtop to charming effect, and the girls would stay in the pink room or Irene's bed in varying combinations throughout their lives. The days at Irene's whooshed by with the coastal winds. They had the beach at their disposal, never for swimming, but you could play make-believe and *Five Run Away Together*; loiter around the folk dragging their set nets across the shore, gumboots dimpling the sand, boldly calling out "Good day for it!" or "What a beaut!"; search for polished shells and rocks to show Irene. In summer they bottled preserves and pickled cucumbers, boiled marmalade in winter, scrubbed spuds, hung lavender to dry for sachets, and they sang.

On rainy days, the house was a treasure trove of crystals and mysterious books and Irene's prized tarot cards, and if you were on your best behaviour, the jammiest treat of all was being allowed to wait in the hallway when customers called in to have their palms read, or a spread of cards pulled from Irene's deck. Lying on your back, eyes scrunched shut, gripping your sister's hand, as though the two of you formed part of the ritual, or lying on your stomach, motionless as the visitor's car parked outside, only able to see the brim of Mrs Quentin's hat—Mrs Fonseka's crossed ankles in grey pantyhose—Irene's fingernails, the colour of boiling plums. The resinous scent of lemon balm always catapulted Rita back to her childhood, sipping the fragrant tea Irene made for her, with the promise it would send her straight to sleep with sweet dreams. But, Irene assured her, bad dreams were nothing to fear; they're only our subconscious telling us what we weren't ready to face in the daylight.

The kettle rumbled to the boil as Rita arrived. Desire for tea was irrelevant, as Irene believed you couldn't invite a visitor into your house without offering them hospitality, nor could they refuse the offering. She baked this value into the family at every level, and whether a host received you thusly became an enduring indictment of character.

"It's manaakitanga," said Mahalia, at one gathering when the conversation inevitably turned to judgement. "It's our heritage."

"Pffft." Judy didn't take kindly to this usurping of her status as family historian. "It's good old-fashioned country values, that's all."

"It's manaakitanga," said Irene, each syllable chaperoned by the pounding of her stick.

Henceforth, the number of complaints from Judy's direction about not being offered tea while out and about remained quite unchanged. But now she called upon manaakitanga each time.

Rita kissed her grandmother's cheek. "What's the brew today, Irene?"

"Fresh mint. Nothing fancy. If you'd come round yesterday,

you would've got fennel and orange peel. Seems it knocked the stuffing out of me a bit."

"I should come pick your herbs for you." Rita accepted a steaming dove-grey cup from Irene. "Marlon's a keen gardener too, she can help."

"Ach, you don't have to do my work, girl. I can still get out there, it's good for me, but it wears me out for the rest of the day. Now, you know where the biscuits are."

"Go on."

Lifting the fluted lid from that sage-green container sent forth the scent of golden syrup, so sweet it prickled the throat; the tranquillising promise of melted butter; and a tooth-roughening hint of baking soda. Irene's biscuits, called All-In-One Biscuits in the tautly dictated Aunt Daisy recipe book whence they came, were elementary enough with their melt, mix and drop method for the young girls to bake with their clumsy child hands, and for Irene to keep the biscuit container propagated in her old age.

Down came Irene's stick against the floor.

"How long have you had cancer, Rita?"

Rita coughed on her biscuit and raised her fist to her lips. "What now?"

"Isn't that what you were fixing to tell everyone at your mother's birthday?"

"Well, I wasn't exactly telling them I'd won a trip to Hawai'i."

"So it's true?"

"Yep. Ovaries." Rita scratched the back of her head. "What have they done for me lately, anyway."

Intuition is not confirmation. Irene's stick fell to the ground, and she gripped Rita's hands with her own brown, wizened hands, and the honesty of it all made Rita's stomach jump. She was once an infant, then a child, then a young woman, now an adult, and Irene had always been old, and in speaking to her Rita found herself paddling, uncertain, between these ages. So strange to speak freely to Irene about her ovaries, woman to woman, yet still be her grandchild. Still Baby Ree.

"That's no good. I'm sorry, my girl. You'll get treatment, of course. Are the quacks recommending treatment?"

Rita retrieved Irene's stick.

"You surprise me, Irene. Thought you'd be fixing a poultice or casting a spell. Mum's anointed me with so much essential oil, I feel like the queen on her coronation. Walking round smelling like the bloody spice rack."

"Don't give me that horse hockey. Of course you should get all the treatment they offer. We *can* cast a spell to be on the safe side."

"They said surgery first. If that doesn't work, well. You know. It's funny—not funny *ha-ha*, just funny—so many people here have had cancer. So many women. Maybe it's not so many. What's a normal number of people with cancer. I didn't even think about it until it happened to me. Dunno why. Now I'm another one. Look at us go." Rita stopped before she said: *What if no one thinks about me?*

"That's enough. It'll all work out, I know it."

"Y'think?"

Irene wrapped her fingers around Rita's wrist. "I do. I buried a child; I'll not bury a grandchild."

Rita smiled faintly. What the hell do you say to that.

"We talk about the dead, you know. We keep them with us. You won't be forgotten. Just like your father hasn't been forgotten, just like you won't forget me."

Rita ignored the implication. "Mum never talks about her own dad. And when she mentions her mother, all she says is how pretty she was. Like it was a personality trait or something."

"Yes, well." Irene let go of Rita's wrist. "He wasn't much worth wasting your memories on by the sounds of things."

"Anyway, you'll outlive us all, Irene."

"Do you think you're depressed?"

With this tangent, Rita's tenuous grip on the conversation fell from her hands like Irene's stick.

"I mean. I've got cancer."

"No, that's not what I mean. You sit there—day in, day out—like a bump on a log. Is this what you want to do with your life? It's a blessing to have your children home, but surely you want more than this? Why don't you find a place of your own? What about all your friends? What about that Italian . . . thingy? You used to have a bit of spark, you know. I remember."

"I've been away for so long," said Rita. "How am I supposed to move out now. I don't have a job, and I can't imagine anyone's falling over themselves to hire a fifty-something dropout with cancer." She winced. Those words did not sound good.

Rita had plenty of friends back in her day. Like a still body of water attracting wild geese and ducks to its mirror-flat surface, Rita's reticence was catnip to extroverts, and they latched on to her silence and sarcastic asides. But after taking off for Italy and her subsequent abscondings, she lost touch, and her friends moved on, had children, sought company with lives that reflected theirs. If you wanted to pinpoint the moment Rita's efforts to make new connections faded, you might consider the year her childhood friend Erana died. Whether or not this was true, you wouldn't get it out of Rita.

"Listen to yourself, girl. You're still young. Got your whole life ahead of you."

"Everyone's young to you, Irene. I'm not the baby anymore. I can't get away with this sort of thing."

"Spend the rest of your life in that chair if you want," said Irene, "but the world is turning while you sit and turn to rust."

"Living any kind of way round here looks pretty rusty to me. And since when have you heard of depression. Your generation didn't have time for all that. According to Judy, you'd think Big Pharma invented anxiety ten years ago to sell pills."

"Girl, every farmer and his mother from here to Timbuktu was miserable, and we didn't know what to do about it, so we drank ourselves to death or beat our children or drove our cars into trees. Now we've got a name for it, we can do a little better. Judy's not wrong, mind you. She's not right, either. She'll never tell you that though, will she."

Rita's bones felt too close to her skin in the hard wooden chair. Irene looked so content she might as well have been sitting on a cloud. A real power move, come to think of it.

"Can't a person want to be left alone to read their book without it meaning anything?"

"It's boring."

"Are you done?"

"Don't be saucy with me, girl."

"*You* never went anywhere," said Rita, without thinking.

"That's right, my husband brought me here at sixteen and I never saw my people again and this land has been under my feet since 1932, and it's the land that'll stay under my feet."

"Didn't you ever want to leave?"

"You ask too many questions, girl."

The corners of Rita's mouth twitched. "No, I don't. But, okay. Never mind."

"Let's not quarrel. I've said my piece—I won't shatter like a dropped plate if you disagree. Do with it what you will and be it on your own head. Now, shall I pull a tarot card for you, while I'm awake?"

Rita weighed up her options. She didn't wish to leave on a sour note. And a 102-year-old deserved to be coddled.

"Fine. A single card. Let me, you stay put." She placed the cards in front of Irene. "Alright. What's the story, morning glory."

Irene took a deep, centring breath which merged into a yawn. "I'll know if you're not thinking of anything. Humour your wise old nannie."

Rita closed her eyes. *What comes next? What should I do? What do I want?* To cook lunch every Sunday for friends round a table—ice cream—a fireplace—*oh Christ, now I'm just describing home.*

Her palms tingled. Probably numb from holding them parallel to the table. Another of Irene's cunning tricks to make the procedure feel more momentous. But still. A sign's a sign. Let's get this over with.

"Stop." Opening her eyes, Rita chose the top card. Before she could turn it over, a muscle in her thumb spasmed, and the card fell.

"Gah. Sorry." Rita picked up the card. "Right. Who's he when he's at home."

Irene nodded with the fulsome gratification of having foreseen this coming from the moment Rita walked in the door. "The Knight of Pentacles. Of course."

"Does it make the card reversed, since I dropped him? He's sort of diagonal, really."

"Up to you, girl. What does the card's energy tell you?"

"Ah, just read me up and down for this Knight guy. I'll choose the one I like best."

"As you wish." Irene had no need to consult her tarot books, having read and reread their words, and carried their information across generations. "In short—since that's your style. The clever Knight of Pentacles is slowly getting to where he needs to be on that horse of his. But look," she pointed at the knight. "His armour can be a trap. He's too hidden away. He needs to forgive himself and others for not being perfect."

"And reversed? Let me guess, it's not looking good?"

"Reversed, the Knight of Pentacles suggests inertia, stagnation, waiting around for things to happen instead of making them happen. He's a dull pessimist." Irene snorted. "Ring any bells?"

The little man on the card, hand-drawn by her grandmother decades before Rita first drew breath, seemed to ridicule her. She wished she could throw the pentacle at his head. She settled for covering his face with her hand. Him and his stupid horse.

"You know, I think it fell more upright than diagonal."

Irene raised her palms. "It's out of my hands, girl. The card finds the person, the person finds the card. Take what you need and leave the rest. And now, I'm having a nap because I am tuckered out. Can you please put away the cups and fold the cards up in the scarf for me?"

"Of course." Rita carried the cups and two plates over to the sink. She rinsed them in a little soapy water and dried them with a clean tea towel from the third drawer down, washed her hands, bundled the tarot cards in their silk scarf, and returned them to the shelf.

Irene banged her wooden cane against her bedroom floor. She might want another biscuit, or she might be about to pop her clogs. Either way, you heeded the call with haste.

"While you're still here—my music—could you?"

Rita picked up the CD next to the boombox on the table opposite Irene's bed. Irene wasn't easy to buy for, but this Christmas gift from the family in 1999 was a definite success.

"*Kathleen Battle sings Mozart*," Rita read aloud. "Good for her."

She kissed Irene's cheek. The sound of 'Vorrei spiegarvi, oh Dio!' pursued her out the door. Rita unlocked her car, kicked the tyre, locked it again and walked back into the house.

"D'you mind if I sit here and listen? I'll be quiet. You know how—this reminds me . . ."

Belly pressed against carpet. Face warmed by the fireplace. Burning hot but you can't move away. Records playing while her mother trilled along from the kitchen or pedalled at the trundle sewing machine. Shutting her eyes and letting the world pass by. Falling asleep counting blue flowers on the wall while Irene's wool-encased footsteps padded round the house, steady as a heartbeat. The symphony orchestra in Auckland, marinating in the sound, her entire body tuning to A with the orchestra, playing records in her grotty flat, Italy—

"I know, girl. You take your time."

"We should go for another drive one of these days, Irene."

"That sounds fine to me."

Irene fell asleep within moments. Beside her, Rita shut her eyes, listening to Kathleen Battle. When she opened her eyes, her vision was wet and blurry. She left, pulling the front door closed as slowly as she could to not make a sound, and drove the short distance back home.

☾

Wally taught Bufty to drive, and later Marlon and Judy, and Marlon taught Jayne and Rita, cackling as they bunny-hopped over the back roads. Judy kept her foot to the floor, yelling expletives at both the deserving and the blameless. Marlon slammed on the brakes if she saw so much as a brittle autumn leaf pirouetting across the bitumen. Jayne drove with dopey caution, slowing to a halt when she changed gear, remaining in second on the open road "just in case". Bufty had an unstable détente with the gearstick and would propel the car into reverse in the middle of town, to the girls' humiliation. All in all, the advent of automatic transmission was a blessing to the Gordon family.

Several times a week, Rita slipped away for an hour or so in her red Cortina. No fixed destination in mind, unless Bufty caught her leaving and called, "Pick up a loaf of bread!" as Rita backed out of the driveway, more to ensure she'd come back than for lack of bread.

When you drive, you're not where you're going. You're not where you've been. You're only where you are, in the unanswerable middle. No one can drop in uninvited or ask questions. If Young Bunratty remarked, "I caught up with Rita Gordon today while I was doing jobs in town," he meant he drove past her, and Rita lifted a finger off the wheel, and he lifted a finger in return. Rita permitted Irene on these aimless jaunts, the pair contained yet in motion, the road moving backwards as they hurtled forwards, the low sun winking through the filigree of hedges and branches wrapping the land.

She arrived home to Bufty nursing a stockpot of dog bone soup, its cobby bacon bone bobbing as lentils and barley dissolved into the broth.

Bufty raised an eyebrow.

"How did it go, hmm? Did you tell her? You know, about the cancer?"

"Mmhmm."

"And? How'd she take it?"

"Over the moon."

"Yeah, yeah. It must feel good now it's no longer a secret. Like removing an underwire bra at the end of a long day."

"Sure." Rita kissed her mother's steam-moistened cheek. "Smells good. Aren't we too hot for soup? I know Stevie's not menopausal yet—"

"Speak for yourself," said Stevie, on the couch with her laptop. "But who could tell in this heat? It's at *least* perimenopausal. The change is gonna come, to dishonourably misquote Sam Cooke."

"Oh, it's far too hot, but this isn't for us." Bufty wiped her hands on her frilly apron and rested the wooden spoon on the pot's rim.

"I'm fixing some little dinners for Rachel Phillips—you went to school with her, remember, she was a Loomis. Well, she's moving back home to look after her mother, Mrs Hetty Loomis, remember her? She and I went to school together, she was an Uprichard . . . anyway she's positively perforated with dementia and can't look after herself. I ran into Young Bunratty at the supermarket, and he told me he'd seen Rachel driving her around—of course if you want the scuttlebutt, you ask *him*—and it's evidently placing a great strain on Rachel, but at least she has her nursing experience, and her three girls are all quite grown up . . . I suppose that will be them one day, taking care of her . . ."

Bufty had long given up on being blessed with any grandchildren from Rita. But few mothers are immune to the lure of a passive remark on the subject of their childless offspring.

"You always said Mrs Loomis was a—"

"Oh, that old rip can go straight to hell, fast-post," interrupted Bufty. "But I'll still make her soup. If you can't be neighbourly and help the less fortunate, you're no use to me."

Stevie looked up from her writing. "Very good, Nana. What Would Jesus Do, and all that."

"Never mind him, this is What Would Bufty Gordon Do?, a question more people should ask. We could solve a lot of the world's ills this way, mark my words."

"And so say all of us." Stevie closed her laptop. "Right, no more exertion. Must be cocktail hour." She batted away the two flies milling about her face. "Were the flies always so populous? I'm sure it wasn't this bad when I was a kid."

"That's the countryside for you, my love," said Bufty.

A shroud of dust loomed over the fence, lurking in the febrile air with no wind to disperse it.

"Give me a break," said Bufty, "shut the place up, Rita, where are the dogs—oh here they are, right behind me, no bacon for you sorry, Roger—bloody Murphy's at it again. S'pose we can turn on the cold air since we're shutting the place up."

Rita closed the French doors and tugged the windows.

"That nefarious man." Bufty stirred the soup with more vicious energy than before. "First they sprayed the paddock so the grass died, then they planted maize which grew a foot taller every time you turned around, like the bloody day of the triffids, and then they chopped it all away again and sprayed it. The mercenary sod. I put a cover over my vegetable garden, but I'm sure the chemicals are getting through."

"Is he aware the spray gets all over our house?" asked Stevie.

"He's aware," said Avery, coming in from the study. "Though butter wouldn't melt in his mouth. He reckons it's the safe kind of glyphosate. Their house is protected by the trees and they only spray when the wind's coming this way. Must be a coincidence, right?"

Was it—the glyphosate—but surely they'd all—not just her? But. It was already happening. Rita stretched her hands out to Roger, who climbed onto her lap and made her feel slightly less like she was going to fly headfirst into the cobweb on the bay window.

The one charitable thing Bufty would say for their neighbour Murphy was that every December he'd let Wally chop down a pine tree from the back of his property. The second charitable thing she'd say for Murphy was that since Avery moved in, he'd passed this tree-chopping privilege on to her without fuss. But even a thicko like Murphy could take one look at Avery and know she could swing an axe with purpose. Then, out came the decorations from the cupboard in the study, in drawstring bags made from an old tobacco-leaf print quilt cover, rustling and clinking with apricot and gold Mardi Gras beads, Bufty's mother's paper lanterns, bushy gold and silver tinsel, inquisitive red-breasted robins, silver trumpets, red apples, gold baubles fastened to the tree with pipe cleaners, their original threads long disintegrated. Finally, the multicoloured lights blinking from the moment Bufty got out of bed in the morning. Christmas was no time to quibble over the electricity bill.

Bufty placed a lid on the pot and switched off the flame.

"Now, Flossie Doll, you're driving to Jayne's on Monday, but are you staying up this end long? I'm not sure how much time off they're giving you down in Wellington, and I'm sure you won't want to be around here over New Year's. But of course, you can stay as long as you like."

Stevie tipped her head from side to side.

"I'm here for Chrimbo, after that, I'm not sure."

"It's all hunky dunky, however it shakes out. We'll always have a bed for you here." Bufty turned to Rita. "Do you want to cook dinner, bub? Nothing stodgy, I think, in this heat."

Rita's eyes lit up. "Sure."

For all that she loved to read restaurant menus and pore over cookbooks and entertain ideas of gelatine-set appetisers and flambéed desserts, when it came to dinnertime Bufty reverted to cooking the sort of hearty mid-century country fare that you'd eat before ploughing a six-acre paddock by hand. Food for people who went to bed at 7:30PM. Rita, who always cleared her plate as a child because that's what you did, had less patience for old-fashioned food in adulthood. Taking charge of dinner neatly avoided pallid boiled vegetables and contributed to the household in one fell swoop. It meant putting up with a lot of "Now, what do you call this, bub?" but it was worth it to consume seasoning and ingredients that hailed from further afield than England's dampest villages.

"Anything in mind?"

"You only just asked me, Mum."

"Oop, so I did. Shall we put on another Christmas record? How about Doris Day?"

☾

Avery lay like a craggy island rising from the sea of oatmeal carpet, Glenn's knitted socks pointing towards the ceiling, following a video on her phone propped against the skirting board. Her legs drooped to the right, then left. Jimmy Stewart followed the movement, to see if it was a game he could be involved in.

Roger sat next to Stevie on the couch while she typed, occasionally stopping to cup his chin. Rita curled like a fist around *The Heart Is a Lonely Hunter*, her eyes sliding between the wasps sleeping above the red curtains and Stevie's face.

Her niece's presence still surprised her, so incongruent amongst all this sleepy smallness.

"So, gents," said Stevie, pushing her laptop shut. "What's on the menu tonight? A little espionage, a car chase, ferrying verboten items across state lines, general skullduggery, perhaps culminating in an orgy?"

"Well, we've got biscuits." Bufty approached, carrying a tin tray with four small gold-rimmed goblets filled with Stone's green ginger wine, and a plate of Squiggles.

"It'll be biscuits, then a quiz. If we're lucky, an episode of a TV show about a nun who solves crime." Rita did not look up from her book.

"Oh, it's not very good, is it, that show?" Bufty lowered the tray under Stevie's nose. "But that's the thing about English accents, isn't it? They make even the bad TV shows seem high quality. Did you find that, living in London?"

Stevie did not know how to answer the question but took two biscuits and a goblet.

Avery pushed herself up on her haunches.

"Ta, Buf," she said, taking a ginger wine. "Squiggles, what is this? High days and holy days."

"It is the silly season, and they were on special. They're not as good as they used to be though, are they?"

This was a favoured subject amongst the Gordons, a subject they mined regularly and with gusto.

"In fact," said Bufty, "biscuits just don't taste the same altogether. I don't know why I buy them when I like to bake. But I see that little 'On Special' label and bam, away I go, sucked in again. Don't get me started on Gingernuts. You used to know the difference between Griffin's and Arnott's blindfolded, and now they're the same. And they crumble in your tea in seconds. Seconds! You used to have to soak them for a *full minute* or you'd break your teeth, now it's like a sponge. A full minute!"

Avery, Rita and Stevie murmured in tacit agreement and reached for more biscuits.

"Did you have Squiggles in London, Stevie?" asked Bufty. "This ginger wine is tasty, isn't it? Really hits the spot, as they say."

"Not at Tesco, no, but you'd be surprised what those diplomats can get their mitts on."

Bufty opened her laptop. "Oh, here's a trick—a man in Florida, high on meth, put his penis in a toasted sandwich maker."

Just as chickens take themselves to bed without being trained, thanks to the mechanisms of their innate circadian rhythms, Bufty possessed an elemental drive to read out the most appalling stories syndicated into the local news sites each night after dinner, with no sense of the effect it might have on those listening.

"I didn't know they ate toasted sandwiches over there! Fancy that. Just like us. Hang about, they've included a little picture, it's a sandwich *press*, not a quicksie iron like ours. I suppose that makes all the difference . . . Goodness, America has gone downhill, hasn't it?"

"Is it the actual machine in the photo? The one he flattened his penis in?" asked Stevie. "With said penis still cooking?"

"No, my love, only a stock image." Bufty looked put out, as if this was yet another sign of declining journalism standards.

"Just like us. Minus the meth, I s'pose," said Stevie.

"I shouldn't think so," said Bufty. "Our postman is on meth."

"Not much else to do in the countryside," said Rita.

"Why do you think the mail is so unpredictable? Though it gets here in the end, I'll give him that. I think he waits till there's enough built up to make the journey worthwhile. Which is most infuriating, because I'm waiting for your little present to arrive, Stevie, now I know you're going to be here . . . you'd think the meth would make him move a bit faster, wouldn't you?"

"He's probably just bad at his job," said Rita. More than one house had blown up in the area over the past twenty years. But your own mailman?

"Never let the facts get in the way of a good story," said Stevie.

"We came up with that saying," said Bufty.

"No, we didn't," said Rita.

"His wife's definitely on meth though," said Avery.

"It's a ruthless world to live in these days," said Bufty. "There but for the grace of God go we, isn't that right, Avery? Now, shall we do a little quiz?"

"Correct as always, and I thought you'd never ask." Avery removed the Trivial Pursuit book from the mantle, where it was resting on top of *Modern Philosophies on Ancient Religions*. Avery left such recondite books lying conspicuously around the house in the hopes someone might ask her about them and kick off a debate.

She knew, however, to be forthright in matters of philosophy. She might say to Bufty over the morning cuppa: "You could speak of loving a good steak, or you could say a child is good, or a gift you have received is good, or that God is good. But you're not speaking of the steak's behaviour, and the child may act in a way that is not good after you praise them, and the gift may be acceptable but not great, and with all this in mind, what do we mean when we say God is good? And can He even be truly described?"

And Bufty would try to not topple over on the spot.

Or Avery might roll over in bed, wide-apart eyes glinting, and ask: "If God is unchangeable, did God have a choice in creating the universe?"

And Bufty would quake and say that she'd better go to the library to study for a bit first.

"You don't have to study," Avery would tell her, "I want to hear what's in your head. We can talk about this, you can talk to me about movies, I'll know as much about them as you know about the Bible, and we can both learn from each other. You don't have to pretend to be scholarly around me, and besides, the more I find out, the more I have to learn."

And Bufty, who couldn't resist making a person feel appreciated, would say perhaps God didn't have a choice in the matter, because if it *had* been planned, he might've done it a little more efficiently, since it took so long for the first creatures to evolve and become recognisable to us today, and for homes to have electric washing machines and hot water. If he'd had it in mind that we should be as we are now, he should've done it, rather than taking millions of years for evolution to catch up. "Of course, I don't know where Adam and Eve fit into all this . . ."

And this would astound Avery. "There, see, you'd knock all my books and their supposed wisdom into a cocked hat. I don't even know how to answer that question."

"I'm sorry!"

"No, it's fantastic, it's the essence of philosophy. Now, tell me about what that Vivien Leigh is up to these days."

"Not a lot, truth be told."

☾

Bufty was about to push off for bed when Rita grasped her gauzy white dressing gown sleeve.

"Irene reckons I should get the treatment. If the surgery doesn't take."

"Righto." Bufty plucked a bauble from a drooping pine sprig, attaching it to a sturdier clump of needles. "That's that, then. Switch off the tree before you hit the sack, will you? I like going to bed with them still on, seeing them in my peripherals, it's so jolly and homey. Turning them off for the night makes it feel like Christmas will soon be over for another year."

"Sure thing, Mum."

Though Bufty could talk a big game about The Family Bladder—cast iron, camels spoke of it with envy, could survive forty days and forty nights in the desert with nary a call from nature—she was no match for the persistent dripping waters of Time, and so she increasingly woke in the night to use the bathroom. The absorbent pads in the bottom drawer—just in case—were an unsightly reminder of her mortality, but the package as yet remained unopened. Mostly because Bufty never went far away enough from home to necessitate such forward planning. She'd ordered the pads online after a close call while laughing at a *Fawlty Towers* rerun on the telly, but she noticed—one couldn't help it—people much younger than her putting them in their trolleys at the supermarket.

During one such perambulation down the hall at 1:30AM that same night, Bufty saw the Christmas lights twinkling in the lounge. Rita must've forgotten to switch them off. She touched Diana and Whetū's frames as she passed. How many times had she studied Whetū's photo, searching for clues? Did dimples sink into her cheeks when she smiled, was her bladder made of cast iron, did the family's praiseworthy ankles originate under the hem of that skirt? Did she ever fall in love with a woman?

Rita sat at the kitchen table, the coloured lights reflecting off her tears. Bufty flew to her side with the speed of a fifty-year-old.

"My baby! What's wrong?" She embraced her daughter. "Is it the *cancer*?"

"No."

On the table was a plate, empty but for crumbs and smears, their colour not visible in the dark, their scent a distinct orange-red.

"I was craving spaghetti on toast. The way you used to make it for us. So I picked some up yesterday when I went for a drive, and . . ." Rita lowered her face into her hands. "It's not the same as it used to be. Must've changed the recipe. Watered down the sauce. I don't know. Foul. Too mushy to twirl on your fork. It's . . . It's not the same as it used to be.

Like the biscuits. It's all changing, and I'll never get it—that spaghetti—back." She pushed the plate away. "Still ate the lot, though. Can't waste it."

Bufty patted Rita's shoulder. "Two world wars and a depression, it's true."

"Dunno what came over me. Overtired, I guess. Sorry to wake you."

"Nonsense, I was up on my little nightly visit to the latrine. Are you *sure*-sure you're alright?" Bufty removed the offending plate and sat in the chair by Rita. "It's okay to have a little cry. We're all here for you, we love you."

"Here for me in my time of tragic spaghetti?"

Bufty saw this was as much as she would get.

"The very one. Why don't you head off to bed before we wake the whole house up, and I'd better get the Christmas lights. In the morning, we can throw the can in the recycle bin and send an angry little email to Watties, give them a good seeing-to. Once upon a time you could slide the spaghetti out of the can in a cylinder—*shup*! Now I wouldn't give it to the dogs."

The lights from the tree, with no other reflective surface to land on, found their way to the white fabric of Bufty's nylon dressing gown like sliced strawberries and kiwifruit pressed into the hand-whipped cream on a pavlova.

"You go first, Mum. I'll wait till your door shuts. Then I'll turn out the lights."

Chapter Eight

Erana Milner
Breast cancer
1 July 1985

It was already quite a day. The sirens woke Avery and Bufty at 6AM, undulating yowls announcing a fire at the aerosol factory. Bufty hadn't been inside the factory for several years, not since the girls were at school and she picked up hours to help fatten the coffers, but she could shut her eyes and the building would rise around her: the telephone exchange with its tangle of cords, the small padded metal chairs which curved round your back like a courteous gentleman guiding you into a room, the smart corner offices, the narrow hallways, the chugging and whistling of medium-scale industry. The villagers stood in the street, red and dun Swanndris over dressing gowns, a wall of steam from mugs of tea raised like shields, saying "love a man in uniform" and "someone's head'll roll over this" while their children rarked around in their gumboots or bare feet.

Roger, a German shepherd once named Humphrey Bogart, leaned his weight against Avery's legs. Barbara, a workshy huntaway who was fired from her job at Rube Barley's farm, barked at the fire engines.

"Thank goodness it didn't catch fire later in the day," said Avery.

"You know I live in fear of that factory blowing up," shivered Bufty. "But it would get the six o'clock newsreaders to show. Imagine if Angela D'Audney saw me without any blush and powder? I would die right there on the spot. Do you think I should go inside and get dressed in a little outfit, just in case?"

Bufty heard the phone ringing over the sirens and chatter.

☾

Wiremu Milner did sharemilking for the Murphys and lived with his wife Delwyn and their three daughters in the small house at the back end of Murphy's farm, close enough to the Gordon homestead that you could hear a mother's voice calling you for supper from either direction. Their eldest girl, Erana, befriended Rita without ceremony the moment their paths crossed. They recognised each other as equals. Both inscrutable. Both content with their lot in life but not in any way that you could guess how. The pair sat on the Milner's porch like old men, observing the minimal world drifting by as they drank their Arcoroc mugs of sweet tea. The milk tanker drivers honked their horns at the two girls as they passed, and the girls would lift their chins in acknowledgement. When it was cold outside, they'd read the *Encyclopædia Britannica* and memorise facts or draw pictures. They shared a secret notebook where they wrote words they liked the feel of: *Decatur, reliquary, Rock Island Line, Baltics, fricative.*

At twenty-seven a lump appeared under Erana's arm.

"How much do you drink every day?" asked Dr Codlin, peering over his clipboard like a peeping Tom looking over the fence into your bedroom.

"I don't drink," she said.

"And how many children do you have?"

"None . . ."

"Did your mother smoke when she was pregnant with you?"

"Did yours?"

The doctor's nostrils flared. "Breast cancer is unlikely in a girl of your age. Are you sure the pain isn't a bruise from someone hitting you? Your father, maybe, or your boyfriend?"

"I want a scan," said Erana, clenching her teeth.

Dr Codlin's nostrils retreated, and he scribbled illegible words on his clipboard.

"I felt a lump. I know what that means." She stretched her eyes open wide and leaned forward. Let him think she's scary. He'll give in.

The lump was breast cancer. Vaulting from one lymph node to the next with the unstudied velocity of a picked-clean ham bone hiffed over the fence to the dogs.

☾

Avery came back into the house with Barbara over her shoulder to find Bufty on the floor sobbing, cradling an empty jar to her chest, the phone swinging from its curly cord.

"That was Delwyn's sister on the phone. Erana—in her sleep last night—an infection. Oh, why didn't I buy more teabags? How are we going to tell Rita? Where's her Christmas postcard? It'll have her address . . ."

Avery let Barbara jump from her arms to the floor. She squatted beside Bufty with a clicking noise from both kneecaps and pulled her in close. Barbara ran back out the door to bark at the fire trucks.

"How can you stand losing a daughter? How could this happen to such a lovely girl—such a lovely family—it just spread too far, and they couldn't—what am I going to *say* to Delwyn and Wiremu when I see them—"

Bufty wept into Avery's towelling dressing gown, leaving a glutinous trail of snot.

"Oh, look what I've done. I'm sorry. I'm sorry there's no tea. I'm sorry Barbara won't shut up. I'm sorry, I'm sorry, I'm—"

"Don't you worry about me, my love. I'll get the ginger wine." Avery kissed the top of her head. "A nip will do us good."

"I'd better get a pot of soup on for them," said Bufty, staggering to her feet.

Outside, the sirens continued blaring.

The Milner family invited Avery and Bufty to the third day of Erana's tangi. Bufty's eyes welled from the moment she got out of the car, and when she realised no one would tell her she was making a scene, and when she saw Erana laid out calm and shockingly present in her coffin, Bufty wept, open, noisy and damp, into Avery's shoulder.

"Isn't it nice the way they do it?" said Bufty to Avery later that week, over a cup of tea and Gaylene Glossop slice. "All the togetherness, none of it over too quick. I wish our funerals could be like that. Our way feels a bit cold in comparison, doesn't it? Of course, you did a smashing job with Wally's send-off, but I was in such a fog, and it was all over before I could come to."

"Nothing's stopping you," said Avery. "When it comes down to it."

"Oh, we're not like that," said Bufty, not entirely sure what she meant by those words. "Which marae would we go to? I can't show up at the gates holding Whetū's picture like it's a plane ticket. We'd get laughed at. Or worse, they'd think we were making a mockery."

"What about Irene?"

"Oh Irene, the high queen of mystery. Besides, if I've never been on my marae, how do you think she'd feel? She did once tell me her teacher hit her across the knuckles with his wooden pointer when he heard her speaking a little bit of the language, and she only knew a few words. He told her not to say she was Māori, not to anyone. They don't do that anymore, do they?"

"Not in those exact words, I suppose," said Avery, taking another piece of slice. "If you ever wanted to, sort of . . . explore all that . . . I'm here for you."

"Maybe one day," said Bufty.

Rita returned home one week later. She visited the Milners, wept with them, told them if she could have cut up her own body and given it to Erana to replace the cancerous parts, she would have.

Bufty wanted to ask Rita if she was doing okay, wanted her daughter to cry in her arms. Instead, when Erana's birthday came around, Bufty picked a bundle of flowers from the garden—anemones, carnations, gold-lipped freesias—and left them on the kitchen table. That afternoon, they were gone. From then on, if Rita was living at home, Bufty would pick flowers and leave them on the table. Rita would take them. And that quiet system was a kind of communication they could both live with.

One day, Rita asked if Bufty only picked the flowers when she was home. Bufty gasped. Of course not. She and Avery delivered flowers to Erana and talked to her about Rita whenever they visited Wally's grave. Rita's face broke into a smile. She hugged her mother. Bufty sometimes forgot that Rita had dimples at all. As a child, Rita would stop her smile just short of where the cheeks puckered, like a raindrop falling into a puddle, but fighting it made her look like a chipmunk stuffed full of acorns.

After primary school, Erana and her sister had both left to board at Baradene. So she got two memorial cups in her honour. The factory site never operated again after the fire, nor did any new business take its place.

Chapter Nine

The twins knew you had to, when establishing a bar, commit to being a summer hotspot with a poky outdoor area optimistically called a beer garden, or a winter retreat with shadowy corners where the sun couldn't hurt you. They, unsurprisingly, chose the latter energy for The Chariot.

Blue-green shapes floated in Rita's vision, remnants of the midday sun outside the dim bar. Mahalia slid a high stool over beside her. Diana, behind the bar, poured Jameson into three rocks glasses. Rita raised her eyebrows. Diana tilted her head.

Sun's over the yardarm. It's five o'clock somewhere. You live with your mother. Insert validating aphorism here.

The persuasive scent of extruded potato spirals sizzling in fat wafted closer. Mahalia handed Rita a red New World tote bag. Inside, Rita found a knitted beanie of feather-soft yarn the colour of iron sand.

"Dad made it for you. Apparently you skipped the queue in his Christmas knitting—Mum says he was up till 2AM finishing it," said Mahalia. "No seams, see. It's a cotton-bamboo blend, so it won't hurt your head. Mum was in denial. First she said you might not need one. Then she reckoned the colour should be bright and jazzy. Cringe. We told her black or nothing."

"It's jumping the gun," said Diana, "but you know how Dad is. Eager beaver alert. And if you don't end up needing the treatment, no harm done. You've still got a hat out of it."

"And you won't have cancer," added Mahalia.

"Better and better," said Diana.

Rita ran her hand over the beanie, over the cables uprooting its stitches. Neat. Even. Nowhere in the neighbourhood of jazzy.

"Jeez. He's talented, your old man. Tell him I said so. This could be from a shop." She pulled the beanie over her short dark hair. "Don't have much of it to lose, do I."

"Hey," said Mahalia. "The op might sort you out."

"It will or it won't," said Rita. "Not much I can do." She picked up a lighter sitting on the cash register, flicking it with her thumb. "Guess I can take up smoking again if it doesn't. In for a penny, in for a pounding."

"There's always wigs," said Diana, sweeping her fingers through the flame. "Blondes have more fun."

"Blondes, redheads. They're all having more fun than me right now."

"This'll help." Diana lined up the rocks glasses in front of Rita and Mahalia and retrieved the curly fries from the kitchen.

"To good health," said Mahalia and Diana in unison, lifting their Jamesons.

After a pause, Rita laughed. "Bravo."

Someone outside pressed their face against the front door and rapped on the glass.

"Bugger off, we're not open yet!" yelled Mahalia.

☾

Wally knocked the wall out between the kitchen and the sitting room after Judy was born, "so we can be all together", and lucky he did, because later when they bought their first Philips K9 TV, Bufty wouldn't miss a single minute of broadcast if she was preparing food or drinks in the kitchen. It was a real event, even Irene would come around to watch *Bonanza, Hogan's Heroes* or our Nyree Dawn Porter in *The Forsyte Saga*. Between the stove and the fireplace, the heart of the home stayed snug through the frostiest winters.

On those days, Bufty might say to her shivering, red-faced daughters arriving home from school in their matching blouses and clamdiggers handmade from old sheets and bedspreads, "What if we go to bed with nothing *but* pudding tonight, girls?" And the girls would whoop and jump and swing each other in circles. Bufty would make apple shortcake, served with cream from the top of the milk bottle—the best apple shortcake for miles around, because Bufty added a fragrant dot of ground cloves, while other mothers only used cinnamon. She might push the boat out with a queen of puddings, and the girls would beg to whip the egg whites with the rotary beater. Or—best of all—steamed pudding with treacle from the big green tin, sitting in its bath on the stove for hours and hours, till you were frenzied with waiting. During the lean times, Bufty simmered squat dough balls in syrup or served up cornflakes with evaporated milk and tinned peaches, all received with rapture.

On those frosty nights, after the dishes, everyone dizzy with the smug repletion that comes from eating sugar when no one else is, the girls might say, "Tell us what it was like when you were growing up!"

Wally, reading in His Chair, might be prevailed on to tell the story of Irene teaching him to ride Robber Baron, the nag she rescued from Old Bunratty's farm. And the girls would prod each other's arms because they knew what was coming.

Irene had no money for a car. She found out from Old Bunratty's wife Edith that he was fixing to shoot Robber Baron for hound tucker and persuaded him to give her the horse for a modest price.

"That moke's neither use nor ornament," said Old Bunratty, "dead on his feet." But Irene, who was lifted onto a horse at age five by her Aunty Merry, had a good feeling about Robber Baron, and her yard had ample space for a superannuitant horse to eat grass and bask in the sun. Under Irene's care, the hitherto lethargic Robber Baron acquitted himself like a horse half his age. Now Irene could trot into town when she had errands to attend to, tying the horse to the hitching post outside the general store, laying her hand on his snout to say, "I'm ready", his gait so steady she could hold the reins with one hand and her parcels with the other.

Old Bunratty was ropeable. He drove back up to Irene's house, shook his fist at Robber Baron and demanded Irene give back the pestilent horse. She refused: fair's fair, a deal's a deal, and Old Bunratty spluttered and fizzled till his whiskers stood on end, and he accused Irene of casting a spell on Robber Baron. "Maybe I did, maybe I didn't," said Irene, "maybe I'm a better hand with horses than you. Will that be all, Mr Bunratty?" And Old Bunratty thundered that his wife would no longer be seeking Irene's services, and Irene said, "We'll see," because, despite his bluff and bluster, Irene knew who held the most influence in that household. When Old Bunratty refused to budge, Irene pulled her shovel from where it was shunted into the earth near the front door and made chase, Robber Baron stamping his hoof in support.

The girls loved that part: their dignified nannie besting a grown man. They'd play-act the scene, one in the role of Old Bunratty and one playing Irene, and with each iteration the insults she hurled grew more fanciful and Bunratty's roaring more shrill.

The girls would say to Bufty, "Now tell us about when you were our age, Mum," and though Bufty had so many stories, the more she told, the more she concealed. That was her skill, to be so open and so hidden at the same time. So she would tell them about putting up blackout curtains in the war, and the warden marching past to make sure no one had any lights on. About going to the movies with her mother and sister every Saturday, about the time they took the train up to Grey Lynn to stay with her mother's aunt, and a thunderstorm cut the power at the Adelphi, but a group of American GIs in the audience got up and led everyone in a song, and even performed a soft-shoe dance for the crowd, and Bufty got to hold one of the torches they used for a spotlight and felt like a film star herself, and a soldier who looked like Gene Kelly gave her a real American dollar coin which she still had, sitting on the hutch dresser next to the Princess Diana mug. Only once did Bufty tell the girls about spending Christmas of 1953 volunteering on the phone exchange for twelve hours straight after the catastrophic rail disaster at Tangiwai, and her and Wally eating bread and dripping, instead of the roast she'd planned, in bushwhacked silence. Jayne didn't sleep for days after that story, and Bufty never spoke of it again.

Sometimes the girls would ask, "Did you know each other when you were young?" hoping to catch their parents out in revealing romantic fairytale notions, as if they wouldn't hear the same reply, that Wally left school at fourteen to work as a carpenter, by which point Bufty would've still been at the little school. And Bufty would say everyone in the village knew of Irene, some tales apocryphal, some not exaggerated enough—but she never crossed paths with Wally till the factory.

"You couldn't help noticing her as soon as you saw her—or heard her," said Wally. "She turned heads." It wasn't even a big factory, she'd say, but it was the biggest thing to happen around here since anyone could remember, and Wally looked so dashing she assumed he must've moved down from the city. To think, a man like that, growing up right here in the village!

"Tell us about your Aunty Elspeth," the girls would say if the mood seemed right, and if it was, with raindrops hitting the roof so hard their noise rose over the fireplace crackling, so you felt for all the world like a storybook mouse living inside a tree trunk with a matchbox for your bed and a soft petal for your blanket, then Wally might hold his thumbs and index fingers up to his eyes like spectacles with his pinkie fingers splayed and ask, "Ladies, surely you aren't using such a familiar term to refer to *The Very Proper Mrs Elspeth Coventry*?" And though they'd heard it so many times they could mouth along, the girls still burst into giggles every time Wally imitated her high, priggish voice: *fye-nan-see-al matters* and *conserves* and *being cul-tee-vated*. Aunty Elspeth was the mother of an old friend of his father's family, who, despite this tenuous connection, would sail up unannounced in her Humber Snipe with Rawdon the driver who never spoke a word, to make backhanded judgements on Irene's ability to raise a small child.

And Judy would spoil it by asking where Mrs Coventry was now, and Wally would put down his mimed spectacles and say simply that her husband and son were both killed: one in Crete, the other shot down over Holland, and she went quite mad soon after.

Jayne hated hearing how these stories ended, and sometimes she would wake in the night and climb into bed with Marlon and Judy, weeping at the plight of these long-gone souls. Marlon, eyes still glued closed from sleep, would gather Jayne in her arms, and Judy would roll over and scoff. Judy reckoned these tragedies could only happen to old people from long ago and thought Jayne too sensitive by half. Jayne, who cried listening to doo-wop records! Who wept in Bufty's lap while 'Pretty Little Angel Eyes' by Curtis Lee spun round, crying "Why does it make me feel so unhappy, Mum?" and Bufty explained that it was a happy song, but as she listened, the progression of the notes made her heart ache a little too.

Folks dissected Bufty's child-rearing peccadilloes from one end of the road to the other and twice on the side roads, and when teenaged Jayne fell pregnant, and when Rita ran off to Italy, there was more than one dinner table discussion that ended with, "Well, she *would* let those girls have pudding for dinner . . ."

Chapter Ten

Tarns Fuffer
Cervical cancer
11 August 2001

No one would wish the life of Mish Fuffer on their worst enemy. He lost both daughters to cancer. The old Smith Road claimed his wife when she rolled her Nissan Pulsar full of groceries into the ditch, leaving milk, blood and tomato sauce mingling in the chipseal. And the poor sod's name was Michelle.

This handle, in fairness to Mish, evolved as it passed hands from one illiterate ancestor to another, disembarking from migrant ship to new land, settling at the currently accepted spelling in 1871. One hundred years later, Clarence Heightsmith suggested over an amber pint of bitter at the Cossie Club that Michelle was "a girl's name . . . a *poofter's* name", and Mish hoisted him by his collar and asked, "Which one is it, mate, girl or poofter? Can't be both now, can I?" Upon reflection, Clarence conceded neither option was particularly pertinent, but it was too late to stop Mish's fist from connecting with his jaw at high speed. Though that punch put an end to further defamatory remarks, Mish lived his life henceforth unequivocally rejecting the trappings of girliness, as he saw them, just to be safe. He ate mince on toast for breakfast, chewed the marrow from chicken bones, wore stubbies year-round, and greeted friends and strangers both with "Who's this prick?" But his rakish, off-handed charm gave the impression that not a single high-born soul dwelled on this earth for whom it couldn't be a reasonable salutation. If he asked, "Who's this rooster?", *then* you swam in shark-infested enemy waters.

Tarns was in Jayne's year, neither friend nor foe, and she married straight out of high school to Joe Glossop, content to be a farmer's wife and mother to three boys, providing a home away from home for baby Janine after her sister Sharon's death. You might pity Tarns Fuffer, too: mother dead; her golden sister's beauty preserved in amber while she, the homelier one, trundled along; and, as discovered during a routine check-up while trying for a fourth child, the bearer of accelerated cervical cancer.

Stevie, staying with Bufty in the spare room at the time and travelling up to Takaanini for her hairdressing course, fixed Judy, Jayne and Marlon's hair for the funeral as part of her practical. Marlon, with her propensity for using rubber bands as hair ties, posed a challenge.

"It's no reflection on you at all," said Marlon kindly. "You don't have to include my photo in your assessment."

Mish Fuffer had blue eyes and a jaw like the front of a ride-on mower. Casseroles and pasta bakes were foisted upon him by the single and spoken-for local women even though he'd killed a beast for the freezer just a month prior. Judy fixed three Tupperware containers of meatballs and brought around a tray of steaks, which she fried up for him the evening after Tarns's funeral.

"Let's face it, anyone can make a casserole," she told him, working slabs of butter into a billowing mass of mashed potatoes as the steaks rested. "And homekill is fine for the day-to-day. But a man needs rare beef in times of crisis, and a woman to cook it for him. D'you know what I mean?"

Mish, despite the haze of grief, knew exactly what she meant.

The Sharon Fuffer Memorial Cup for the school prize-giving was changed to the Fuffer Family Memorial Cup.

Chapter Eleven

Where other isolated village churches lost their congregations to idle secularity and dwindling rural populations, the church down the road from the Gordon homestead chugged along in peaks and troughs thanks to its atypical provenance. Some hundred years prior, a forward-thinking group of Protestants built the modest church under the auspices of a board of trustees comprising Anglicans, Methodists and Presbyterians. The church would offer worship for everyone, in perpetuity. Except for the Catholics, who had to fend for themselves elsewhere. The initial board of trustees felt they could only do so much reaching across the table. With changing times and priorities, and a drop in Presbyterians and Methodists, the trustees decided in the mid-70s to only hold their service on the third Sunday of the month. By this point Avery and the Methodist Father Leo were alternating services, with discomfort arising from their mutual aversion; after he shot off to impose himself upon the unlucky people of the Chathams, Avery had the pulpit to herself. For the rest of the month she worked as a lay minister, roving the greater province wherever she was needed.

The one exception to this burgeoning pastoral apathy was the annual Christmas service. Locals would arrive half an hour early to get a good seat, their children bunched cross-legged in the aisle and latecomers crowded in the lobby. The after-match function took place in the village hall across the road, hotly anticipated by those who considered bringing a plate to be a combat sport. Every December Avery's commanding sermon astonished the crowd, and every January they guiltily ignored their resolutions to go to church more. Avery didn't mind, saying she didn't work on commission, and she'd declaim as heartily to one person as she would to a packed house.

Rita folded programmes for the service at the long kitchen table. The oil diffuser burbled on the hutch dresser, shooting fragrant steam into the air.

Avery lunged forward with one foot propped against the couch, limbering up for the service. Even for two people as happy in their own heads as the present company, Avery's imposing stance prompted Rita to fill the silence.

"Good line-up. No 'Away in a Manger' this year?"

"Thank you!" Avery rubbed her kneecap and thrust her hips deeper towards the couch. "The way I see it, we've got about forty minutes from go to whoa. I don't want to get too bogged down and maudlin. The congregation's attention span only lasts so long, so Manger got the chop."

"Fair dues."

Decades in the pulpit had honed Avery's precise order of service. Much as she loved the Nine Lessons and Carols, you couldn't waste it on this weddings-and-funerals crowd. In a nod to it, however, the service opened with 'Once in Royal David's City'. Next, lift the mood with your gutsy, stirring carols—'Joy to the World', 'O Come, All Ye Faithful'—and wait for Bufty to bring up the alto. Allow for plaintiveness in the middle section with 'The First Noel' and 'Silent Night'. Avoid the hazardous songs—you don't need the congregation tittering through the *pa-rum-pum-pum-pums* or going off the rails in 'Carol of the Bells', but you could swing for the fences with 'O Holy Night', which stirs the emotions, and you can feel like Whitney Houston, God rest her soul. Then set aside good taste—after all, it is the silly season—by finishing on 'Rudolph, the Red-Nosed Reindeer'. That gets the kiddies pepped up, and while secular, it conveys that the meek are blessed and shall inherit the earth, in a roundabout way. Done and dusted at a good clip, so we can be eating Mrs Nadine Van der Hoek's brandy truffles and drinking a milky tea by no later than twelve minutes past seven.

"Those lunges, Lord smite me down where I stand!" Bufty stuck her head through the French doors and fanned herself with a gardening-gloved hand. "Are you finished in the bathroom? I'm popping in to have a little wash. I'll get you to zip me up after. Or not!" Behind her, Jimmy Stewart spun around in circles and Roger lay on his back rolling from one side to the other.

"I think I hear someone arriving," said Avery, blushing. Rita folded her paper a little faster.

"Yep," called Judy from the back door.

"Yep," called Rita.

Life was a combat sport for Judy, who sailed in carrying numerous gifts for the church tree and a plastic-wrapped plate of star-shaped shortbread, dipped in dark chocolate with a white chocolate squiggle piped over the top.

Judy placed the biscuits on the table where Rita could see them.

"Sissy's not coming tonight—seeing that boyfriend she refuses to talk about—so boo sucks to the anti-butter brigade, I've made my famous shortbread."

"That's a shame about Sissy, but either way your mother should have bagsed enough VIP seats when we decorated the tree this morning—it's not what Jesus would've wanted, but you know there's no talking her out of it." Avery stretched her hands towards the ceiling, rested her other foot against the couch and resumed her lunging.

"Marlon's on her way with Glenn. The twins said they'd be here, they're bigger heathens than any of us but the bar's shut on Mondays, so no excuses. Now, Jayne's shop is open late tonight, so it's a no from her. Mind you, why anyone would need to go Christmas shopping for a wedding dress, let alone after 5 PM, is quite beyond me. And speaking of, Peter's wife insisted they drive up to Manukau to go late-night Christmas shopping, which—" Judy raised her hands and shook her head. "Let's just say he's made his bed and is now lying in it. But Pete and Neil should be there. I rang them both, sent a reminder to the group chat, and texted them today."

Judy picked up a folded programme. "Where's Stevie hidden, is she coming along tonight? Looks like a decent line-up, Avery. Ah yes. *Once in royal* . . . hmm!" Judy interrupted her own singing. "No 'Away in a Manger'?"

"Too maudlin," said Rita.

"Hmm."

"I made Russian fudge," added Rita.

"Hmm."

"Someone's here!" called Bufty from inside the bathroom. "I'll be out in a minute!"

"Knock-knock!"

"Door's open!" Judy and Marlon's voices were so alike that Judy could've been replying to herself.

The dogs wreathed Marlon and Glenn's ankles as they walked in, wet noses pushing against hands, hoping to secure a scritch behind the ears.

"Would've been here sooner," said Marlon, "but there was cattle on the old Smith Road."

"What do I always say?" said Judy. "You've got to come down the Breem Road."

"Ben sends his apologies," continued Marlon, "his boss is putting on a bit of a do tonight for the team. But he's knitted us three nifty beanies for under the tree."

"And I made a couple of merino lace baby blankets," said Glenn, crouching to pat both dogs, Roger on his considerable upturned tummy, and Jimmy Stewart on his flanks.

Judy unfolded one of the blankets. "Glenn, you've done it again. Who could imagine those burly hands that fix my toilet could produce such fine-spun lacework?"

No Gordon was in any danger of being rich, but Marlon's branch got the closest thanks to Glenn's plumbing business. Both Glenn and Marlon hoped Ben would take over once he got his Master Plumber certification under his belt. Either way, with the price of merino yarn it was fortunate both father and son were in a well-paid line of work.

"Has anyone talked to Irene today?" asked Marlon.

Rita raised her hand. "She sounded a bit tired. Passed on her best wishes for tonight."

"No digs about Jesus?"

"Nope."

"Bloody hell," said Judy. "Only took 102 years, but the old girl's getting soft."

"She said she knew we'd sound better during the hymns than anyone else."

"There you go," Marlon mimed shooting a bow and arrow towards Rita. "Irene's still Irene."

"Goodness, everyone's here, yes, kia ora, kia ora." Bufty appeared, tugging at the beaded neckline of her purple tunic. "Ave, can you zip me up, please and thank you?"

Marlon took a programme from Rita's pile. "Great line-up, Avery. I just love 'O Come, All Ye Faithful'."

"Should rename it 'O Come, All Ye Unfaithful' for this lot," giggled Bufty, as Avery zipped her dress.

Several notification alerts sounded off simultaneously around the room.

"The twins messaged," said Glenn, holding his phone at arm's length, "Let me see, they're—"

"Going to meet us at the church," read Judy.

"Why do you have to . . . I mean, we're all here," said Rita, stacking the programmes back into a neat pile.

"Ah, they've made churros in the deep fryer at the bar," said Marlon, "and chocolate sauce with scotch in it. Very continental."

"So they have! I thought they didn't like cooking," said Bufty, fixing the clasp on the string of pearls around her neck.

"They don't cook much, it's true," said Marlon.

"But when they do put in the effort—well," finished Glenn. "What was it, the other day when they came round? Handmade noodles! From scratch! No middle ground, those girls."

"I'm going to put my clown suit on, and then I'd better head off," said Avery, waving as she went down the hallway. "Ta-ta, see you all soon."

"Isn't that scent in the diffuser magical?" said Bufty. "It's a special Christmas blend, they sent us a little bottle because we're such loyal customers. Frankincense, myrrh and orange. The gifts of the Magi, and all that."

"Let's face it, the day you can locate three wise men around here there'll be red bluebirds," chortled Judy. She glanced at her watch, slender and gold with a purple face, her sixtieth birthday gift from Pete, Peter and Neil. "Right, we better get this covered wagon on the road. Marlon, what are you bringing for a plate?"

Between Judy gathering up the programmes; Marlon sending Glenn out to the car to get their peanut brittle; Stevie emerging from the hall, swinging a leather jacket over her shoulders; the dogs scooting back and forth, affronted that they weren't receiving attention; Bufty deciding at the last minute to change her lipstick and everyone remembering that they still had to put their shoes back on; no one clocked

Rita sitting unresponsive while her family eightsome reeled around her. Why would anyone notice that.

Marlon leaned on the back of Rita's chair and pulled her sensible blue slip-ons over her heels. "You okay Ree? Up-diddly-up, we'll be late."

Rita was not okay. Her custard-soft bones liquified beneath her skin. A distant and unsettling pain was forming. Like someone had taken sharp scissors and snipped the fine membrane at the base of her belly button.

"I feel a bit . . . crook."

Marlon leaned over. Rita's face was blotchy. Sweat pasted her fringe to her forehead.

"Let's get you lying down," said Marlon, "here, I'll help you."

Bufty walked in from the hallway. "Oh! My baby! What's happened? Judy, call the ambulance!"

Marlon lifted Rita's arm over her shoulder. Together, they hobbled over to the couch. Rita collapsed into its ochre cushions.

"I'm fine," said Rita, unconvincingly. "Just need to rest my eyes."

"I'll call Avery," said Bufty, pacing the room. "We'll cancel it—"

"Don't do that, Mum," said Marlon, placing her hand on Rita's forehead. "Is that someone pulling in? Stevie, can you fetch a cool facecloth?"

"Hello! Only me!" called a man's voice.

"Neil, thank goodness," said Judy, "is Pete coming?"

"He's there already—hello Bufty, don't you look bonny," said Neil, kissing her cheek. "If it isn't Stevie! Goodness, you haven't aged a day. How is . . . was it—London? The Ministry and all that?"

Stevie handed Marlon a wet cloth. "Back for the holibobs, I am. Good to see you, too."

"Anyway," Neil continued, "I've got Lego for under the

tree and a packet of biscuits for the table. Cripes, Rita, you alright there?"

"Why don't you take the bickies back home," said Judy, patting his hand. "I've made my shortbread stars, you can go in on those." The annual Christmas Service after-match function was no time for packaged biscuits. Imagine people thinking her ex-husband couldn't fix a plate!

"I'll stay with you, Rita," said Bufty, "someone unzip me."

"Keep your clothes on Mum, I'll stay, you can't miss the service," said Marlon, "Avery needs you there, it'll be a bust without you to lead the carols."

"It's true," conceded Bufty, "Nadine Van der Hoek makes fine truffles, but she's no singer. Though clearly, no one close to her has let her in on this yet."

"No, I'll stay," said Judy, looking sadly at her shortbread stars. She wouldn't get to see everyone demolish them. Well, Christmas is a time of giving, after all.

Stevie removed her sunglasses. "I'll stay."

The room fell quiet.

Judy folded her arms. "Why are you wearing sunglasses inside?"

Rita lifted the facecloth. "She can stay."

"Fine," said Bufty, "We'd better scarper, look, my phone's on, I love you, and we're just down the road. And if you need to call 111, just get in the car and start driving to the hospital, by the time the ambulance gets all the way out here—"

"Yep," croaked Rita.

"Now, where's my handbag—"

"You can leave the medicine cabinet at home, surely," said Judy, straining under the weight of her mother's leather bag as she passed it to her. "We'll only be gone a tick, and it's a bloody tight squeeze in the church as it is. That bag is like an extra person."

Bufty, lifting the straps over her shoulder, shook her head. "There's no talking me out of it, Judy, you never know when someone will need a biro or a tampon. Now, can you get the

Gaylene Glossop slice from the fridge? I've already put it on a little plate."

The farewells, mottled and overlapping, plaintive and practical, continued down the hallway until only Stevie and Rita remained, silent.

Stevie dropped the sunglasses back over her eyes. "Let's get pissed."

Chapter Twelve

Darrelle Hoare
Bone cancer
2 September 1988

Bufty's voice rose over the hum of the vacuum cleaner as she worked her way a cappella through the libretto for *South Pacific*. She wore a pink-and-blue floral housecoat, her hair in a jade-green scarf tied at the forehead, apricot-scented Nutrimetics emollient barding her face. Rita lay on the couch in a baggy Meat Puppets t-shirt over her underwear and odd socks, eating cornflakes and evaporated milk from a coffee mug with a teaspoon. Sitting on her legs, watching Rita intently, was Roger. To Avery, immersed in a volume of Maya Angelou poetry in the bay window, Bufty vacuuming and singing the last lines of 'Dites-moi' was as a whisper in the background.

"Local vice squad's here," murmured Rita to Roger. His ears quivered, but he was not to be distracted.

"Knock-knock!" called Hetty Loomis, who had walked in through the wide-open back door.

She tried again.

"*But I'm only a cock*—Oh my stars, Hetty, I didn't see you there!" Bufty motioned at the vacuum cleaner. "I must look a fright! We weren't expecting company!" She mashed the switch with her heel.

"Yes, I gather," said Hetty over the vacuum's long sigh into silence. "I've got my niece's raffle tickets to sell you. How many shall I put you down for?"

Bufty froze. Rita continued chewing.

Avery shut her book and slid off the window seat. "Cuppa?"

Hetty surveyed the room. A dog, sitting on the furniture. *That Rita*, half-naked in broad daylight, thinking she can waltz back into town from Italy like a bad penny to lie slugabed ignoring her elders and betters. Bufty, looking like the Wreck of the Hesperus. And as for that mannish Avery, Hetty didn't even trust her to make a cup of tea.

"Rita made neenish tarts this morning," said Avery, sloshing water into the jug. "Would you like one?"

"She did indeed!" Bufty pulled the vacuum cord tight to stop her hands trembling. "That'll be nice, won't it, a little homemade neenish tart?"

"Hmm. Homemade . . . that does sound novel."

The picture printed on Rita's black t-shirt wasn't identifiably lewd yet still appeared threatening to Hetty. But—neenish tarts, much easier bought than made—perhaps the girl had her uses after all.

Rita fed the last spoonful of cornflakes to Roger.

"Well, I never," wheezed Hetty.

"I'll go wipe my face." Bufty sensed Avery's pained glance. "I'll only be a tick—Avery will fix your tea, and we can have a nice little sit-down." Jittery, unsure of the order of her words, she considered hiding under her bed. Rita shot off the couch, cradling Roger, and shut herself in the study.

Bufty and Avery drummed up as many pleasantries as they could muster and dutifully purchased a raffle ticket in aid of the new chapel roof at the niece's boarding school. Invigorated by two neenish tarts—faultless, she had to admit—Hetty Loomis revealed the real reason for her imposition.

"Now, I suppose you've heard Darrelle Hoare is dying." Her smile did not meet her small, dull eyes.

Avery touched Bufty's leg under the table. *Steady*.

Bufty had known Hetty Loomis since she was an Uprichard. You could never let an Uprichard get the better of you. Even if she had got the better of you.

She forced a warm smile for Hetty. "Of course, I knew she'd been indisposed. She's over in Gisborne with her sister, getting sunshine and rest. Just the ticket, I should think."

"She's got weeks on the clock, if that. Bone cancer is a beastly one to beat. It'll be a blessed miracle if she sees Christmas. Though I doubt she will."

How did Hetty come by all these details of her friend's health while she, the real friend, was in the dark? But Bufty was not about to press Hetty, not with that pompous look on her face. It was already too hard to bear.

Not wry, worldly Darrelle! Not cancer! Bufty met Darrelle at the aerosol factory when she was seventeen. Together with Nan Smith and Mary Flint, also townies unaware of Bufty's past, they became "The Set", sitting side by side, connecting calls between the main plant in Panmure and the men in their factory. To them, Bufty was a dear, pretty, stout-hearted country girl who made them laugh. They organised the kitchen tea at Irene's the week before Bufty's wedding and stood by her side as bridesmaids. Darrelle and Jonty Hoare were unable to bear children, but she became a treasured aunty to the girls, who greeted her as if Santa Claus had slid down the chimney whenever she visited.

Darrelle reached out first after Avery moved in, coming round with a bottle of schnapps and confiding in Bufty that her beloved aunt had been what you might call *a confirmed spinster*. Summarily frozen out of the family for living with another woman, this aunt had moved to America with her partner five years ago and Darrelle had never seen her since, though she wrote her covert letters.

"To tell the truth Buf, in boarding school we were all in love with at least one of the older girls, they practically wrote it into the prospectus. I was absolutely *gone* on Marianne Sutcliffe, she had long, chestnut hair—not brown, mind you, chestnut—and she could outrun anyone, and she had this dimple in her chin . . ."

"Gosh, Darrelle," said Bufty, "you paint quite a picture. Are you sure you're not, y'know, one of us?"

"The dreaded L-word, you mean?" Darrelle poured another nip of schnapps into Bufty's glass. "No, I like Jonty as he is, though I do sometimes wonder what Marianne is up to. Ann Hammond accosted me in the supermarket the other day, asking if I'd heard about you and Avery. She and her sisters were in the boarding house with me, and she mooned over the older girls as much as anyone else. Ann was obsessed with Joy Fairweather, and why wouldn't you be with a name like that. So, I told her not to be so bloody bourgeois. She nearly dropped her carrots."

With Darrelle on board, Nan and Mary had followed. Though perplexed by the logistics of lesbian life, shunning Bufty was no fun at all.

"Well, best be off, these raffle tickets won't sell themselves," said Hetty, having sufficiently set her cat amongst Bufty's pigeons.

"I must call Darrelle's mother for her sister's number," fretted Bufty, watching Hetty's car pull away from the driveway. She flapped her hands. "Oh, that woman! And me looking all done up like a dog's dinner! It's as if she *tries* to drop in when it's least convenient. Why isn't she at home doing her own bloody vacuuming? It's Saturday morning!"

"Oh, undoubtedly," said Avery, "this was no accident."

"That menacing look in Hetty's eyes, when she's about to tell you she knows something you don't, oh it gives me chills," said Bufty. "Like an apex predator preparing to devour. I'll never forget that terrible day when—" She paused, seeing

Rita enter the room again. “Ah, yes, that is, when she called in right after I had Marlon, and said, ‘Oh, Bufty, you do keep a *very smudgy bathroom mirror*, don’t you?’ And I said, ‘You need to get your eyes checked Hetty, I always polish my mirrors’. As if I’d had time to worry about the bathroom mirror with a screaming newborn.”

“That’s all Hetty’ll ever amount to.” Avery hunkered back down into the bay window and draped a knitted afghan over her knees. “A busybody prying into everyone’s lives, because if she pried inwards for one minute all she’d see is an empty, cracked vessel.”

“Honestly!” Bufty picked a pastry crumb from the tablecloth and ate it. “You could travel to a monastery in the middle of Timbuktu and consume a bran muffin in perfect silence and the next day there’d be a telegram from that whited sepulchre asking if you were keeping regular. She must’ve heard about Darrelle from her daughter, she’s a nurse up at Middlemore.”

“Those neenish tarts impressed her though,” said Avery, “bravo Rita, saving the day.”

Rita, now back on the couch, ran the pendant from her necklace back and forth over her fingers.

“Pearls before swine,” she said.

Bufty rang Darrelle.

“Poppet, I’m so sorry you found out like this,” said Darrelle. “I’m not hiding it from you on purpose, it’s just so ugly and pitiful that every time I talk about it, I feel like screaming. Everyone either avoids me because they’re too scared to look me in the eye, or they mope like I’m already dead. What I want more than anything is for you to come stay, and we’ll gossip and laugh, and stay up talking long after we should be in bed like the old days, and for the dreaded C-word to not pass our lips once the entire time.”

Rita drove her mother to Gisborne, the back seat of the Cortina filled with five containers of homemade biscuits. Bufty only stopped talking to sleep, her head lolling against the window, and they arrived one and a half containers of biscuits down.

Darrelle's funeral was two months later. Bufty wrote a letter to the aunt in America to let her know.

Chapter Thirteen

"God, have you seen this line of ants here? Marching two by two, hurrah, hurrah?" Stevie stepped back from the stove. "Should I kill them?"

Each black dot linked to form a purposeful chain, snaking across white tiles embellished by Irene with hand-painted poppies.

"No point," said Rita, still lying on the couch. "Mum's tried everything. They'll outlive us all." She pushed up the damp cloth covering her eyes, squinting at the rush of light. "Least they don't say much. Avery calls them our load-bearing ants."

Stevie opened the cupboard above the bench, hooking her thumb into the flat steel latch. "Are you quite sure you don't want a green ginger wine? If Nana's wisdom holds, this stuff will just about cure . . . uh, what ails you." She wiggled the bottle.

"Fair dues. A nip."

"Blimey, Nana's got heaps back here, what is she up to—even I only get Cointreau from duty-free which, let me tell you, is not as exciting as this lot make it sound, although I suppose you know that . . . fuck me, Chambord! I haven't had Chambord in donkey's. Shall we?"

"It's barely alcoholic, isn't it?"

"Sixteen percent, it says."

"Christ," said Rita.

"So it's basically Capri-Sun," said Stevie at the same time.

"Knock yourself out," said Rita, "I'll stick with ginger. And—I feel like a dick for asking, but—could you grab me some water too, please?"

"Happy to," said Stevie, filling a cup from the tap and leaning over the bench to pass it to Rita. "If I'm honest, I'd rather be with you than with everyone at the church, all those people from *round here* looking at me, asking questions about my life, and telling me I've gotten taller."

"We're from round here," said Rita.

"Yes, and we're about the only sane ones, and even that's pushing it. Here we go—green ginger wine for you, Chambord for me, clink clink! Since you're couchbound, I might even take this opportune moment to steal the La-Z-Boy . . ." She wrenched the lever to raise the footrest and leaned forward, elbows resting on her outstretched legs. "You were always my favourite, you know. Bloody sorry about the cancer."

"Cheers," said Rita, tilting her glass towards Stevie.

"My favourite, aside from Nana, of course." Stevie drained her glass of Chambord with a juicebox-clearing slurp.

Rita didn't answer. Not silent out of rudeness. She could tell Stevie wanted to say more. Stevie, no slouch at observation herself, knew Rita would never outright ask you anything, but damn it if she couldn't give you enough rope with all that silence if you weren't careful.

Doris Day stopped singing, the needle resting at the centre of the record. With the absence of her voice louder than its presence, Stevie leapt to her feet, lifted the needle and turned the record over.

Stevie held up the record sleeve and imitated Doris Day's smile. When that didn't get a rise out of Rita, she said, "You know, as of late, I'm not *quite* happy as Larry working for the Ministry. Well, that's not it precisely—"

The landline rang.

Stevie lifted the needle again and took the phone off its cradle.

"Ahoy-hoy? Sorry, I can't hear you—right, right—I'll put you on speakerphone." Stevie pressed a button. "It's Nana," she whispered. "They're about to do 'O Holy Night'."

Bufty's voice swooped down the phone line as the congregation reached the crescendo. Rita could smell the polished kauri pews, could picture Avery swaying in front of the oak and burgundy damask reredos and the banners hand-quilted by local women back when it was your duty to know such skills.

She pressed the cloth against her eyes. Tears spilled over the waterline. "Christ's sake."

"Yes, that's why they're singing. It's especially delicious taking the Lord's name in vain at Christmas, isn't it?" Stevie shielded her voice from the receiver with her hand. "A real seasonal treat."

The song finished, and they heard Avery's voice in the distance through the phone line until Bufty hung up.

"I won't tell anyone you cried," said Stevie, "if you don't tell anyone what I said."

"You didn't say anything."

"Exactly."

"No, but really. You told me nothing."

"Preeeecisely. Scout's honour, dyb-dyb-dyb, dob-dob-dob."

"Alright, alright." Rita lowered the cloth back over her

eyes, even though it had, by this point, become warm and damp instead of cold and damp. "Give it a rest. How about some Johnny Cash Christmas next."

Chapter Fourteen

Aunty Sweet
Non-Hodgkin lymphoma
5 June 1991

"She's a high-spirited girl, Bufty," said Principal Fitzwallace. He turned to Miss Crisp, the school nurse, his shoulders creeping towards his ears. Though out of his depth, he didn't want Miss Crisp to know; nor did he want Mr Jock Williams to get wind of the upper hand being there for the taking.

Miss Crisp raised a Pall Mall Menthol to her sloping chin. Her face was as grey as her serge skirt, and every bit as severely fashioned.

"Your daughter is a high-spirited girl," Principal Fitzwallace repeated feebly. He longed for the taupe handkerchief in his breast pocket. He could sense a heavy sweat droplet forming at his hairline, with more queued behind it.

"She talks too much. Is that what you're saying? Is she talking back in class? That's not how I raised her—"

"No, no, Mr Williams, that's not—that's not what we're getting at here. Bufty is exemplary, favoured by all her teachers."

"Well?" Jock Williams folded his arms. Being near the high school wound him up. He'd left all that business to his wife and avoided it however possible now she'd gone. Being in the principal's office called to mind the beatings and dressing-downs of his own short-lived schooling.

Principal Fitzwallace's hands clasped and unclasped on his desk. Jock tensed, as though expecting once more the cane's hot sting to stripe his calves.

"Your daughter is behaving a little . . . out of the ordinary. She's always been independent—fleet-footed—hearty—"

Principal Fitzwallace knew he was losing his prepollency.

Miss Crisp took a full-bodied drag from her cigarette. "The kind of girl who holds open the door for you." She emitted a puff of smoke towards Jock, onto which he could've drawn two dots for eyes and a line for a mouth and it wouldn't've looked much different from the person behind it.

"Exactly," said Principal Fitzwallace, fortified. "We are concerned Bufty's plucky nature and close friendship with Miss Avery Manrose may veer towards the *irregular*, bordering on . . . you might say . . . *turpitude*."

Coincidentally, Jock Williams had of late suspected that Avery Manrose wielded undue influence on Bufty's life. He was too unsophisticated and incurious and, to his defence, ill-travelled, to grasp any subtext in Principal Fitzwallace's words; it simply rankled him no end that Bufty wasn't around to fix his dinner and keep house.

"It's not uncommon for young girls to experience a certain contumacy when their mothers have . . . that is . . . are *no longer with us* . . . perhaps what she requires is a role model, some moral guidance, to see off any such *corruption* . . ."

Bringing up the wife was the final straw. Jock was not inclined to bow and scrape before some poncy, edge-you-cated rooster, some ghoulish nurse, telling him how to raise his daughter, and he relayed this sentiment in as many words.

Principal Fitzwallace noted the vein pulsing like a siren at the ex-boxer's temple. He was not inclined to die with his boots on and pushed the matter no further.

"Bufty's going to take a job at the new factory soon," said Jock, prodding the principal's plywood desk so hard his fountain pen bounced in its holder. "Can't imagine why she'd want to stay round this shanty when she could make good money and support her father. And with her face, some fellow'll snap her up lickety-split. So, you won't have to worry about her high spirits for much longer."

"A consummation devoutly to be wished," said Principal Fitzwallace, content that he'd explicitly imparted his desired message. "Good day, Mr Williams."

Jock Williams suspected the principal had insulted him—consummation, my eye! He tugged his hat down and stomped back to Bufty, who was squirming in the front seat of the brown Hillman Minx.

"Heedless girl," said Miss Crisp, stubbing her cigarette out in the heavy square glass dish on Principal Fitzwallace's desk. "The kind to carry her own books—and read them, too."

"That will do, Miss Crisp." One got the impression, not wholly unfounded, that she had a list of phrases at the ready for impressing upon parents that their daughters were altogether unnatural.

"The type to eat an apple on a cold day," muttered Miss Crisp as she walked out the office door. "Not afraid of bees."

Jock slammed the car door and pulled a carton of Capstans from his breast pocket. Bufty folded the rough material of her school skirt hem over and under her fingers and waited for him to yell or wallop her across the face. You had to be prepared. If it didn't happen, it was a good day, and if it did, at least you weren't surprised.

He took a drag from his cigarette, then let it dangle from his lower lip like a loose tooth. The smoke smelled like wet, muddy boots and singed flour sacks, but it was a familiar smell. Not safe. Familiar.

"The old muckety-muck reckons you talk too much."

"Is that all?"

"Couldn't make hide nor hair of what he was going on about, so I left him with a flea in his ear for wasting my time and said you'd be well shot of the place. Though if I were you, I'd cut out right now. Can't imagine what they're teaching you in there, but it can't be better than having an honest job."

He laughed, and Bufty laughed with him. It was a good day, after all.

☾

Principal Fitzwallace's meeting with Bill Manrose about his daughter Avery was equally productive.

"Self-reliant," rasped Miss Crisp from behind her cigarette smoke. "Knows which way the wind is blowing. Fires a rifle without a buttstock."

Bill Manrose was far more widely read and travelled than Jock Williams, who, to be fair, had little spare time left over after pursuing his next gin. He'd observed Bufty and Avery's friendship and reached his conclusion with more largesse.

And though not pugnacious like Jock, Bill Manrose had a backbone, and he regarded Principal Fitzwallace frankly.

"My daughter has never laughed so much, never been so happy, since becoming friends with Miss Williams."

"We're not in the business of concerning ourselves with such trivialities as the happiness of children, Mr Manrose."

"Be that as it may, I see nothing amiss. Let us be gentlemen, forget this disagreeable exchange, and conduct ourselves accordingly. Good day." Bill stood, placing his hat atop his head, and left.

"The kind to play the chukka with two mallets."

Principal Fitzwallace drew the handkerchief from his breast pocket and held it to his forehead. "That will do, Miss Crisp."

☾

While Bill Manrose cherished his daughter, who had her mother's eyes and his love of books, Jock Williams, on the other hand, was a boorish sot who'd taken too many hits to the head and pretended that was the reason he failed the enlistment medical examination. His instability grew like black mould slithering across the ceiling, and it wasn't long before his wife Clara secretly renewed correspondence with Aubwyn, the fellow she used to go steady with before marrying Jock. The more distant and infatuated with her past she became, the more Jock drank, until one day Clara left, and a note on the kitchen table remained. By anyone's standards, it was abominable to abandon Bufty. But Clara was not a bad person. Just the wrong woman at the wrong time, who'd had it up to here with living in the unglamorous middle of nowhere married to a coarse brute with Clark Gable's ears but none of his charisma. Bufty's sister Sweet had married, and Bufty wouldn't be far behind—as Clara wrote in her note—and perhaps Bufty would like to visit, when things worked out.

Bufty did not want to do that.

"Tell them she died," said Bufty to her father on the Monday morning after Clara left, glancing out the door to check if Avery had pulled up in Mr Manrose's blue Vauxhall. Kids often rode horses to school, three or four astride, and a bus putt-putted from the surrounding villages into the town each morning. It was terribly grown-up to arrive in a car. She wished Avery would drive her miles away from here, not to school, but far across the seas to America. Or at least to Auckland.

"You can write a note. I'll take it in today to excuse me from school. We'll say she died on Saturday, and we're having a private burial this week. They'll forget about it all soon enough, and so can we. That's what I'm going to do. Well, I'll do it if you will."

Jock patted around in his pockets for a scrap of paper and pencil stub.

"What about the gravestone?"

"We'll say we took her back to Onehunga and buried her there. I'll go to school today, put on a bit of a show, get it over with, and we'll lie tomorrow, and that will be that. I'll ask Avery to collect our paper and the milk, so no one suspects."

Jock's jaw tightened at the mention of Avery. "The death notice in the paper. People look for those."

"We'll think of something."

"What about Sweet? Can't have her looking like a stunned mullet when people pass on their condolences."

"I'll write and tell her the plan. She'll understand. She probably won't even care."

"What if Clara comes back?" Jock angled away from his daughter, big shoulders around his big ears, wearing the same shirt and trousers as when he found the note, looking like a pile of rocks that had slipped from some high crag to the dust below.

Bufty fidgeted with her blouse. "I've fixed you a sandwich for lunch. Cold sausage and plenty of mustard. It's in the larder." She dropped a quick kiss on her father's shoulder. "Avery's here. You'll feel better for eating."

Jock watched her get in the car, gesturing high and low as she talked to Avery, waving about like a sapling in a gale. He rubbed his cramped calf muscle, and for the first time, as Bufty left in another father's car, he saw his daughter as a whole, capable human being, instead of a good-looking financial burden at worst, and a manifestation of his virility and God-given rights as a husband at best. He'd forget about this moment by the time another bottle emptied. And the moment came too late. But it happened.

Bufty yearned for her father's approval, yet counted down the days till he would drink himself to death. Glimpses of a real father revealed themselves with maddening rarity when he wasn't spending all the food money on grog, or seething at the kitchen table, icy resentment trapped inside him like a forgotten child playing hide and seek in a refrigerator.

If Bufty resented her mother and sister for skipping town, she never let on. What was life, after all, but muddling from one scrape and strife to the next, and gussying it up with a coat of paint so your neighbours would mind their business? She knew the local mothers and fathers were not the Greer Garsons and Walter Pidgeons of the picture theatre. They were imperfect, violent, up to no good, and their daughters got put in the club and their sons got drunk and fell off cliffs, and their dogs ran into paddocks and ripped open sheep throats with their teeth, and a car couldn't so much as pull into a driveway because they'd gone the wrong way without the neighbours building a cheap novel's worth of narrative around the innocent moment. You take the best of your sorry situation and tell the story you want people to hear, because if you leave it too late, they'll tell it for you.

☾

Bill Manrose didn't mind if bubbly Bufty stayed for days at a time. She went out of her way to help, picking flowers for the table, gathering fallen peaches from the yard, or bringing buckets of windfall fruit from the tree of someone she'd charmed while walking Fred the dog. He taught her to play the piano, which she picked up in a trice, and lent her books from his library. It did not pass him by that she brought out a side of his daughter usually only reserved for animals. Something carefree, yet protective.

Jock Williams died six weeks after Bufty turned seventeen. There was no funeral.

"Come stay with us for a bit," said Sweet. But Bufty got in the way at Sweet's house in Drury, reeling from Avery's recent departure for St Swithin's Theological College and unable to placate the fractious babies that refused to sleep. Sweet grew impatient with Bufty's wanton displays of emotion and told her to go stay with Clara and Aubwyn in Wellington.

There, she was even more in the way, dazed with longing for Avery's safe familiarity. Only the train journey lifted her spirits, watching the world slip by, no responsibilities, imagining herself a noirish vamp carrying reckless secrets. She considered lowering her voice like Lauren Bacall when the attendant asked to see her ticket, but she was worried people might think she was acting cheap.

Upon returning home, Bufty scrubbed the little house from top to bottom. She boiled and aired her father's clothes, donated the passable garments to the church for distribution amongst the needy and burned the rest. She considered throwing away Jock's remaining gin. Instead, she took his place at the kitchen table and drank. Was she more of a failure for not saving her father, or for not being able to find kinship with her mother? Or for feeling about a girl the way you're supposed to feel about a fellow? *How could parents be so careless with someone they brought into the world on purpose?* She fell into a nightmare-stained sleep with her life in tatters around her ankles.

The next morning, Bill Manrose knocked on the door.

"Special delivery from Avery," he said, placing a box on the ground and touching his hat. Judging by the snuffling and agitation, the box contained something alive and excited to be so.

Bufty opened the box, and a tawny German shepherd puppy sprang out, pressing itself against her shins. There was a note on its collar.

My name is Roger. For my blonde namesake, Ginger Rogers. I'm your new friend and confidante, and I shall keep you safe while AM is away. Nota bene: I'm a lady canine, who has undergone all the necessary personal veterinary procedures!

Bufty sobbed into Roger's dense fur, warm and bristly as a father's chin, forgetting her temple-crunching hangover.

"Oh, Mr Manrose! She's the most beautiful creature I've ever seen. Please come over for dinner this Sunday. I'd love to have you."

Bufty excelled at her new factory job because she had to, and it was fun earning real money and feeling grown-up. Maybe if her mother had a job to give her a sense of purpose and income, she might've not been so listless and overcast to make running off with a man called *Aubwyn* a worthwhile option. Then again, her daughters could've surely diverted her.

The bank sent a letter. Her father had accrued gambling debts. The house was to be foreclosed. And that was that. Clara had told young Bufty and Sweet that her family came from wealth and grandeur until her father squandered it on drink and gambling. By the time Bufty cottoned on that there had never been any great heights to fall from, and that it was more embarrassing altogether for her grandfather to have frittered away not much at all, and for Clara to have married a carbon copy of him, it was too late. He left only a few chattels and an ability to gloss over the truth for Bufty to inherit.

Mr Manrose invited her to stay at his house in Avery's room. Breathing deep into Avery's pillows, trying to imprint any remaining trace of her onto her skin, Bufty slept better than she had in years.

Wally Gordon asked her to marry him. Mr Manrose died of a heart attack. The lingering scent of Port Royal pipe tobacco was all that was left of him, like a cross between burning paddock stubble and the lapels of an oilskin jacket when you lean in for a welcome hug. And soon that was gone, too. There was so much to take in, and it didn't stop coming.

Bufty and Sweet barely talked to each other at all. Both had small children to look after, and children make it easy to let the time slide past without anyone else noticing. No one noticed—possibly not even Bufty and Sweet—when they started talking to each other again, either.

Sometime after Jayne was born, Sweet showed up with a bottle of apricot brandy. She and Bufty shut themselves in the study and resurfaced six hours later, red-faced and tearful with laughter, bottle empty.

After that, Aunty Sweet was around a lot more. You'd hear her in the kitchen asking where the sugar was and Bufty singing back "where do you keep the su-u-u-uugar", setting each other off into howls of laughter, turning any conversation into a song, both pretending it had always been this way. And at Sweet's funeral after her short battle with cancer, and her unveiling, and every family gathering from then on out, Bufty perpetuated this little myth, and eventually, with no one left to vouch or dispute, it became the truth.

Chapter Fifteen

"Are you feeling better? We brought a plate back for you," said Mahalia.

"There would've been a brandy truffle, but it rolled onto the road on the way back," said Diana

"I'm okay. Not hungry, though," said Rita.

"You have to eat something," said Marlon.

"I'll have it." Stevie took the paper plate from her cousin. "How'd it go? You must've damn near blown the roof off with 'O Holy Night'."

Avery filled the kettle. "Everyone did an outstanding job. We topped last year's gift collection, too. Cuppa, anyone?"

"Who wants Grand Marnier?" asked Diana at the same time. "Stole it from the bar."

"Grand Marnier?" Stevie looked impressed. "Pa-rum-pum-pum-*pum*."

"I'll just make a big one." Avery dropped teabags into the silver pot. Diana set out rows of Arcoroc mugs and liqueur goblets.

Bufty bustled into the living area, pulling off her long, spangled earrings and massaging her earlobes. "Didn't our singing sound good? You should have heard my harmonies on 'Joy to the World'." She squeezed Diana's shoulder and kissed her cheek. "I'll have a little nip alongside my tea, bub. How are you feeling, Baby Ree?"

Rita shrugged, but shuffled to sitting so Judy could drop onto the couch beside her.

"The kiddies were well-behaved, mind you," said Judy, placing Rita's feet into her lap. "I was quite pleasantly surprised. And never mind 'Joy to the World', how about my harmonies in 'Rudolph, the Red-Nosed Reindeer'? I know Nadine Van der Hoek didn't see *that* coming."

"*You'll go down in history*—like Rachel Hunter!" chorused Marlon. "Weren't you twins clever coming up with that line years ago, and everyone went with it? Do you think the kids these days even know who Rachel Hunter is?"

"Yeah, real genius of us," said Mahalia. "You had the audience in the palm of your hand, Avery."

"It's called a congregation," said Avery, crouching by the tree, "but I'm happy to call them anything at all when they show up in droves like that. Don't mind me, my lumbar is shot. Glenn, can you hand out the drinks for me? It should be steeped, and there's Bufty's fruitcake in the tin on the fridge."

"I always thought Christmas cake was revolting," said Marlon. "And as soon as I turned thirty it's like a switch went off, and now I can't get enough of it. Isn't that silly?"

"Wasn't it funny when that fly landed on Bev Murphy's head when she was doing the reading, and she didn't notice?" said Judy. "And god, remember Aunty Sweet's Christmas cake fried in fat on Boxing Day? Even I couldn't face it."

"I know, and how about Rob Heaphy showing up?" said Marlon. "He used to be such a hunk before he got on the hard stuff, didn't he? I never thought I'd see him again. Old Mrs Heaphy sure looked beside herself, and fair enough.

I suppose Christmas is the time for prodigal sons . . ." She glanced at Stevie, who tapped her nose.

"That's right," said Judy, "he was on the bad stuff, I mean the *really* bad stuff. I see he still hasn't located any of the teeth he lost."

"And there but for the grace of God go we, isn't that right, Avery?"

"That's right, Buf."

"There indeed," continued Judy. "Now, I haven't brought back any shortbread stars, Rita, because of course everyone snaffled them up straight away. Even Janice Ormondson, with her face like a fiddle, put away three." She patted her sister's feet. "Sure you're okay?"

Rita gave her the thumbs up.

"Here we go, no milk for you anymore, right Bufty?" Glenn automatically took the tea to Bufty's usual armchair and corrected himself when he realised she was in the La-Z-Boy. The room felt a bit thrown off with Rita on the couch.

"Correct and correct, Glenn, we refuse to give a single cent to Fonterra," said Bufty, "devious swines, the lot of them."

"Ruthless pack animals," said Diana.

"Slippery bastards," said Mahalia.

"They're not very nice, are they," said Marlon.

"Overpaid townies," said Judy.

"Can't trust 'em at all," said Stevie.

Everyone looked at Rita.

"Fascist Tories," she said.

"Amen," said Avery, "and may Rik Mayall rest in peace."

"How *are* you doing, Baby Ree?" asked Marlon.

"You look better than you did before," said Judy, "less green about the gills."

"Yeah, nah," said Rita. "I guess I'm better for a lie-down. It's weird. Since finding out about the cancer I feel like I get the wind knocked out of me in a second. Most days I'm fine. And then. Not fine."

She paused. *That's enough of that.* "The singing was good."

Stevie, on the floor, rested her head against Bufty's knee.

"Thank you for staying behind with her, Floss," said Bufty.

Marlon sat in Bufty's armchair. Mahalia and Diana took seats at the kitchen table, with Glenn on a folding chair beside the Christmas tree. Next to him, without uncurling from child's pose, Avery took cautious sips of Grand Marnier.

"So, what *have* you been up to since you've been back, Stevie?" asked Judy.

At the same time, Bufty raised her hand. "Speaking of how much we hate Fonterra—look, we were thinking—just a little thought, that I'm going to run by you, to see what you think—"

"Spit it out, Mum," said Rita.

"What if we made this year's Christmas . . . vegan?"

"But it's only a week away!" squawked Judy. "What about my trifle!"

"I'm sure you can work it out," said Bufty, "she's your daughter. I've felt wretched ever since Sissy made us watch that YouTube video about what they do to cows, and she's put up with us eating meat every Christmas for so long."

"Not that she put up with it quietly," said Judy.

"I—*we*—thought it would be nice. And, if I'm honest, I think it might be good for Rita, what with—" Bufty waved her hand at Rita "—everything."

"Hey, don't blame me."

"We're in," said Diana, "can't remember the last time we ate meat."

"Except for that steak last night," said Mahalia. "Stood there behind the bar eating it while all the customers watched. Some old guy asked where she got it from, and she was like, 'Where'd I get *what*'. It was crack up."

"Okay, except that."

"Hey, I'll try anything once," said Glenn.

"Byron spoke of man being a carnivorous production,"

said Avery, "though he was probably shickered on laudanum at the time."

Judy reached over the back of the couch for the bottle of Grand Marnier on the bench and topped up her glass. "I suppose I am used to it," she said, pressing her index finger between her eyebrows. "Well, what's the story then? What rabbit food are we supping on this Christmas?"

"Sissy mentioned the Lim Chhour supermarket up in Auckland," said Bufty. "They do a mock duck—isn't that something? I don't even know how to make real duck. She says filo pastry is vegan, and suggested duck-pesto pies since our basil is growing like the clappers."

"No roast, though," said Judy. "You can't distract me with pesto."

"Of course we'll roast potatoes, carrots, all that will be the same."

"A mushroom gravy," continued Avery, "Bufty found a neat recipe online."

"No ham . . ." said Judy.

"Minted peas, beans with almonds, Uncle Tom Cobley and all," said Bufty, "Sissy said she'd make a sticky date pudding and vegan ice cream."

"And I'll bring my trifle of course," said Judy.

"Marlon, you're bringing your potato dish—can you maybe use coconut cream?"

"*Bring me flesh and bring me wine*," sang Marlon. "Sure, why not?"

"Twins, did you have anything in mind?"

"Booze," said Mahalia.

"Or choux farci," said Diana. "A whole stuffed savoy cabbage. Very rustic."

Judy played her ace. "Don't get me wrong Mum, but what about butter? We can't have Christmas dinner with *margarine*."

Marlon hissed and held her index fingers up in an X as though warding off a vampire. Judy pointed inside her mouth and pretended to gag. Avery, heels pressed together in Baddha Konasana, did an exaggerated sign of the cross.

"You're right," said Bufty. "Margarine is disgusting, I won't desecrate the baby Jesus on his birthday. Butter it is. I'll buy the poncy stuff, at least."

"I'm sure Sissy will be pleased to have something to be aggrieved by," said Marlon.

Bufty laced her fingers, raising them to her heart.

"Oh, but we'll have to have a little roast though! What was I thinking?"

Rita's eyelids fluttered. The wasps, still side by side above the red curtains, grew fuzzy and receded as the words washed over her.

"Let's face it, she was no better than she ought to be."

"Of course, her mother's cousin was a Chiswick."

"The boy racers think it's a bloody road. It's not, it's a driveway."

"There's no one good on the right and if they were, they'd be on the left. Note that I didn't say Labour."

"Araucana, Red Shaver."

"We made our own fun, mind you."

"Oh, that was Kane, who worked at the Lido, we called him Lidocaine, because he was so boring—"

Chapter Sixteen

Sue Dijkstra
Breast cancer
6 May 2010

"Don't get me wrong," said Judy, "but Sue was a real—"

"Bully," said Marlon.

"Airhead?" said Jayne.

"No, that's you," said Judy. "Sue Dijkstra, on the other hand, was a—"

"Bitch," said Marlon and Judy—Judy barking the word, Marlon whispering—and they both laughed in surprise.

Once it got out that Bufty Gordon had shacked up with another woman, with the sod on her poor long-suffering husband's grave still damp, young Sue Ormondson spearheaded the high school persecution campaign against Judy. Which turned out to be a damp squib, as the words flowed off Judy's rhinoceros hide like mercury zipping across a Petri dish.

Foolish Sue! To undermine Judy was one thing, but to deride her mother, and to direct not a little of her contempt towards Jayne and her baby—that meant war. Jayne lived on another planet altogether and saw the good in everyone, so most of it went over her head. But bloody-minded Judy stayed ready and spoiling for battle.

"I can forgive someone *looking* stupid, or *being* stupid," Judy would say, playing to the back row, "but let's face it, both is too much. For god's sake, Sue, pick one." And she'd laugh, uproarious, then Sharon Fuffer would join in, and the rest of the class—who flowed like water to fit whichever container had the strongest walls—would join them in laughing at Sue.

No one misses a trick like children, especially not Janice Ormondson eavesdropping on her mum and older sister in the hallway after her bedtime. And so, the news made its way to the primary school soon enough. Janice told Erana not to eat lunch with Rita, or she'd "turn you lezzy". Rita strode right up to her, close enough that she could smell the egg sandwich on Janice's breath.

"Don't tell on me," bleated Janice.

Rita was no grass. She punched Janice's fleshy upper arm. Hard.

"If you cry, I'll do it again. And if I hear you talking about my family one more time, I'll punch you every single day for the rest of your life." Rita cracked her knuckles, lip curling in disgust to reveal teeth like tombstones. She was the first kid in her year to have all her adult teeth come in. Janice still had two baby teeth and was too sooky to pull them out with a bit of twine and a slammed door.

"Rat fink," snarled Rita.

While local parents were hacked off about their children learning such immoral terms as *lesbian*, they couldn't stop foaming at the mouth with gossip and conjecture behind closed doors, and so their children absorbed a lifetime's worth of ideas about lesbianism every dinner time.

The storm passed, but Judy neither forgot nor forgave, quite comfortable settling in for the long haul with a grudge. Indeed, such was the potency of Judy's self-confidence that the bullied became the bully, with little encouragement.

When Sue married Stu Dijkstra, she didn't dare have their first dance to 'Forever and Ever' by Demis Roussos after Judy insisted his music belonged to her. When folks passed a card and envelope around the factory for Sue's maternity leave farewell, Judy told Pete she'd divorce him on the spot if he signed or donated. Pete, not to know this portent would be amply fulfilled soon enough, meekly bowed out. Sue barely spoke a word as treasurer of the PTA meetings when Judy was chairman. Sometime around 1992, it seemed they might reach an impasse, but it got back to Judy that Sue had said to Trish Battie that "you'd think Judy Gordon *enjoyed* getting divorced", and it was all back to square one.

Would Judy have stood by her mother so staunchly without Sue attempting to overthrow her authority? Did she remember her horror at Jayne's pregnancy, and her certainty it would bring their family name, such as it was, into disrepute? Judy would say, "It's okay for me to call you a pregnant tramp, but I'll run over anyone else who says it," and that was as far as her self-awareness went.

By the time Sue was diagnosed with breast cancer, her children had left school, and she and Judy only crossed paths at the supermarket or the annual Christmas service. Sue's nerve never recovered enough for her to sit anywhere close to the front pews. Not that the church had many pews to choose from.

"She did go out of her way to compliment my ginger loaf at the last Christmas service after-match function, mind you," said Judy. "Maybe it was her way of trying to make amends. Not a very impressive effort, which is to be expected, but it was nice of her to say so."

And though she still bore the grudge, Judy no longer went out of her way to say that Sue was a snake in the grass.

Chapter Seventeen

"Well now you're *really* home," Stevie told herself, burying her head under a granny square blanket as 'Albatross' by Fleetwood Mac sneaked through the half-inch gap below the door in her mother's spare bedroom.

As best she could, Jayne made the flat her own with fresh flowers, fringed scarves thrown over the couch, framed pictures of her family and far-off destinations, a yellow paisley tablecloth and yellow candlesticks bearing tall burning tapers, her record player and guitar, rattan placemats, pottery bowls filled with flat glass gemstones in turquoise and cobalt, and a wind chime by the front door. But she couldn't push thumbtacks into the Spanish-Cream walls, her neighbour's neighbour's neighbour blocked all the sun, and the kitchen only had two convection elements and a mini oven. No number of shawls and teen-girl tchotchkes could distract from being wedged cheek by jowl in the arse-end of Hamilton, or the fact that her landlord could turf her out at any second. There was one measly corner shop and no footpaths to get there. *You might as well live in the country*, thought Stevie.

"Is that you Stevie? Jug's hot."

Stevie pulled back the blanket. Whoever sold this slender bed to her mother lied about it being a king single. Pulling on socks from her suitcase, she weighed up whether it was cold enough, despite being December, to put on trackpants underneath the stretched-out and sagging Snoopy t-shirt she slept in. No need to stand on ceremony here. She padded out to the kitchen bare-legged, laptop in hand.

"Good morning, starshine. Have you had a coffee yet?" Stevie kissed her mother's cheek and placed the laptop on the bench.

"No, I was waiting for you."

"Let me make it, Mum, you go sit down. I see you've still got the old mugs. Not too bad at it, was I?"

"Of course, I love them," said Jayne. "As if I'd ever throw out anything you made!"

Stevie brought two pottery mugs of black, sugary coffee into the small lounge and sat on the couch beside her mother.

"Gosh, it's good to see you again, bub, I'm still not used to having you here in front of me. When do you have to go back to Wellington? Are they sending you overseas again? Sorry, too many questions. It's been so long, hasn't it!"

"You know . . . I was thinking about maybe . . . I've not been having the best time . . . of course, London is *London*, I'll always love it, but . . ."

Stevie took a deep breath. The phone rang.

"Now who could that be? I'll go get it—hullo, Jayne speaking. Hullo, Mama! I'm putting you on the speaker-phone. Stevie's just got up; we're having a coffee together. She made it."

"Oh, decided to join us, have you, Flossie?"

"It's only 8am, Nana. How are you, anyway?"

"How am I? Well, your father's dead!"

"Ron?" gasped Stevie.

"Not Sal! Why, I talked to him the other day," said Jayne.

"No, your real father. Father Leo."

No one spoke. Only the crackle of the phone line filled the space.

Jayne's hands trembled. "Dead?"

"As a doornail."

"How did he go?" asked Stevie.

"Hit by a car," said Bufty. "Which unfortunately didn't take him out, but then he had a heart attack, and by the time the ambulance showed up from town with a defibrillator—goodnight nurse. They've no idea who was behind the wheel, I haven't heard if they're investigating further. I'm sorry to invoke his name, but I saw it on Facebook and didn't want you to find out like that. His family's on there calling him a good man of faith. My eye. Mind you, they're deleting the cheeky comments as soon as they appear. Love a bit of stoush from the pitchfork mob in the morning!"

1973 had been a turbulent year for the Gordons. Wally went to the quack about his persistent cough and came back with lung cancer. Betty Grable, Veronica Lake and Bobby Darin died. Bev Murphy ran over another family cat. And Jayne, at seventeen, fell pregnant to Father Leo, the local Methodist minister. "Him being Methodist doesn't sit right with me," said Bufty to Irene, and though neither of them held allegiance to any denomination, Irene got the gist of Bufty's sentiment, and Bufty could not have elaborated her point further if pressed. Father Leo didn't lack for admirers with his square, bearded jaw and long, nut-brown hair, as if doing his level best to resemble Warner Sallman's romantic portrait of Jesus, but as far as twenty-nine-year-old married men who sleep with teenagers go, he was fairly spineless.

That left the delicate matter of the *on dit*, the curtain-twitching busybody wives and surprisingly gossipy farmers, and the family's public image, which had been Bufty's life's work to keep afloat. Any other year, Bufty might've packed Jayne off to Aunty Sweet's, padded her dresses and given birth to a surprise younger sister, but Jayne was already showing, and who would believe Wally had it in him with his deteriorating health? Coping with his decline put enough stress on Bufty without having to feign a geriatric pregnancy.

Irene had special tea at the ready to "Take care of things." No questions asked. But a trip to the doctor established that Jayne was too far along for the conventional bud-nipping methods to be fruitful.

So Bufty asked her daughter what she wanted, and Jayne, with all the maturity life had thus afforded her, said if she had to have a baby she hoped it would be a girl, and she wanted to never speak to Father Leo ever again.

"I'm sorry, Mama," said Jayne, her eyes rimmed with red. "Do you ever feel like a chicken in the road, and all your feathers are falling out? Sometimes it's like I'm watching myself in a dream, like I'm not even here at all."

Bufty hugged her daughter and felt Jayne's growing stomach pressing against her own, where all too recently Jayne grew. "Nonsense, bub, you're perfect, and we'll raise this little baby with love, and Father Leo can go to hell, and that's all there is to it. Now, we'd better tell your father."

You didn't have to worry about Wally yelling, cursing, beating Jayne or banging on Father Leo's door with the butt of a hunting rifle in the way other local fathers might have done upon receiving such news. But Wally was so adoring of his daughters, and so sick, that his potential disappointment was as unbearable to Jayne as any other response.

"You'd be surprised what he can cope with," said Bufty. "Go on, bub. Get it over with."

Wally squeezed Jayne's clammy hand.

"Mum had me when she was your age, you know. We'll find a way, we always do. Your baby can't go wrong with all these stroppy women in its life."

"You'll be there too, right Dad?"

Wally hesitated. "I just can't wait to meet my first grandchild."

"And you won't run off and kill you-know-who?"

"I'm not running anywhere at the moment, kiddo. Besides, it's not me he should be scared of."

Without telling Jayne, Bufty and Irene approached Father Leo in his office at the Methodist church in town to ask for a little upfront financial support in exchange for their silence on the matter of his pending child.

"Talk all you want, it's not mine," smirked Father Leo. He rotated the Good News Book of Psalms on his desk. "She's a girl of easy virtue. It could be anyone's."

Bufty gripped her skirt with white-knuckled hands to stop herself from doing something extremely godless to the bridge of his nose. Irene held Bufty back, and pointed at Father Leo's smarmy face.

"You'll be sorry," she said. "I'll make it so."

Though scornful of this mad old woman and her slapper daughter-in-law, Father Leo took the precaution of decamping with his wife for missionary work in the Chathams till it all blew over.

Irene never cast any kind of dark spell on Father Leo—or so Bufty thought. Irene knew about the world's dark energies and said whatever you put out would come back to you threefold. And if this is how bad life got when Bufty was trying to do good, what the hell would it be like if evil intent came back to her three times over?

Irene admitted, after a few restorative ports, that she wouldn't give Father Leo the steam off her piss to warm himself with, and the strength of that conviction may well have set wheels into motion, perhaps heard by some ancestor with too much time on their hands and a yen for pettiness the afterworld couldn't fulfil. How else could Father Leo explain how he couldn't go one month without being mugged or clobbered in the street by a drunk, even in those secluded islands where he pushed his dogma onto unwelcoming locals? And the harder he prayed, the more violence followed, with this hit-and-run death a natural culmination of all this bloodthirsty energy.

Though Jayne's baby's paternity remained a secret, and you wouldn't dare speak on it with any of her sisters around, perhaps locals put two and two together and sought vengeance for poor fallen Jayne, so sweet with her angelic singing that would bring tears to your eyes. Perhaps Father Leo made one too many enemies after dipping his wick all over the region. But the people of the Chatham Islands didn't know his past. And Irene never seemed surprised by his misfortune.

On his return in December 1977, Father Leo won the meat pack at the Combined Churches Christmas raffle and sent a glib prayer up to the Lord for his luck turning around at last. And as soon as Father Leo stepped outside, a pack of youths fell upon him, shoving him into the wall and stealing the meat pack. The crowd within—who offered the faintest applause when he won—and the two passers-by on the street maintained they saw no young men sauntering off, brazenly eating chipolatas plucked from a plastic-wrapped tray still cold from the chiller and smelling of efficient, edible death. Father Leo's win was not recorded in the end-of-year newsletters of any of the participating churches.

And so, Stevie was born and loved without question, and the Gordons raised her all at once, and Wally met his grandchild, though the strength in his arms gave out too much to hold her. And all this mattered more to Bufty than what anyone said about how or where the child sprang from. And people stopped asking, or alluding to the scandal of it all, because before long another disgraced girl swallowed a watermelon seed, and another surprise baby was born to an older couple.

"I'm a bit lost for words, Mama," said Jayne. "But I appreciate you calling, truly."

"I'm lost for words too, love. That man has been dead to me since 1973, I'm only surprised he even had a desiccated heart beating beneath those cowardly bones to fail on him, and I wish I knew who ran him down so I could pick them a bunch of flowers."

"Thanks, Mama, that means a lot. Look, I've got to get to work soon so I can't chat, I wish I could, but . . ."

"Alright, I won't keep you," said Bufty. "Bye now, love you both so much. Oh—do you want to tell Irene, or should I? Why don't you do it, as a little treat, if you have a minute? She's been waiting for this day."

"Okay, Mama, I will. Love you too."

Jayne held the phone without hanging up. The dial tone grew louder in the silence. Stevie removed it from her mother's hand and pressed the END button.

"Alright?" she asked.

"I don't know." Jayne raked her fingers through her hair. She kept it in two long braids each night and pulled them undone during the phone call, letting each plait fall into zig-zag waves. "Like Mum said, he died to me a long time ago, too. The way I see it is that you and I were destined to meet someday, and if that's the time it had to happen, well, so be it. We had our struggles but I wouldn't trade my Flossie Doll for anything in the world."

Stevie never met Father Leo face to face and held few illusions about his character. She waited for that pinprick of longing—to learn about her relatives, their quirks and inherited physical features. She was still waiting. The capacious Gordon family and their combined army of motherly outreach saw off—or at least distracted from—any nagging despondence at her father's rejection.

"Are you glad? Deep down? That he's—" Stevie drew her finger across her throat and stuck out her tongue.

Jayne's mouth crept into a half-smile. "A little. Isn't that naughty?"

"Not a jot, Mum, your spite is well-earned. That man was the scum of the earth, and I inherited nothing from him, as far as I'm concerned, it's all you. I was like Jesus, appearing out of nowhere to Mary."

"Isn't it funny, that's what I used to imagine to comfort myself . . . if it can happen to Mary, it can happen to little old Jayne Gordon . . ." Jayne looked up at the popcorn ceiling, its frothy points sparkling in the low morning sun not blocked by her neighbour's property. "Do you know, I've been having so many dreams that you were here, that we were all together. Sometimes in a big sunny field, I'd see you laughing with Irene, and I'd run through the grass and hug you both. Sometimes we'd be at Irene's Beach, or round the dinner table at home. And I'd wake up and wonder if it was a dream or a memory, and if you had any memory of it happening too, as if my dream-self talked to your dream-self. Even though it was all in my head, and while I was sleeping, you were awake on the other side of the world. And now you're really here, and it feels like another dream."

"I have dreams like that too, Mum. All the time. I'm really here now." Stevie put her hand on her mother's. "Irene. It's time."

Jayne dialled Irene's number, letting it ring, envisaging her grandmother's slow walk across the hallway.

"Hullo, Irene? It's me, Jayne. Stevie's here too, I've put you on the speakerphone. You'll never guess what I just heard from Mum. Father Leo's dead. It was a hit-and-run, then he had a heart attack. We thought you might like to know."

Irene's laughter rose from the phone. Cracked, hearty, rare as hen's teeth.

"I know. It's about bloody time."

"Hey Mum," said Stevie, as Jayne hung up the phone. "Just when did Irene's driver's licence expire . . ."

Chapter Eighteen

Lorraine Hooker
Kidney cancer
15 September 2004

It didn't take much. In 1947 Mrs Reginald Blewitt breezed into church on Sunday with glass beads glued to the rims of her spectacles, an effect she thought very dainty and becoming, and for weeks the village talked about it as though she'd stood stark naked with one leg propped up on the church pulpit and bellowed, "Come and have a go" to the reverend.

With the factory bringing new blood into the area, people had to adjust their commitment to insularity. At least, that would've been the logical development. Instead, they relished the influx of scandalising potential. One look at Lorraine Hooker from Takaanini, the new teacher here with her factory worker husband in 1962, her curly hair flowing free as her peasant skirts and loose blouses, and remarks like "Well, Hooker by name . . ." were passed around with only a cursory nod to discretion.

She was a storybook teacher, governing with love, all papier mâché and experiments with baking soda and vinegar and silly songs sung in a round till the waves of overlapping verse made you light-headed, and once a year, without warning, she taught the children how to make ice cream from scratch. Bufty, herself easily swayed by ice cream and song, respected these teaching methods and loved seeing Jayne at last blossom at school. One day, Jayne came home in tears because she'd accidentally called Mrs Hooker "Mum", and she was sorry and felt awful, and Bufty dried her tears and suggested pudding for dinner. The other local parents, resentful from enduring the strap and a gruel-slop diet of reading-writing-'rithmetic, said Mrs Hooker would lead their children down a bohemian path of indolence and ruin. But she persevered, and by the time those pupils grew up and became parents, her classroom was every child's North Star.

Her kidney cancer diagnosis came in 1992. She stayed robust through treatment and remission, and doctors declared her cancer-free by 1995. A new tumour grew in 2002. Mrs Hooker retired in December 2003, too frail to manage a classroom any longer.

A memorial cup in her name was engraved in time for the 2004 prizegiving, and Jayne sang 'You Are My Sunshine', Mrs Hooker's favourite classroom song, at her funeral. After thirty-seven years of teaching, she was the longest-serving staff member. She held this title until the school closed in 2009.

Chapter Nineteen

Despite the late afternoon humidity swelling every last air particle till they hung fat and saturated like grains of rice, Irene held her hands beneath the hot tap as she washed the dish-soap bubbles from her last cup of tea, and the water ran, steady and soothing, over her skin. She'd already opened the front door and thrown the swampy mint leaves from the base of the cup back into the garden. A more careless person might've rinsed the cup under the cold tap and called it a day, but not Irene. Whoever used it next wouldn't want the smell of mint lingering.

The teacup, a modest dove-grey thing in a set of four. These cups once belonged to her Aunty Martha, who in turn gave them to Irene when she left home for this house, a new bride at sixteen. On her first day in the house, Irene dropped one of the teacups and cracked it clean in two. A sinister omen, she feared. Her husband Albert was on a farm miles away hammering fences into clay soil and wouldn't be home till long after sundown. Beneath her verandah, the west coast wind whipped the ocean into stiff peaks, ran its fingers through the sand and cavorted in the tussocks.

"I'm scared!" she cried, and the wind sucked the voice right out of her and flung it into the sky. That's enough of that. No time to feel pity for one's self. There was wood to chop, and a cold supper to prepare and leave on the bench under a cloth, so Albert could eat as soon as he got in.

That night Irene dreamed of a figure with the faces of all her aunties, meshed into one, yet with each aunty distinguishable, telling her it was good luck to break something in a new house, to scare out the old spirits, to show you're in charge. The two broken pieces stood for the past and the future, and she held them both in her hands, and she could mend the cup and her life just as easily. Then the figure became her grandmother, Ruth. Tangible. Walking towards her. Slowly, deliberately.

"We're far away, but we walk with you," said Ruth. She curled her fingers around Irene's wrist. "You are us, and we are you. There is power within you. Do what you must to keep walking, and we'll find you again one day."

Irene woke the next morning with the sun, one hand around her wrist, brain thrumming with purpose, Albert snuffling under the blanket. She would never see her grandmother again while awake.

This dream planted a seed that grew boundless and evergreen. And when Albert dropped dead of a heart attack in the middle of a sodden paddock on a job with a shearing gang, leaving her alone with a newborn baby and her little family cracked in two, Irene clung to her attempts to find meaning in the world, because they gave her consolation, purpose, even hope. Above all, Irene was practical, and she needed to get by.

The good ladies of the church pitied her—all alone with a baby, still a baby herself—and dropped by with meals and handmade clothing for Wally, welcoming her to the church for solace and community. And Irene took their gifts but demurred their religious overtures, resolute and self-possessed. Instead, Irene made ends meet with tarot readings, dream interpreting, palm readings, herbs and tinctures, whatever she could come up with, and the customers flowed, even—if not especially—the good ladies of the church. They told each other they'd have to travel for days before meeting another person like Irene, and this effort would be too committed to heathenish practices in the Lord's eyes, whereas dropping in on Irene down the road was informal, indeliberate. No snake oil merchant, Irene ordered books from overseas, memorised their words and wrote letters to the authors. And so, while Irene's audience was small, she had no competition, and without competition, she became the local authority on all such matters relating to the unknown.

Irene's name still carried respect, and there were families for whom she had read tarot for three generations. Initially, her clientele were all women—sure, they were even more laconic than the men, but their defences were easier for Irene to break through, to relate to. As the years passed, a gruff farmer, hat in hand, might approach Irene's front door and shyly request her predictions. Would they have a good calving season? Would they hear from their boy in far-off lands defeating the Huns? Buttoned-up folk who would sooner self-immolate than articulate a single emotion willingly accepted therapy by stealth under Irene. "It never hurts to hedge your bets," she told hesitant customers. "If you believe in the Lord, then perhaps the Lord is guiding my hand towards the right card." All you needed was the right line to get people's fences to drop, and that one usually did the trick.

Irene placed the dove-grey cup back on its shelf, next to the other three in the set, one with its jagged, glued edges clinging to each other. She opened a drawer next to the sink and pulled out an old greengrocer receipt and a pen. She wrote a few lines, tucked the note under the pepper shaker on the kitchen table, walked out to the verandah, and from her straight-backed wooden chair she watched the tide below roll forwards, backwards, always already.

Presently, Irene walked inside, leaving the verandah doors open, and took the hallway into her bedroom. She turned on the electric fan, opened the window, and skipped to track three on the *Most Beautiful Opera Ever!* CD in her boom box. As Delibes's 'Flower Duet' played, Irene smoothed her pillowcase, turned down the yellow candlewick bedspread, lay in her bed, lifted the bedspread over her chest, and folded her hands beneath it.

Irene took a deep breath and died.

Ten minutes later, the twins arrived with the week's groceries, Mahalia whistling, Diana calling Irene's name. The door was unlocked. Bizet's 'Pearl Fishers' Duet' filled the house.

Mahalia picked up the note, read it and handed it to her sister.

I want to be cremated. My will is in the drawer by my bed. No funeral. I love you all and I'll always be here with you. We all will.

Diana peered over the verandah and shook her head at Mahalia. They followed each other into Irene's bedroom.

The twins bordered their great-grandmother, both resting one hand on her still-warm, starched shoulders, until their eyes met and passed a question back and forth. Diana nodded and went out to the hallway. She called the local doctor, who advised her on a death certificate. Diana ducked her head back into the bedroom. Mahalia rolled her hands: get on with it. Diana took her phone back out of her pocket. Irene's hallway was the only spot in the house where you could get even a bar of reception. As such, there was an air of sanctity to the confined space.

"She left a *note*?" shrieked Bufty. "Do you mean she—"

"No, Nana." Diana held her phone away from her ear. "It's just a note. She died in her sleep."

"But it's so unexpected!"

"She's 102 years old, Nana."

"And it's so close to Christmas. She can't miss Christmas! Look, I'm coming over, don't go anywhere."

"Tell Avery or Rita to ring the aunties, and then come straight out. We're not going anywhere. Irene sure isn't. I've talked to the doctor and I'm ringing the funeral home after this, it's all taken care of. Love you, Nana."

Mahalia unscrewed the lid from a slender tube of apricot-scented moisturiser on the side table and massaged it into her great-grandmother's hands.

After talking to the funeral home, Diana put away the groceries. Two tote bags, all useful stuff for feeding crowds of visitors—milk, bread, a carton of eggs.

Irene must've known they'd be the ones to find her. That they could shoulder it. Everything was easier with two of you.

The music stopped, and all they could hear was the exhalation of the tide and the squalling gulls.

Chapter Twenty

Margery Dick
Bladder cancer
18 July 2000

The irony of the doctor not listening to the school nurse! But, "Cobblers' children go without shoes, and so on," said Bufty, "and that's the way the bongo bingos."

"Poor old Bert, it's knocked him for six." Avery hung up the phone and resumed making the tea.

"Margery Dick was the type of woman whose ghost walked around behind her," said Judy at the kitchen table eating a yo-yo biscuit.

"She griped about her stomach every Sunday," said Avery. She placed the silver teapot on a circular cork mat next to the biscuits. "I should've done something."

Fair dues, God himself would scramble to keep up with Margery Dick's list of vexations—whether balking at Christ's unhygienic blood during Communion or shifting seats to avoid the sun freckling her milk-white wrists through the leadlight windows.

Dr Codlin said the pain in her stomach was trapped wind.

Margery Dick rose in her seat, back arched, nostrils wide as a provoked cobra's.

"I have *never* had wind in my *life*."

To her abject shame at having to acknowledge the bodily functions against her will, Margery also suffered from ferocious and unrelenting urinary tract infections.

Dr Codlin reproached her for—oh, she couldn't even bear to listen to the words—*not urinating after sex*. He asked her, most impudently, if she'd been engaging in intercourse with multiple partners.

"That is *none of my business*." In her shock, she did not register her misapplied words. As the running joke passed from student to student over the years went, Mrs Dick was so uptight she couldn't even speak her own surname aloud. Cruel, yes. Barely an exaggeration.

A student could merely stage-whisper "cramps" to Mrs Dick, a legendary easy mark, and she'd whisk you away. The school budget only allowed for two squelchy, plastic-coated mattresses in the sick bay, and often students feigning a cough or a migraine—"cluster migraine", for added flair—would find the beds already claimed by spotty fourth-formers traumatised by gym class. Or worse still, they'd find that Mrs Dick had the day off, and in her place stood the dreaded locum nurse Mrs Butters, with her sinewy arms folded, the medicine cabinet locked, and a sceptical face that only the most savage and bloodied injuries could shift towards something approaching sympathy.

Margery showed up to her next appointment, still afflicted with the scorpion-sting of cystitis, stomach still aching. Dr Codlin said she needed to drink more water, and he chalked up her persistent infections to stress. All part of the ageing process for a woman over forty, he concluded.

"I'm thirty-nine! If I'm a day!"

At each appointment she would implore Dr Codlin for a scan, an ultrasound, a radionuclide cystogram, any kind of referral.

"I know what I'm talking about. This is not regular behaviour for—" she dropped her voice "—a *bladder*."

And Dr Codlin would repeat his lines about stress, or wind, or drinking water, and would send her away.

Finally, Margery brought in reinforcements. Bert Dick was peevish and blustery about having to ask for time off from his sharemilking rounds at the Bunratty farm—they had stock to move and Young Bunratty was not best pleased to be a man down. All it took for Bert's suspicion over his squeamish wife's flouncing to subside was the effrontery of another man's suspicion. Bert's sunburnt hands crashed onto his thighs as he told Dr Codlin that his wife *would* have a referral for a scan thingamabob and he *would* arrange for it to be done double quick and if this did not come to pass, he *would* speak to the doctor's higher-ups, fist-first.

Dr Codlin booked a scan.

Margery had late-stage bladder cancer.

Quite treatable if detected early.

She died eight months later.

More skilled than most at bunking off gym class, the twins almost always got into the sick bay while a spare bed remained; side by side, staring down whoever lay on the other mattress. They could lose an entire school day by swapping in and out, pretending to be each other. The twins had impressed Mrs Dick by offering her a Kurols lozenge during one such stint, and they took to plying her with them on every visit.

Her death devastated the twins. When they excused themselves from class to go wallow in their loss, Mrs Butters, waiting at the sick bay, sent them back without so much as a Panadol.

Avery led the funeral on a vivid winter's day, and the sun poured through the windows as they sang 'Jesus Lives! Thy Terrors Now', Margery's favourite hymn. The twins held hands and wore dark glasses throughout the service, having gotten written permission from Marlon to take the day off school, though she thought the sunglasses were a bit much. People might talk. She knew the twins would give rise to talk round here whatever they got up to, but every time they proved her right it felt like realising it all over again for the first time.

When Avery ran into Dr Codlin in the toilet paper aisle at the supermarket the day before the funeral. She passed on, helpfully, that Bert Dick had told her that if he ever ran into that godawful doctor he'd shoot him in the face and use his body for hound meat and after that, he'd send his hounds to piss Dr Codlin back onto his own doorstep, and not a soul would question the doctor's absence, let alone miss him. And as such, he might want to steer clear of the funeral. She couldn't save Margery, but Avery lifted her chin a little higher as she steered her cart beneath those fluorescent lights.

Chapter Twenty-One

"Me here."

"Rita? Are you alright?" Marlon tucked the receiver between her ear and shoulder. "You never ring. Is it the cancer? Can you hear me? I'm out in the garden. The reception's a bit pakaru out here." She angled the hose at the base of her runner beans, scaling two long bamboo stakes.

"Yeah, Glenn said. Look—I'm fine. It's Irene. She's dead. This afternoon. Went to sleep, didn't wake up. The twins found her at home. They're still there. We're gonna head round just now."

"Right. Right. Okay. Goodness, I've imagined hearing those words more than once, but . . ." A thick, pubic thatch of parsley had sprung up below the beans, and Marlon realised she still had the hose trained upon it and it might all drown. How silly to worry about parsley at a time like this. So silly, silly, *silly*—her eyes filled with tears, and she shook her head. "I'll be right over. Let me get changed first though, I'm sweating like a horse, and I've trod in something unspeakable that Moggy deposited between my rhubarb and the aspidistra."

"Good-o. Can you call Jayne and Stevie when you get inside?"

"Of course. Does Judy know?"

"She will in a minute."

☾

"Hullo, Jayne speaking."

"Hello, you. It's me, Marlon."

"Hullo, you! I'm putting you on the speakerphone, Stevie's here beside me on her laptop. What's up?"

"Oh, Jayne. Rita rang. It's Irene. She's gone."

"Dead?" whispered Stevie.

"This afternoon, the twins found her in bed, looks like she drifted off to sleep one last time, no struggle. Gosh, those poor girls, can't imagine how they must've felt. But if anyone can handle a dead body, it's my babies."

"No!" Jayne wrapped her fingers tight around Stevie's hand. "Is Mum okay?"

"You know how she is. Anyway, you'd better get here," said Marlon. "The rest of us are gathering to sit with the body."

"Man . . . I know she was a million years old, but I thought she'd be here forever," said Jayne, wiping her tears with her arm. "Is that silly?"

"Not silly at all," said Marlon.

"I'll drive," said Stevie, as Jayne hung up the phone. "God, this must be what it'll be like when the queen pops off. You know, Operation London Bridge and all that."

"Just don't go mentioning the queen around Mum," said Jayne, "that's the last thing she needs right now."

☾

"Judy Harada-Hemphill residence, Judy Harada-Hemphill speaking."

"Yep, me here."

"Christ on a bike, what are you doing on the phone, is someone dead?"

"Yep."

"What!"

"Irene. Just now. In her sleep. The twins found her."

"My god. The old girl finally did it. Are you there?"

"Soon."

"Right, I'm coming over. Don't get me wrong, but you lot couldn't organise a punch-up in a honky-tonk."

"Good-o."

"Do the other girls know?"

"Yep."

"Did you ring Jayne before you rang me?"

"No, ding-dong, Marlon's ringing her."

"Alright, calm the farm. I'm coming over—and Baby Ree?"

"Yep."

"Love you."

"You too—love you too. See you in a bit."

☾

Bufty and Avery arrived with Rita. Bufty eased herself down beside the bed and rested her hand on Irene's shoulder. Rita, on the other side of Irene, did the same. Mahalia leaned against the windowsill. Avery, in the doorframe, crossed herself, then shoved her hand in her pocket.

"She looks so peaceful," said Bufty. "Really something, isn't it? A dead body. Just like that."

"She looks like you've just told her she's in the right," said Rita.

"I can't believe I saw her yesterday, and now she's never going to tell me she's right ever again," whimpered Bufty. Avery stepped forward and placed her hands on Bufty's head, and Rita reached across the bed for her mother's free hand, creating a wreath of arms around Irene.

Diana passed around Irene's handwritten note.

"Oh, she would be contrary to the last." Bufty shifted off her knees to lean against the wall. "Di, can you please fetch me a cushion from the lounge? Now I know Irene never favoured the church, but . . . I mean, we have to have a funeral. We have to!" She glanced over to Irene, instinctively leaving a pause for her to reply. "Well, we just have to."

The doctor arrived to sign the death certificate and advised them to gather everyone in so they could get Irene out as soon as possible, given the heat.

Judy and Marlon arrived together, and Marlon moved her car so the doctor could leave. Avery boiled the jug.

Irene lay still as a beech log. The women interlaced fingers, kissed cheeks, squeezed shoulders, wiped tears, first in reverent silence, soon relaxing into their normal speaking voices, as though it were a family party. The only unusual thing being Irene lying down instead of upright, and equally rigid either way. They couldn't leave Irene unaccompanied, and they couldn't bring cups of tea into the bedroom with her, but they needed to plan their next moves, so they all ended up squashed in the hallway, calling over each other to those keeping vigil in the bedroom.

"We *need* to have a little funeral," said Bufty, stamping her foot against the hallway rug with its faded pattern of cabbage roses. "I don't mean a full noise church affair of course, but we have to mark the occasion. I don't care if she didn't want a fuss. It's bad enough that she died alone, she can't go into the next world alone too."

Marlon, standing next to her, read the note again.

"I think she wanted a bit of fuss, Mama, just not, you know, a *funeral*-funeral. We could get together here, once she's cremated . . ." She gasped, and tears filled her eyes. "I'm sorry, where's one of those handkerchiefs you always cart around? But yeah, we can bring her back home, where she wanted to be, and we can be here with her, with each other. Maybe say a few words, have a sing, not a funeral, but—something."

"It doesn't seem right," said Bufty, pulling an embroidered handkerchief from her bag for Marlon. "At 102 years old . . ."

"I think Marlon's right," called Judy from the bedroom, "and let's face it, I never think anyone but me is right, and with good reason. Irene died alone, but if she'd wanted to die in front of us, she would've done that instead. We can have a bit of a ceremony, just a special time for us to all say our piece—to say goodbye. I think that would be fine. And don't get me wrong, but funerals are absolute daylight robbery, and I don't feel like spending my share of the inheritance on a funeral she doesn't even want. And you *know* she could haunt us if we don't listen to her."

"Has anyone heard from Jayne and Stevie?" asked Marlon, accepting a cup of tea from Avery.

"On their way," said Rita.

"What about Sissy?"

"I called her," said Judy, "she won't be far away, s'long as she's not caught up in the city traffic."

"I feel like I should be cleaning," said Bufty, gripping her shirt hem. "Or boiling the jug, or—oh, I don't know! I don't know."

"All you have to do is be here, Mama," said Judy. "Like Marlon said. We'll be here when she goes, and we'll be here when she comes back home again. Irene's homecoming, that's what we can call it."

"Now, that is lovely, Judy."

Jayne arrived half an hour later, face puckered from crying, Stevie behind her, eyes hidden behind sunglasses.

"I haven't missed her? She's still here?" Jayne rushed into the bedroom and dropped to her knees beside the bed.

"She's not going to pop out for a pint of milk," said Rita.

Stevie stood beside Rita. Jayne dropped a kiss on Irene's shoulder. Bufty leaned against the doorframe, barely reaching halfway up. Her daughters inherited their height from Wally; she was three apples tall and none of it legs. Fortunately, some ancestor's neat ankles kicked their way through the genetic stampede to her and her daughters. Food and shelter are both fundamental, but the assurance of a well-turned ankle kept you warm at night.

"I think we should sing for Irene," Jayne said. "I think that would be nice."

"I agree," said Bufty.

"Yep," said Rita, hugging Jayne.

Jayne fetched her guitar from Stevie's car. She pulled at the strings with her thumb, turning the knobs to bring it into tune for 'The Wayward Wind'. Judy and Marlon joined in, and Rita and Stevie and Bufty and the twins. Sissy, just arrived, walked in singing and crying, and Avery ducked out to the verandah, her tears falling onto the railings.

☾

After Wally died, Bufty had suspected her bereaved mother-in-law wouldn't immediately take to Avery.

"The hardest thing is living it," reasoned Avery as Bufty lay face down on her bed, sobbing into a pillow, "the next hardest thing is telling people." It could all only go up from there, and even if it didn't, at least you'd got the hardest part out of the way. So, Bufty went to talk to Irene, fair and square.

"You're confused, girl. You've lost your husband. It's made you all bamboozled."

"I *am* confused," said Bufty. "It's terribly confusing! But it doesn't make it any different, and I'd be more confused if I didn't feel this way. You know I loved Wally; we were mad for each other. This doesn't take away from us, even though it might seem like it does. It's just the strange way I am. I didn't wake up in the morning and say, 'I'm going to be a homosexual' for the fun of it!"

"I don't care if you live with a woman," said Irene, startling Bufty from the tirade she was quite prepared to continue with for several paragraphs more.

"W-what?"

"Couldn't care less. Takes all kinds, this world, and I suppose if we weren't meant to be queers, nature wouldn't have found a way. Besides which, men aren't the heroes they'd like you to think, and you'll have as decent a shot of it with a woman by your side. No, I'm not going to take against something because the church frowns on it, believe *me*. I know you think it's a great debasement, but it takes more than that to shock old Irene."

Bufty blinked, the wind significantly removed from her voluminous sails.

"But c'mon, girl. A *minister*?"

"Avery's not like that at all, oh, I can't even tell you—there's no fire and brimstone, it's all about kindness and goodness." Bufty grasped Irene's hands, her eyes pleading. "Truly and honestly. I wasn't raised churchy either, you know that. She's different. She's good."

"Hmm. Never heard of any good coming from someone of the cloth." Irene's tone implied that Bufty might as well have taken up with an axe murderer and, furthermore, committed to joining them in their chosen profession. But she could see the face of someone in love. "People will talk, you know they will. They won't understand it. Not everyone is sensible like me. They'll talk about the girls too. Can't you wait a bit, keep it quiet-like? Don't go borrowing trouble."

"The girls are fine," snapped Bufty. "Jayne's hippy friends are rather excited, the boys all look like girls and the girls all look like boys, so nothing much bothers them, it's quite lovely. Judy and Marlon are big girls, and Rita wouldn't blink if I told her I was off to hunt rhinoceros in the Serengeti."

The wind billowed in Bufty's sails again.

"And I'm surprised to hear you concerned by talk, when not so long ago people talked about you, strange old Irene up on the cliffs with her magic and fortune telling, and we had to watch out or she'd cast a spell on us."

Bufty clapped her hand over her mouth. "I'm sorry Irene, my father would have clipped me round the ear so fast I'd be spinning if I spoke back to him like that. I'm so overwhelmed, it's all so much. If people talk, be it on my own head, but please don't let's change anything about us. You're the leader of the family, the girls need you—I need you."

"A minister . . ." Irene rubbed the bridge of her nose. "The only one you can trust is the bishop on a chessboard, and I've got my eye on him, too."

"Please, Irene. You're like a mother to me."

There was a pause.

"Ah, come here, girl." Irene opened her arms and Bufty fell into them, sobbing tears of such emotion she couldn't place it—ecstatic, remorseful, petrified, grateful, all the colours at once.

Later that week, while perusing dress patterns in Clifford's, Irene overheard Mrs Keel and Mrs Erskine, with no regard for volume, talking about Bufty and Avery. Upon hearing the word "bent", Irene marched up to the pair, obsidian eyes bulging.

"I'll thank you to never talk about my daughter in that manner again," she said, forgetting to include the distancing 'in-law', "unless perhaps you'd like me to discuss *your* business in public too? Perhaps we could start with your husband's little problem, Mrs Erskine—but I wouldn't do that, because I was brought up right. Perhaps I was wrong to assume two good ladies of the church would also be brought up right—but I will leave the assuming to you, since it's more your style. Now, I ought to go pay for this pattern—although perhaps I should thank you for it, Mrs Keel, since you were so happy to buy my services last week. I shall certainly think of you as I'm driving my needle through the fabric. Good day!"

Irene turned on her heel and paid for the pattern, warmly greeting Renny Clifford behind the counter while his good eye darted around the store apprehensively and his glass eye stayed fixed straight ahead. and she marched away into the sun, heart racing, cursing herself for using the word "perhaps" too many times. She rode Robber Baron back to her house as hard as the horse's mature bones would allow, ate three biscuits from her tall green container, walked into the hallway and rang Bufty.

"Bring Avery around for afternoon tea."

Irene shook Avery's hand, gripping her forearm and kissing her on the cheek. She acknowledged Avery's sound job with Wally's funeral, even though she thought little of The Church, and church funerals.

"Why, in the 'Canticle of the Sun'," said Avery, "St Francis of Assisi spoke of Brother Sun, Sister Moon, Brother Wind and Sister Water. He and the earth were on the same wavelength. Look at your cards. A man is walking. Standing on a hill. Sitting on a throne. They could all be scenes from the scripture. You interpret cards, I interpret the Bible. That's all it is. We're not so different, you and I." Avery pointed to Irene's copy of *Siddhartha* and said she'd love to analyse it with her, and approval flashed across Irene's eyes.

And Bufty could exhale and unclench at last.

"But why the church, Avery? Are you telling me you believe in God? Really? A bearded man up there telling us what to do?"

Bufty's buttocks re-clenched. Even a woman like Irene couldn't flat-out *ask* someone if they believed in God.

"If I'm honest, I don't know that I believe in God every single day," said Avery, and Bufty nearly fainted dead away in her chair. "But I believe in faith. I believe in a higher power, and I believe in exploring it. I believe in what my instincts tell me, and I believe in learning from all those who have gone before me. This faith is part of me—I could no sooner shake it than I could the colour of my eyes, and I couldn't explain it or them to you either. But they're there. 'My highest ambition is to be what I already am', said the Monk Thomas Merton, and I hold that true and dear in all areas of my life, including my faith."

"If you're so intellectual, why'd you become a reverend? I see you squirming, Bufty, but I know you philosophical types love questions."

"It came to me in a dream," said Avery, "when I turned sixteen. Three dreams, one after the other. So indisputable—they spoke right to my very heart—and it sounds strange, but I knew my dreams were a sign, a call, and I needed to take that call."

She leaned back in her chair a little.

"On the first night, I dreamed I stood in a vast, shimmering body of water, soft as the back of a dog's ears against my legs. Birds swooped around me, swallows, ospreys, herons, but I felt no fear. The setting sun was so enormous, so incandescent, pouring warm, radiant light across the water like a footpath, and fish leapt out of the water to greet the birds, their bodies obscured by veiling luminance, so they appeared as leaping shadows. I felt entirely at peace, basking in the beauty and warmth. On the second night, I dreamed I walked through an endless green meadow, the grass soft as sleep itself against my bare feet. A flock of lambs appeared, all following me where I walked. One lamb, smaller than the rest, leapt into my arms, and the lamb's wool was so warm against my skin, and its eyes so trusting, and as we walked, the flock of lambs began leading me rather than me leading them, and every animal you could name appeared behind us, walking shoulder to shoulder, prey with predator, predator with prey. On the third night, I dreamed I sheltered from a thunderstorm in a tremendous hall, its soaring ceilings and walls decked in vividly hued paintings of angels and commoners alike, the lowliest as beautiful as the highest, and from each wall hung blue velvet curtains, soft as flour, and I unhooked one of those curtains and wrapped it around myself to keep warm, and a queen appeared, wearing a dress of the same blue velvet as the curtains, her eyes bright as candles, and I thought she would admonish me and throw me out into the storm, but instead she tore down the blue velvet curtains and gave them to me, and then she disrobed with no shame for her nakedness, and she told me to go out into the street and give people the curtains for blankets, and to sell the blue velvet dress for money to feed the hungry, and she was so entrancing and munificent that I wept, and she wiped away my tears with her long hair, and I awoke weeping and so happy at the same time, and I knew then what I had to do with my life. Does that make sense?"

"God yes," said Bufty, enraptured, face streaming with tears, and no clue what Avery was talking about but more in love with every word.

"I understand," said Irene, and Bufty's shoulders lowered.

"But how does your God feel about you being a lesbian, hmm?"

"Irene!" yelped Bufty, feeling like a badminton shuttlecock lobbed between uncaring opponents.

"So the eyes of man are never satisfied," quoted Avery, not bothered in the slightest. "I knew I was different. That I couldn't live fully, as my true self. I think God was showing me in these dreams a way to be myself, or at least, another way I could be different. As if the more different I became, the easier it would be for people to comprehend. And now it all feels like one part of me, not disparate or incompatible."

"Your lot colonised my lot," said Irene, getting in one last dig. "How do I know you're not going to try and con vert me?"

"So they did, and I've no plans to continue in that not-so-grand tradition."

By the time Bufty worked out they were having a ball, it was all over, and Irene and Avery were out in the garden picking herbs together for a fresh pot of tea.

And since the good ladies of the church still wanted to have a spiritual bob each way with Irene's palm reading and tarot cards, they kept their gossip behind closed doors, and even then in hushed voices, in case Irene might guess by the look in your eyes or the furrow of your brow that you'd been speaking ill of her family. Much as Avery adored Bufty, she knew life together would've been one hell of a Sisyphean battle without Irene's influence.

☾

The soft voices, sliding into easy harmony, floated out the French doors to where Avery stood, floated out over the waves into the sky.

Stevie combed Irene's hair and fashioned it into two braids, white as sun-bleached driftwood and every inch as long as when she'd played hairdresser on Irene as a child.

"Don't s'pose anyone's got a hair tie on their wrist?" Stevie ran her fingers through her short, bleached mop. "Nana, you must have something in that Mary Poppins bag."

Bufty fished a packet of hair ties from a zipped pocket in her handbag.

"Yes, you can borrow these Irene, but I want them back, wink wink." Bufty's eyes brimmed with tears again. "Oh, I hate to think of her all alone at the crematorium. It's not right."

"If she stays here any longer, the heat might get the job done for us," said Rita, fanning her face with the CD case beside the boombox.

"What if we send something of us with her?" said Stevie. "So it's like we're there while she's . . . y'know, waiting."

"Toenail clippings?" said Rita.

"We could all chop off a lock of our hair, and put it in her pocket," said Jayne, pushing Rita's shoulder. "Although I suppose the burning hair will smell gross."

"That'll be the least of her worries," said Judy, appearing in the doorway.

"True, silly me. What if we write her a note?"

“I was about to suggest that,” said Judy, “but yes, that’s not a bad idea.”

It took a good ten minutes and much back and forth to workshop the message, but eventually Marlon, whose handwriting was the neatest, wrote *We love you Irene* on the back of the twins’ grocery receipt, and the family signed it, and Bufty folded it seven times, kissed it, and tucked it into Irene’s sleeve.

The funeral director arrived and prepared Irene to leave the house. Bufty, who till now could only make discomforted tearful noises without release, wailed in earnest. Jayne continued to strum her guitar as the Irene they knew left her front door for the last time. Rita dropped onto the couch, sinking the points of her incisors into her tongue, trying to return to the present moment. Jayne sat cross-legged beside Rita and stroked her hair.

“How are you feeling, Baby Ree? Still funny from the other day?”

“Just today-funny,” said Rita. “It’s all so weird.”

“Now, I think we should—” Marlon mimed flicking water at her face “—and eat. How about we order a Chinese takeaway? Any objections to A1?”

“I prefer the *A1*, mind you,” said Judy, “their chow mein is better.”

Chapter Twenty-Two

Statistically, the holiday season sees an uptick in natural deaths, for reasons scientists can only but speculate on, whether it's fuelled by Yuletide excess and strain or simply the logical endpoint at the closing of another year. Be it correlation or causation, the province encasing the village was no stranger to these statistics, and the soonest date the family could secure for Irene's cremation was four days away. Five days before Christmas.

These four days provided the Gordons time to plan and process. But the phone rang non-stop, and Bufty let no thought enter her head without uttering it, and Jayne, staying in the study, wouldn't stop playing her guitar and irrigating the place with her tears, and Judy and Marlon kept appearing at the door to launch into their double-act floor show of domineering and appeasing. The dogs fawned for attention, and Stevie's black-polished nails clattered across her laptop keyboard and directly into Rita's temples. The wasps sleeping on the wall taunted her with their serenity, the Christmas lights jerked from one colour to the next, the fridge whirred at the top of its lungs, a fly caught in a web in the upper corner of the bay window bucked back and forth in its gluey prison, unable to be heard over everyone's voices, baying for its life.

Rita decided to take a drive.

She tapped the Cortina's steering wheel. Her short nails made no sound against the leather. Up ahead, the young man driving his John Deere veered left and waved her on. She honked the horn in gratitude as she overtook him, with enough space before the elbow leading into the town. Turning the corner, Rita found herself behind another tractor. She tapped her fingers against the steering wheel again. Driver number two didn't offer the same courtesy as his earlier compatriot.

"Well, Irene," Rita said. The bubbling tar-seal ahead seemed to warn her from approaching further. "I guess I wanted to say . . ." She cleared her throat. No. Communicating feelings with the dead just wasn't going to work. And now she felt like she'd had to answer a knock at the door wearing only a bath towel. In her own car.

A parking space awaited her in front of The Chariot. Rita saluted the empty passenger seat. *Thanks, Irene.*

Mahalia, methodically removing crackers from a box of Chicken Crimpy Shapes and licking off the flavoured dust before eating them, raised her eyebrows in greeting. Rita returned the expression, and through further eyebrow raisings and half-gestures, Mahalia offered her aunt a shot of Jim Beam—*yes?*—and Rita accepted—*twist my arm*—and Diana, writing on a clipboard, also accepted a shot—*'tis the season.*

They tapped the shot glasses together, then against the bar, and threw back the rye. Rita shook her head involuntarily at the liquor's bite, like the kickback of a rifle. Mahalia popped the lid off a Tiger and offered it to Rita along with the box of crackers. Diana returned to the kitchen with her clipboard.

Rita's vision softened as she sized up the backbar, moving from bottle to bottle, bagsing the ones she might, hypothetically, take with her in a supermarket sweep-type situation. *Cointreau, of course. Expensive. Frangelico, no. Not much of a hazelnut fan. Other people like it, but you don't want to encourage visitors. Drambuie? Don't mind if I do-ie. Midori? Never again, after that party in the garage where Aunty Sweet let her—*

"My dog likes you."

Rita glanced around. An old man at the end of the bar gave her a gummy smile.

Had he been there the whole time? Was he even so old? As a kid, anyone over twenty was ancient. Past it. Until you hit fifty and realise you're only getting started.

"My dog likes you." The man lifted his coffee. A white line ran around his pale blue eyes, and undisciplined grey curls retreated from his high forehead.

Rita lifted her beer. "Cheers."

Mahalia pointed at a sign behind the bar, that read 'Your dog is welcome. You might not be'. She filled a plastic takeout container with water and gave it to the old man, who placed it on the floor next to his chair.

Rita turned around. Behind her, panting steadily like an idling ride-on mower, sat a German shepherd. So, the old man wasn't talking nonsense. A little embarrassed, she held out her hand, and the dog sniffed it, followed by a cautious lick.

"What's your dog called?" asked Rita, as the dog pushed its nose into her palm. "Quite a beauty."

"Rita," he said.

"Rita! *There* you are!" called Bufty from the doorframe, patting her forehead with one of Wally's old blue checkered handkerchiefs.

"For Christ's sake."

"So she is. Hello, twins!" Marlon walked in behind her mother. "Goodness, it's dark in here."

"Shut the door, Mum," said Mahalia, "were you born in a tent, air-con doesn't grow on trees . . ."

"We wondered where you'd got to!" Bufty leaned against the bar. "Ooh, a little beer might be just the ticket, isn't that right, Marlon? It's hot as Hades out there. I don't usually drink beer, but when it's very hot, or I've been working hard, there's nothing like it, is there? And we have been working hard on this funeral for Irene. Not that it's a *funeral*-funeral, I know, I know." Bufty shut her eyes, remembering the foam on her dad's mugs of ale, savoury and altogether unpleasant—but she would never wince when he gave it to her. The act of giving itself was enough to make up for the foam's stale taste in her mouth.

"Oh, hullo, puppy, whose dog is this? What a Bobby Dazzler! Could be twins with our Roger." Bufty tickled the German shepherd behind the ears, and it licked her knee.

"That's my dog," said the old man. "She's as good as gold. May I recommend you the coffee? They always serve it good and hot!" He raised his cup again.

The twins didn't like making coffee, but they weren't stupid. They kept a filter percolator on a hotplate, with free refills. It filled the air with an inviting scent, there was no dicking about with steamed milk and latte art, and only a few seconds separated the request and the consumption.

Marlon's eyes lit up. "Coffee *has* to be good and hot, doesn't it? And what a handsome dog you have. Now, something soft for me, as the designated driver—ginger beer if you have it, Mahalia. No ice, please."

"It's better with ice, Mum," said Mahalia. But she complied. "Is Stevie coming?" She opened another Tiger for Bufty.

"No, couldn't persuade her, she's busy on her laptop and said she'd appreciate the peace and quiet. And Jayne's napping."

Rita took a long drink of beer, the burning cold liquid pushing the scream back down her throat.

"My condolences on your loss," said the old man. "The only way to not die, you know, is to live."

"Have we met?" asked Bufty. You rarely ran into someone this old without already knowing him, his mother, his mother's mother, and whether she took her tea with milk and sugar.

"Everyone knows Irene," said the man. His dog stopped lapping at its container of water and approached Rita again.

"True enough," said Bufty. "Ooh, are those Chicken Crimpys, Mahalia? Mind if I—? It really is the best flavour, isn't it?"

Turning around, Rita found the dog staring at her. Its eyes were like grandaddy firecracker marbles in the dim lighting. Rita looked away first.

Chapter Twenty-Three

Wally Gordon
Lung cancer
12 January 1974

The black fly, poised on a glossy red snooker ball, rubbed its paws together. With a short, buttery click, the white snooker ball hit the remaining balls clustered on the green baize, jolting Roy Killphillip back into the present, and somewhere between these two moments the fly disappeared, and now the red ball had disappeared too, into the corner pocket. Unbeknownst to Roy Killphillip, thumbs hooked into his belt loops, the fly landed on his head.

"Right-ee-oh. One port, five gin and tonics," said Harry Bundle from behind the bar. "This one here is watered down for young Rita over there. The rest, I spilled some in the glass."

"Excellent! Thank you kindly, Harry!" Roy pondered whether to ask for a tray to ferry the drinks over. *Better not.* Trays were the realm of waitresses and weak arms. A man should be able to carry six drinks at once under his own steam. Roy bent his knees, pressed the glasses into his torso, and took a step backwards, then a step sideways, then a step forwards. Could he, the drinks and his masculinity make it to the table before the condensation slid the glasses from his hands, sending liquid tumbling all over his cords and to the carpet below?

Harry Bundle, unperturbed by this scene, continued polishing a glass with his apron, the same glass he'd been polishing since the funeral after-match function kicked off. Roy staggered over to the leaner table where The Girls stood with Bufty and Reverend Avery, and, tongue escaping from the corner of his mouth, eased the drinks from against his torso to the table, not losing a drop.

"Here we are, ladies! This one's yours, Rita, don't drink it all at once!" He wiped his wet hands on his cords and leaned against the table. The fly, forgetting its earlier journey, departed from Roy's head for the snooker table once more.

Two things announced themselves about Roy Killphillip when he entered a room: first, he was exceptionally tall, and second, he had no indoor voice. If anything, people said, his voice was more cacophonous *before* the gelignite explosion.

"Thank you, Roy," said Judy, patting his hand. "That's all."

"Ok then! Catch you on the flip side! And you girls look terrific today—including you, Mrs Gordon! My condolences to you all!"

Bufty's eyes twinkled. "He's a cad, isn't he?"

Roy raised his fingers in a salute, turned around, and made his way towards the other young men slouching over a leaner in the corner of the Cossie Club.

"Oh, Roy—wait a second, Roy!" Judy fluttered her fingertips at him.

He turned around and, in three long strides, returned to the table, thumbs back in his belt loops.

"Did you ask how the tab is looking?"

Roy raised a finger to his lips.

"According to Harry, somebody came and put another $25 on it. They asked to be kept hush-hush, but just between us I'd go give Principal Griffiths a great big kiss if I were you!"

Judy mirrored his gesture. "Secret's safe with me. Thanks, Roy. That's fine."

Jayne and Marlon turned to each other, eyebrows raised.

"Well, la-di-dah," said Marlon.

"The girls are looking good!" Roy called as he walked away, fingers in the shape of guns. "Looking good!"

He pointed at Bufty and mouthed *you too*, the drop into silence presumably out of respect for her having buried her husband that day. But you never could truly be sure what was going on up there in Roy Killphillip's head.

Bufty removed her hat and fanned herself, wrinkling her black crimplene shirtwaister.

"Mind you, he's got such a crush on me," said Judy. "Did you know he's bought a Morrie Thou?"

"Here, take her, will you, Mum?" asked Jayne, extricating her turquoise bead necklace from Stevie's saliva-wet hands. Stevie squealed, her downturned mouth signalling imminent tears.

"Come here, Floss." Bufty slid the baby onto her hip, dipped her index finger into Rita's gin, and held it to Stevie's mouth for her to suck on.

Marlon undid the top button of her ruffled blouse and blew air upwards onto her face. Judy opened her little purse and pulled out a soft carton of Camels.

"Can I crib one off you?" Jayne pinched a cigarette before Judy could say either way.

Judy tapped the carton on the table. "Anyone else, while I'm here?"

"Not me," said Marlon, "I don't think I'm cut out for smoking. It just doesn't suit me! There it is." She mimed dragging from a cigarette and coughing.

"Go on," said Avery, "high days and holy days. If you're offering."

Rita toyed with her drink and watched Judy's lighter pass from one hand to another.

"Giz a puff, Judy?"

"Not a chance, Baby Ree. It's a filthy habit, let's face it."

"That's right," said Marlon. "Put it off as long as you can."

"Oh, let her," said Bufty, her gaze wandering around the room, "life is fleeting."

"Hey now," said Avery, patting Bufty's shoulder. "Why don't we have a toast?"

"Yes, to Dad," interrupted Judy, lifting her glass. "A great send-off for a great man. The best father, a loving husband—"

"That he was," said Bufty. "We were all so lucky."

"Wally Gordon," concluded Judy with a sniff.

"Dad," said Jayne. Their drinks met in the centre of the table.

"Isn't it funny?" said Marlon. "I kept turning around to talk to Dad today, but I think if he were alive and we were all having a party, he would've wanted to be out of the way, not here in the crowd. This wasn't his scene at all."

"I wish Flossie Doll could've got to know him a bit more," said Jayne, stroking Stevie's head. "Do you think she'll remember him?"

"You'll have to tell her stories all about Dad as she grows up," said Marlon, hugging her sister. "Isn't it lucky we took so many photos at Christmas?"

"Be a lot luckier if Dad didn't die," whispered Rita into her gin and tonic.

"Don't get me wrong, but I was surprised so many people showed up today," said Judy. "I suppose there's something to be said for the promise of a bar tab and a free sandwich. I didn't know Dad had any friends at all! Have you met all those men, Mum? Of course, Roy and the boys from the factory came, but that was for me, I'm sure."

"I don't know, bub. Your father kept himself to himself. It *was* a good send-off though." Bufty rocked the baby back and forth. "And didn't you do well Avery, hmm?"

Avery dipped her head bashfully and tapped her cigarette against the pewter ashtray.

"Now, my love, when does Ron finish his shift?"

Jayne twisted her glass on the table. "I don't know Mum, I thought he'd be here already. I guess I'll have to keep looking after her."

"That's what happens when you have children, banana-brain," said Judy.

"Oh, forget it," said Jayne. She was besotted with Stevie. She just had a kooky way of talking, as if she were floating in outer space. Bufty used to say that Judy saw the world through a telescope and Jayne saw it through a microscope, and you couldn't pass a single bumblebee or flower without Jayne stopping to imagine some dialogue between them.

"It's not Ron's fault he's working, he's a good boy, and it's sweet that he takes such an interest in the baby. We can all look after Flossie Doll, she'll be fine—if it comes to it, we can pop her in the car to sleep, or give her to Irene to take home, and we're all here to keep an eye on her. Aren't we, bubba? Aren't we?" Bufty kissed Stevie's head.

Judy drank the last of her gin. "Your round, Marlon. Aunty Sweet read well, didn't she? You both sound so alike, Mum."

Despite the claggy heat of the Cossie Club, Bufty rather looked like a queen surrounded by her courtiers. In years to come, she would hardly remember the funeral, only flashes of colours—a red snooker ball, amber beer—the smell of sweat and cigarettes and linseed oil, and that feeling of everyone watching her.

☾

Bufty could see the bungalow she grew up in from the window by Wally's narrow iron bed at the hospice. Someone had painted the roof dark green, covering up the rust and dirt. Quite becoming.

"Not a bad story, is it?" said Wally between wheezing breaths. "Handsome son of a witch marries a beautiful princess. They magicked a castle, raised four daughters and lived happily ever after. In their own funny way."

"What happens next to the beautiful princess?" asked Bufty, her voice small and far away.

"She does the best she can to keep being happy. She's proud of how hard they tried. And maybe she calls up that fairy godmother."

Bufty lowered her face into Wally's lap and wept.

☾

"I should go say hullo to the hospice sisters," said Bufty, "and see if they want our flowers. Can one of you girls bring Irene over? Smyrna Sneath has her cornered, and no one deserves that on the day of their son's funeral. Here, bub, can you take Miss Flossie Doll?"

"Sure," said Marlon, sniffing Stevie's head.

"I should go do the old how-d'you-do-and-shake-hands, too," said Avery, stubbing the glinting nubbin of her cigarette into the ashtray. "Thus passes the glory of the world . . . will you lot be alright here?"

"We'll be fine and dandy like sour candy, Avery," said Judy. "Us Gordon girls can look after each other." You couldn't ruffle Avery, so she didn't try. But nor was Judy's tone entirely guileless.

"I'll get Irene," said Rita, craning away from the table to see her grandmother. Irene looked all out of puff, like Roger the dog after playing silly buggers, when he'd flop on his back, eyes half-closed but not sleeping. Rita recognised the movement around Irene's eyebrows, arranging your face so you appeared to be listening even though you weren't interested, because you had to be polite. She wanted to protect this woman who was so protective of her, and the urge made Rita's stomach feel all wonky. The cracks in the structure of her life were growing too wide: fathers can die, mothers can be unpredictable, grandmothers can be sad.

Marlon wiggled Stevie onto her other hip. "Why don't you be a sport Rita, and get us another round on your way to Irene? Grenadine for you this time, I think. There's money in my purse."

"See if you can get Roy Killphillip to carry them for you again," said Judy. "He does have such a crush on me, mind you. Go on, stand near him and get him to give you the eye. Lick your lips, arch your back, you'll never have to pay for a drink in your life."

Rita couldn't imagine saying that to anyone, but maybe if she were grown-up and pretty, like Judy and her friends, those words would make sense coming out of her mouth. If Rita had told Judy to lick her lips and arch her back, she probably would've gotten a slap. *It's funny how it all works.*

"Now listen, girls," Rita heard Judy say, as she walked away on unsteady legs. "Do you think Mum and Avery are—you know—"

Chapter Twenty-Four

"Won't you be too hot in jeans and a t-shirt, Rita? And couldn't you wear something smarter? Now, do you have a staying-the-night bag packed?"

The word "homecoming" mollified Bufty's funeral aspirations, but Marlon had to talk her out of writing up and printing off traditional run sheets emblazoned with Irene's face. Bufty was up past midnight making food the evening before, until Rita sent her to bed. Padding about the kitchen in her socks, lit by the Christmas tree, rolling canned asparagus into crustless white bread; Rita could call that peaceful, for now. *Was that Irene out the corner of her eye, spine erect, flame-tipped fingers resting on her cane, watching, watching . . . was that her?* Rita turned to face the chair. Face its emptiness. Its lack of the person who should be there. No one's there. Better get used to it.

Rita licked the butter knife and placed it by the sink. *Let's leave the spiritual visions to Avery.*

The next morning, Rita stood like a cardboard cutout as Bufty scuttled from one end of the house to the other; Avery tailgated, trying to soothe her; Jayne, useless as an ashtray on a motorbike, was verging on tears and ready to be pushed; and Stevie sat typing by the Christmas tree, pausing only to crack her knuckles.

"Have you packed for staying the night, Rita?" Bufty forced pillows into a red, white and blue checked nylon storage bag. "You may want to bring cooler clothes to change into, you'll overheat all dressed in black . . . Now, has anyone heard from Sissy, is she on her way?"

Jimmy Stewart barked twice. The doorbell rang.

"Someone's here," murmured Stevie, not looking up from her laptop.

"Who on earth could that be?" said Bufty, handing the bag to Jayne. "If they're after my credit card details, I will blow my top, I swear!"

Bufty opened the door to a woman around Judy's age with a sweep of sable hair, wearing a trench coat the colour of clover honey over a blouse and slacks. A slim gold chain with a green glass teardrop pendant hung around her neck. The woman smiled at Bufty, as though recognising an old friend in a crowd. Jimmy Stewart, curious but unruffled by the stranger, sat on Bufty's feet.

Underslept and taken aback by this apparition in all her moneyed shades of amber, Bufty forgot her decorum, mouth agape, feeling around in her head for an opening line. The woman didn't mind, perhaps accustomed to having this effect on people.

"How about that? My daughter Rita has the same necklace as you."

It was the right thing to say. The woman at the door grasped Bufty's shoulders and kissed her cheeks.

"Hallo, Bufty. It's brilliant to meet you at last. I'm Sidhal. I'm here to see Rita." Each husky word landed, compelling and deliberate, suggesting a secret known only to you.

"Knock me down with a feather, it's you . . . Rita never

said you were . . ." Bufty pushed up her spectacles. "British?" she concluded tentatively.

Sidhal bounced on her heels. "Guilty. I was born in London but consider Italy my spiritual home, much to the chagrin of my Singaporean parents who relocated to Auckland when I was a teen. You understand how it is."

Sidhal had frequently been asked to disclose her background throughout her life and conveyed these specificities with autopilot offhandedness. Bufty, flustered, did not pick up on this.

"I do hope this isn't inconvenient. Rita hasn't seen my messages from this morning yet, but I know the reception can be a trifle iffy out this way . . ."

Rita appeared behind Bufty, mouth frothy with toothpaste. She removed the toothbrush from her mouth.

"What in the hell are you doing here?" A trail of white, minty spit ran down Rita's chin, and she didn't wipe it away.

"I beg your pardon, you knew I was popping by!"

"No. I didn't. That's a *lie*." Rita dashed to the bathroom, spat audibly, and returned to the scene. "That's a lie."

"Look, you replied to my message two weeks ago: I'd love to see you again, of course you can visit, here's my address, that's a lovely little cat in your profile picture—"

"What's all this then?" Avery, brushing her hair, stepped out from behind Rita. Jayne, eyes wet, still clutching the bag of pillows, drooped like a wilting freesia beside Avery. Roger, under the Christmas tree, sensing this might be his kind of action, tunnelled through everyone's legs to park by Jimmy Stewart.

"*Mum*." Rita glared at Bufty. A sheepish blush crept over Bufty's cheeks, like strawberry jam spread across white bread.

Sidhal put her hands on her hips. "Can someone please tell me exactly what is going on here?"

Bufty pressed her palm against her burning forehead. "Look, I'm sorry, I can explain—Rita, don't get worked up, you sound like Widgeon when he sees the Henry cat across the road. Remember when you couldn't get any messages on your phone, and told me to delete the app, rahdirahdirah? Yes? Well, I found your messages, and . . . I might have sent a little reply to Sidhal here. And with the hustle and bustle of this month, it all got away on me and I forgot, and—oh my Christ!"

She gripped Sidhal's arm, noting the creamy fabric of her coat.

"I somehow forgot for a moment in all the hubbub—you've caught us on the way to a funeral. Now look, I really am sorry about misleading you. I thought I was doing you both a good turn, and I love romance and couldn't resist. I got a bit carried away, is all. And I meant it about the cat."

"Buying a Viennetta when it's not someone's birthday, that's getting carried away," said Rita, eyes raised heavenwards. She wished she could go back in time to last night, making asparagus rolls in the dark. Or better yet, to last week at Irene's house, opera and biscuits and the roar of the ocean, instead of standing here with her brain roaring and Bufty apologising to Sidhal of all people.

Bufty pumped her collar to shoot air onto her face. This woman looked like she'd never known the armpit-crawling betrayal of sweat in her life.

"Why don't you come with us, Sidhal? Do come along, it's not really a funeral, just a day to be spent with family, and you're like family, even though we've only just met you. We've been wondering for years about this mysterious person who purloined our Rita—"

Rita's mouth flatlined. One fancy lady shows up and suddenly we're fine with it not being a funeral.

Tears fell from Jayne's cheeks onto the bag of pillows, nudged along by the F-word. Avery began to suggest a cup of tea but thought better of it. Stevie, roused from her laptop and now standing behind Jayne and Avery, burst into laughter, clamping her hands over her mouth.

Bufty searched Rita's face for a granule of recognition.

"I am sorry, bub. Don't be cross at me, not today. I thought you might like a little drama in your life. You're always sitting there, alone . . ."

"*Mummm.*"

"I don't wish to cause a fracas, believe me," said Sidhal. "I've evidently got ghastly timing, please don't let me keep you."

"Nonsense!" shrieked Bufty, determined not to let this drama slip from her sweaty fingers. "Do come with us, everyone's welcome. Irene didn't want a funeral carry-on, and as you can see by Rita's choice of ensemble, it's more of a come-as-you-are . . ."

"*Oh*!" Sidhal pressed her hands against her heart. "Not Irene, I'm so sorry. I feel I know Irene myself from the way Rita spoke of her. How agonising. Her death must be an unutterable loss for your family." She embraced Bufty.

"It is, it really is, Sidhal. I don't mind saying so."

"A ginormous loss," whispered Jayne, chin resting on the bag of pillows. Rita elbowed her.

"Brobdingnagian," offered Avery.

"Absolutely mahoosive," said Stevie, barely suppressing her giggles.

Sidhal stroked Bufty's hair. "*Mal comune mezzo gaudio.*"

Rita rolled her eyes. "For Christ's sake." She couldn't, however, commit to yelling at Sidhal to bugger off and leave them alone. Nor could she meet her line of sight.

"I've brought a bottle of olive oil," said Sidhal, gesturing towards her Brunswick green Audi, "a bottle of Beaujolais, a flourless almond chocolate cake, a bovolo loaf, et cetera . . . we have a saying in *Venezia*, which loosely translates to, 'It is a greater affront to visit without offerings than it is to show up with a gun and shoot everyone'."

"We sort of have that attitude here too," said Bufty.

Tantrums bored Rita. They were running late. The day would be a hell of a slog, but even more interminable with

Bufty all hang-dog guilty. She didn't want to see Sidhal. But she didn't want to do much of anything.

And she hadn't drunk Beaujolais since 1985.

"Cat's out of the bag," said Rita. "Come along. Why not."

Sidhal embraced Bufty once more.

"Now, I need to change into my dress and then we'll be making tracks. And Sidhal, if you're coming in you might want to hold on to your shoes," said Bufty. "Little Jimmy Stewart here does like to use them for target practice."

"Would you like a cup of tea before we go, Sidhal?" asked Avery, confident in her convictions at last.

"Tea would be superb; do you have any oolong?"

"And you made up that Venetian quote," scowled Rita, stalking away to the sleep-out and falling face-forwards onto her bed. Raising her head, she dug for her phone in her underwear drawer and typed a message into it.

One minute later, Stevie knocked on the sliding door holding a quilted makeup bag.

"For whom the bell bloody well tolls! You didn't even message me for my birthday this year. Don't tell me you want to get dolled up for the ex out there. Nana's already asking her if she's ever met Princess Diana."

"Ugh, no," said Rita, pointing to her chin, under which a red scab coagulated. "Can you cover this up? Got a little overzealous while tweezing, and I don't want Mum to ask me about it all day, you know she will."

"Say no more," said Stevie, unscrewing a tube of concealer. "You're lucky, you hardly need makeup with those brutalist eyebrows leading the way. As for the chin hairs, I swear they came marching out like the ants in the kitchen the day I turned thirty-five. Up-bup-bup!" She lifted Rita's chin and dabbed it with the concealer applicator.

"Must be karma for all the times we sang that Marilyn song 'One Silver Dollar' about Aunty Sweet. Only we changed it to 'One Silver Chin Hair'. Not so sodding droll now, is it."

"I, for one, am pretty amused," said Stevie.

"Yeah well, add my vanity to the list of things you're keeping under your hat, thanks."

☾

They all arrived last at Irene's, behind Jayne and Stevie. The drive was too short for Rita to get her bearings and long enough for the silence to scream at her as the trees and sky and arid grass all blotched into one out the window and Sidhal sat too close to her in the back seat.

Marlon, Ben and Glenn drove in together. Neil rented a van to bring Pete, Peter, Judy, Sissy and the twins. Anne-Marie, the funeral director, was delivering Irene home at 1PM, leaving them an hour to fuss. There wasn't much to do. Marlon and the twins had tidied the house the day before, pushing the couch back and arranging folding chairs. They placed a low table in front of the verandah for Irene's ashes. From the garden they picked lavender, rosemary and lemon balm, now huddled in jars on the table, along with Irene's walking cane and three crystals suggested by Stevie after researching from Irene's books: amethyst for serenity, black tourmaline for protection, moonstone for new beginnings.

Bufty stepped out of the car and raised her arm behind Sidhal, like Bob Hope presenting the next Miss World.

"This," she said, "is Sidhal. *Rita's* Sidhal." Never one to be overburdened with subtlety, Bufty added, "The one she went to Italy with. In 1981. *The Italian.*"

Her sisters' eyebrows shot up so fast, Rita half expected a cartoon dust cloud or screeching tyre noise to accompany them.

Sidhal stood, open and self-possessed, the breeze from the tide below teasing her coat hem. Neither awkward nor combative, she looked like an image from a catalogue. *EziBuy* reckoned Marlon. *Selfridges*, thought Stevie, *at the least*.

"Well!" exclaimed Judy, after a distended pause in which the only noise came from Rita scraping the toe of her boot through the gravel behind Avery's grey hatchback.

"Don't get me wrong," said Judy, starting strong then faltering, "but I didn't know you were . . . not . . . still in Italy?"

Sidhal stepped forward, benevolent as the fairy queens the girls conjured up as children. "You must be Judy, and I can see how you earned your sobriquet Judy the Beauty. I've been back in Aotearoa for some time, but of course, you never truly leave *Venezia*, do you?"

Judy, with no experience to verify this, agreed.

"Thank you for including me today," said Sidhal. "It's a profound honour to mark Irene's death with you all. The stories Rita confided in me evoked a formidable woman. You have my unreserved sympathy."

Sissy leaned over to Judy. "Rita, *confiding*?"

Sidhal, though she ought to have been on the back foot, was so blithely astute that she utterly disarmed the family—as if they should've known all along that she was coming. Should've known that she was A She.

Avery clapped for silence.

"We're delighted to have you here with us on this special day, Sidhal. All are welcome to celebrate Irene's life. On that note, it's going to be a bit of an open home situation,and we could have screeds of visitors passing through to pay their respects. Is all the food in the fridge that needs to be?"

The notion of food and feeding jump-started everyone.

"I've made a cake," Marlon told Sidhal, balancing a tote bag and broad Tupperware container on one arm and slamming her car boot. "I don't know why, I just did."

Sidhal took the container. "Here, let me. I brought a cake too, but I'm sure yours is much tastier—it's inexplicable isn't it, the decisions we make while grieving? But at least we may be certain that there's never a wrong time to have cake."

"Thank you, Sidhal, I hadn't thought of it like that. I'm looking forward to your cake too—so good of you to bring one, you didn't have to at all." Marlon sensed, without turning around, Rita fuming behind her.

Visitors arrived: Ross Lee the pharmacist, loyal acolyte of Irene's homemade herbal teas, who'd rarely had reason to fill a prescription for her; Nina Choudhary and Sue Hipkiss from the fruit and vege shop; Mrs Quentin and Mrs Fonseka, regular visitors to Irene for tarot readings since the 1970s; Jenny Touhou, a nearby neighbour in one of the few houses untampered by developers, she moved back again after her mother passed on and would call in on Irene, who she remembered from her childhood. Seats went to the guests, while the family stood or crouched on the floor. There were too many people for Irene's chair to be left unused, and in the end, with seniority on her side, Bufty lowered herself upon it.

The telephone in the hall rang.

Mahalia caught it.

"She's on her way home."

The family jumbled about, straightening their hems, fixing their hair, as though Irene were arriving revived and in the mood for judgement.

"They're here," called Neil from the doorway where he stood sentinel. Anne-Marie got out of her car carrying a dark wooden box with an engraved plaque on top. Tasteful, not tacky or too costly. A secure lid. Marlon had expressed concern about situating the ashes so close to the verandah.

Bufty took the box. She dropped a kiss onto its lid and led it to the table while Jayne sang 'Pō Atarau', her voice like gossamer, fingers skimming the guitar strings. The girls joined her, parting into alto and soprano.

"You're welcome to stay," said Bufty to Anne-Marie.

Anne-Marie pressed her palms together and bowed. "Thank you, but I've got two more deliveries to knock off this afternoon. It's like Grand Central Station at the crematorium. Merry Christmas and Happy New Year and my sincerest condolences to you, must dash."

Avery approached the table and placed her hand on the wooden box.

"Welcome guests, welcome friends, welcome family. Today we bring Irene back home and, in the process, we come home, too." Her low, hypnotic voice hummed like a vibrational frequency. She spoke without notes.

"Irene was the singular encapsulation of our known history, and the history not yet come to pass. She was the past and future made flesh, united—born in 1916 on the floor of a one-bedroom shack into a world where women were not encouraged to live on their terms, and life dealt her crushing obstacles. Irene withstood them and stood tall, and she provided a furtive glimpse beyond the veil through her gifts. That sixteen-year-old girl from Palmerston North turned into an integral community member, planting roots, growing resilient, refusing to bend or break in the storm. But 'The woods decay, the woods decay and fall', and living on her terms meant Irene died on her terms, and in turn, we must celebrate her on her terms. Today is not a funeral, it is simply a time of communion, where we can tell stories, sing, break bread, share our grief and say goodbye, and to do so is entirely in service of honouring Irene's extraordinary life. And so, our family welcomes Irene home, and welcomes you all."

"*Christ*," whispered Judy to Marlon, "when she's good, she's good, isn't she?"

"I can't concentrate," said Marlon, jittery despite rehearsing her speech three times to Glenn the night before while her cake was in the oven.

Marlon stepped out to the table and touched the box of ashes. "This isn't a eulogy, strictly speaking. But it might be interesting to reflect on what we know about Irene, and where she came from, some of which we learned from her, some from Mum, and still more from Judy's tireless family-tree work."

"Hear, hear," said Judy.

"On the ninth of March in 1916, in a small house in Palmerston North, Irene Arthur was born into a world that looks very different from our world today, or even the world my sisters and I grew up in, which itself seems a faraway place. We were two years into World War I, or The Great War as it was known, with no end in sight and limited information—no TV, no radio, no Facebook. Irene arrived nineteen years after her eldest brother, Wallace, for whom our father was named, sixteen years after her eldest sister, Mary, thirteen years after her other brother, George, and twelve years after the next sister, Rosalie. World War I was disastrous for New Zealand, and few families were not touched by tragedy. This was true for the Arthur family, who lost Wallace in 1916, sharing an unknown grave at the Somme with so many of his countrymen. With this death, and this divide between her and her siblings, Irene was born into a world of sorrow and loneliness, and into a world where—we might deduce—no one hoped for her."

Glenn gave Marlon the thumbs up, and she kept going.

"There is a lot we don't know about Irene's early life, and she held her cards close to her chest. We do know from Judy's research that her mother, Ebba—a name I have to admit I'm relieved didn't make its way down to me—was the daughter of Scottish and German settlers. Irene's father, Walter, was one of fifteen children—astonishingly, all of whom lived until adulthood—born to Ruth, a Māori woman, and Douglas, a Pākehā man whose ancestry leans Irish. We know little about Ruth, where she came from, her parents, even her birthdate is hazy, but she is the source of our Māori ancestry on Dad's side. Not that you'd know it to look at me. Unlike the rest of you girls, I can get sunburnt indoors at midnight. But you could see it in Irene.

"Her remaining brother George served in the Māori Battalion in World War II and, bringing more tragedy to the family, was killed in action at Monte Cassino. Irene often stayed with Ruth and Douglas and their younger children, Aunty Merry, Aunty Tippy, Uncle Fatty and Uncle Ronald, and these were some of Irene's happiest memories. To say this is not to cast any aspersions on her parents; they had lost a son in a war that showed no sign of ending, and didn't need another mouth to feed."

Marlon turned over her printed sheet of paper.

"Irene was sixteen years old when she met Albert Gordon at a dance, and we don't know much about the details—or what he was doing in Palmerston North—but he had the moves, because, needless to say, they married soon after, with our father on the way immediately. Albert brought Irene up here as a young bride, which must've been unimaginably daunting: pregnant and keeping house, her family inaccessible, while our grandfather went out to seek work. Just after Wallace—or Wally, as he was affectionately and enduringly nicknamed—was born, Albert dropped dead of a heart attack while on a job with a shearing gang, leaving Irene at seventeen with a newborn to feed. But this is where the Irene we remember starts to emerge. The sea air and intense dreams guided her towards a mystic life and, despite the religious dominance in the town, she turned this into, if not a lucrative business, enough to scrape by on for her and Wally. And Dad turned out pretty normal—as normal as you can be in this family, anyway."

Marlon waited for laughter, which she received, because people at funerals are secretly desperate to laugh at low-hanging fruit.

"That's where I'll end it but, as Avery said, Irene was our link to the past and future, and it's important today to consider where she came from. She said to me once, when I was staying here and she was putting me to bed, that she didn't know a whole lot about the elders in her family, and so she wanted to give us plenty to remember when we got to be her age. When I asked her what that meant, she sort of clammed up and told me to go to sleep. I just wish . . ." Marlon touched the wooden box. "I wish we could hear your voice again. But we have plenty to remember, don't we?"

Glenn hugged Marlon and kissed her forehead.

Bufty blew her nose with a metallic honk, rose to her feet and pulled a book from the handbag hanging over the back of her chair.

"Don't worry, it's not a Bible verse. That's not Irene's style, is it?"

"None of that claptrap!" called Avery, and everyone laughed.

"I'm going to read a little poem by Yeats, just a couple of verses because it does go on a bit. It's called 'The Tower', and I remember Irene and Avery spending hours unpicking its hidden meanings, all of which went straight over my head. It's my understanding—though I could be wrong, and I still expect Irene to speak up any minute to put me to rights if I am—but Yeats was reflecting on his life, and growing old, and so it feels appropriate."

Avery mouthed the words along with her, and all of Bufty's silliness dropped away as she worked through the poem, only choking up when she got to "The mother bird will rest".

Bufty unfolded a yellowed paper tucked into the back of the book.

"And now, because Irene kept it all this time, here's a little letter Wally wrote to her while at school. It may have been an exercise to practice their penmanship, or maybe he just wanted to write it. Wally wasn't at school for long, as you know, but his spelling shows the makings of a scholar if you ask me . . . I wanted to include this because we're thinking of him always, but especially today, and now he and his dear mum are reunited at last. Irene carried the burden of burying her son—a load I can't even bear to imagine—" and here Bufty hiccupped, but didn't cry. "I'll just read it."

Dear Mother,

How are you? It rained today so we couldn't get a game of ball going. I don't mind, because I like to read and hear the raindrops on the schoolroom roof. Have you made onion pie for dinner? I think that would be nice. I love you.

Your son,

Wally.

"There, isn't that sweet?" Bufty's face pinkened. "His teacher once told him he couldn't knock the skin from a rice pudding, but I don't see how anyone could find fault with such a lovely boy."

"Good stuff, Mum," said Rita, leaning over to touch her hand. The letter had done the rounds before—Judy got hung up on the "I love you" line, saying surely the other boys would've thrashed Wally if they'd seen it. But it sounded different here, read aloud, dead son to dead mother. Untarnished, poignant, harder to poke the borax at.

Judy recounted the story of staying at Irene's for the holidays with Jayne after Rita was born, writing *Jayne took the last biscuit* in the sand, and having a change of conscience at the last minute, and years later realising Irene had probably definitely seen it out the window.

Stevie spoke about Irene and Bufty both taking her in over the years, and about one such time when she and Irene blessed her crystals under the full moon, and Irene gave her a lapis lazuli to keep, which Stevie pulled from her trouser pocket.

"I hadn't thought how I'd wind this up," she said. "But when it comes down to it, what I couldn't be taught by Irene, by Nana, Mum and the aunties, isn't worth a damn and you couldn't find it anywhere else in the world."

Judy blinked back tears. "Well done, Floss."

Rita walked towards the table.

"Here we go," said Marlon to Judy. "Remember her last speech? At the twins' twenty-first? That was a blinder."

Rita shifted her weight from one hip to the other, hands in her back pockets.

"Irene was a great one for sayings. I can still hear her voice: 'stay humble, but never forget your worth'. I know some of us took that last part to heart . . . Judy . . ."

Judy raised her hand, chuckling. "That's me."

"She was a lady of integrity and disapproved of cuss words," continued Rita, "but now and then if the moon waxed or waned to *juuuust* the right position, and she'd been wronged by an onerous scoundrel, you might hear her claim that she wouldn't piss on them if they were on fire. Should this outburst shock you, she'd say that swearing was the universe's little reward for having to pay taxes. And then there were those helpful sayings that were all one word. *Carnafford.* Seems every adult in our family knew that one, hey Mum? But we got by."

Rita could've been doing stand-up comedy. The room reverberated with laughter.

"*Goreadabook*, another exceptional one-word saying, *suffocatetodeath*, how many victims met that particular end in her stories . . . so many sayings . . ." Rita trailed off, breath catching in her throat. "She told us, 'Girls, never forget where you're from, and if you don't know where you're from, wait for your ancestors to tell you because they're always by your side' . . . well, she put it more succinct-like than that . . . I remember after Dad's funeral I told Irene how weird it felt that he was not coming back, and she said that they don't come back, but one day we'll go with them, and . . ."

Rita's words deserted her. Family and visitors alike smiled, encouraging, and a slashing sensation behind her eyes formed the shape of a question: *What will you all say about me when I die? And will I find out soon?* Her knees slackened. She bit her tongue.

And then Jayne appeared on her right with the guitar, singing 'Goodnight, Irene', and Marlon and Judy moved to Rita's left, both resting a hand at her back.

"Join in, everyone," called Jayne. Unable to articulate her gratitude, Rita rested her head on Judy's shoulder and her hand on Jayne's, and she couldn't sing, not yet, but her sisters knew.

The silent lull following the song sent a small wave of relief through Rita. They'd gotten through it.

"If I may?" Sidhal rose from her spot on the floor where she insisted on sitting despite her status as guest.

"Of course," said Bufty, "all are welcome."

Rita rolled her eyes. Only the outside company stopped her from grumbling, but the irritation made her feel more human.

Before her astonished audience, Sidhal sang 'I Dreamt I Dwelt in Marble Halls', her voice bright and smooth as satin ribbon. Few dry eyes remained by the coda, and though Rita didn't join in the thunderous applause, she rubbed her forehead and looked into the distance, and you couldn't hope for much more of an admission of emotion.

"Weren't you a chef?" asked Judy, as Sidhal sat again, knees tucked to the side, in one neat motion.

"No, that was Rita's forte. But she taught me to cook, and I taught her to love opera . . ."

"Rita? Opera?" Judy snorted. "Yeah right."

"Baby Rita only listens to very loud music by the Pixies," said Bufty, "and what's that band you like—the Hot Muppets? Beef Pockets? Something like that, isn't it, bub? They looked like they needed a good wash and a square meal, but they did have that one lovely song, though, didn't they?"

"Yeah, just like that, Mum." This was why Rita didn't tell her family things. Because then they knew things.

"I was never going to be another Renata Tebaldi or Dame Kiri," said Sidhal, "but I could hold my head up high—not that it's a patch on your family's singing—and Rita became quite the aficionado."

"Oh, Sidhal, an opera singer, how *glamorous*." Each additional detail sent Bufty into further spasms of elation. "This is *The Italian*," she stage whispered to Mrs Quentin and Mrs Fonseka.

"Pull yourself together, Mum," muttered Rita, quiet enough that none of the guests heard.

☾

Avery put the kettle on. Judy and Marlon removed gladwrap and laid paper plates on the table. Sidhal found a serrated knife and cut her bread into even slices.

It was good to eat, and to offer the visitors food.

As the afternoon frayed into evening, and the guests drifted home, with the light tinged gold and the sun disintegrating into the water, everything became more liquid and surreal, outside of time, space and how one might expect to feel the week before Christmas. Or at a funeral. Judy moved Irene's boombox out of her bedroom and played one of her classical CDs. Bufty poured her birthday passionfruit liqueur from Avery into all the clean teacups. Neil ducked away in the van and returned with a two-burner barbecue, sausages, buns, vegan patties, tomatoes, onions, mushrooms and lettuce, and proceeded to cook dinner out in the garden. The family dragged their chairs around the barbecue and put up trestle tables and ate off paper plates in the fading heat, leaving the front door open so they could see Irene's ashes.

Later still, Marlon and Jayne lay on Irene's bed, deep in conversation with much gesticulation and giggling. Peter was asleep in the pink room. The twins produced two bottles of honey whiskey, lifted from the bar. Judy and Sissy found Marlon's red and yellow Beatles *1* album in her car, and they goofed around dancing—the Macarena, the chicken dance, bastardised John Travolta moves—and Stevie pulled Sidhal up to dance, and then everyone was dancing, except Avery, who alternated washing and drying teacups and doing lunges, which was a bit like dancing, and Rita, who leaned against the verandah railing, staring blank-eyed over the ocean.

And the sun slipped away below the water, and Avery boiled the jug again, and Neil took Pete, Peter and the barbecue home, and Glenn took Ben home, and remarked with tears in his eyes that it felt odd not to be extending his hand to Irene to drive her home too, and he offered Sidhal a lift but Bufty exhorted her to stay, and to Rita's indignation Sidhal accepted, and everyone left behind changed into comfortable clothes, and Jayne strummed her guitar on the floor by the table where Irene's ashes rested, and Marlon told Avery to sit, that she'd fix the hot drinks, and she made a pot of tea with the box of Bell that Irene asked the twins to buy on their final grocery trip, which should've been a clue, and everyone settled in for the evening, Bufty, Judy and Marlon on the couch, plaiting Jayne's long hair, Stevie on the floor on the other side of Irene's ashes, Rita and Sidhal at the kitchen table with the twins, Sissy on a folding chair, lit only by the brass floor lamp, fat candles sinking into saucers, and the waxing moon rising over the water.

Marlon nodded at Stevie, who was drinking an instant coffee.

"You must feel a bit culture-shocked, hey? Going from London in the middle of winter to all this. Where are they sending you next? Are you allowed to say?"

Jayne reached over the table to touch Stevie's shoulder.

"Go on, babe. Tell them."

"Oooh, tell us what, Floss?" said Bufty. "Is it a promotion?"

Stevie wrinkled her nose. "Okay look, the reason I'm here is—I mean—I won't be going back to the Ministry in the new year."

"Because . . ." encouraged Jayne.

"Because . . ." Stevie stared at her hands, holding the weight of that horrid moment right before The Thing is said. "I've been back in the country since February. I wasn't doing so great at the London High Commission, always two steps behind and cocking up and there was a minor hassle with some nostril candy, not entirely my fault, mind you. They didn't want a fuss and gave me the option to resign or be pushed, so I took the easy way out, which came with a tidy payout, and so I flew back to New Zealand, had a bit of a meltdown, and I've been dossing in with a friend up north. And now, I'm here."

Jayne's face fell. "That's not what you told me the other day! You said you were thinking of leaving."

"Yes well, I was bloody testing the waters, wasn't I?"

"Cocaine!" cried Marlon. "That's illegal!"

"Oh, you country girls," said Stevie, "so naive."

"If it's so illegal, Mum," said Diana, "then how d'you know it's called nostril candy?"

"I watch those CSI shows on TV, I wasn't born yesterday."

"I knew the accent was a put-on," crowed Judy, "didn't I say?"

"Maybe I overdid it a little," said Stevie, "but I think I'm stuck talking like this now."

"So did you even go to London at all, or have you been hiding from us all this time, on the run up north?"

"*Mum*," said Sissy.

Jayne frowned at Judy. *Don't push.*

"I wasn't on the run, and I went to London, for a year and a half at least—"

"You don't have to keep lying to us."

"I was bloody there, Judy! You all saw my photo on the Ministry website! I sent you those Percy Pigs!"

Stevie turned to Bufty. "Nana? I'm sorry. It's a right mess. I wanted to tell you, honest."

"Oh, Floss." Bufty waved Stevie over for a hug. "That painting you did was rather elaborate for someone who'd recently landed in the country. You could've come home, you know, we'll never-ever-ever turn you away. No matter how many scrapes you get into. Isn't that right, Rita?"

"Yep."

Jayne gathered her knees up under her chin, looking

younger than Stevie for a moment. "Was it Heather you were staying with, the one from your course?"

"Yeah, I stayed with Heather, and look, I'm sorry, Mum! I wanted to come home, but I needed to regroup, get my act together, that sort of carry-on, and I couldn't bear to let you all down, and the longer it went on, the harder it was to come clean."

"You haven't let us down," said Marlon, jostling Judy with her elbow.

Judy rubbed her arm. "Yeah, yeah, it's good that you're back. Let's face it, who wants to eat boiled English cuisine, anyway?" She pointed at Stevie. "And if anyone round the way asks after you, we can lie and say you're busy and important. We look after our own here." Judy shifted her hand to point at Sidhal, who appeared not to have noticed.

"I wish you'd told me. I'd never get mad at you." Jayne held out her hand to Stevie, and their fingers intertwined in front of Irene's ashes.

"That's why I couldn't tell you, Mum. It'd be much easier to potentially let you down if you were a massive scumbag."

"What have you been so busy with then, if you're not doing work?" asked Bufty, the picture still not adding up in her head. "Always *tacker-tacker-tacker*."

"Yes," said Judy, "what *have* you been up to? Your payout can't've been that jammy."

"Not cocaine—"

"No, Marlon," said Stevie, "I have not been on my laptop *doing cocaine*. Look, I've been—god, I'll just say it—"

She knew they were all mentally filling in the possible endings to that sentence.

"Get on with it!" said Judy.

"I've been ghostwriting erotic literature."

Even Rita was taken aback.

"You're joking."

"No joke, Judy. I sort of fell into it after meeting a publishing exec at a party in London, you know, the place

I literally lived? And there's a huge market for e-books—positively throbbing—no? Too soon?—and writers can't publish them fast enough. That's why I've been so busy, because I've got a deadline on the twenty-second for a holiday-themed story, *Oh Cum All Ye Faithful: An Unholy Christmas Orgy*."

Judy gripped her teacup of honey whiskey like the ropes of a Burma bridge. Marlon dropped Jayne's hair. Bufty's eyes widened.

"You could take cocaine in your stride, but a bit of blue fiction is where you draw the line? Blue fiction that pays my bills and buys your Christmas presents, I might add." Stevie threw up her hands. "I mean, someone's got to write it!"

Rita rubbed her chin. "Is that all? C'mon guys. I mean, it's gotta be a more honest job than working for the government."

"Fair dues," said Judy.

"So, your cover's been . . . blown . . . from your . . . job . . ." said Marlon, face pink as a peony.

Stevie burst into laughter. From nerves—relief—from shock at Marlon attempting an off-colour joke.

"We Three Kings of Orient Are Horny," said Mahalia.

"Mahalia!" squeaked Bufty, but she laughed too.

"I've got it," said Judy, "Big Dong Merrily on High!"

Bufty's laughter escalated in volume the harder everyone laughed with her, the twins clutching their stomachs, Marlon and Judy hitting each other with cushions, Jayne wiping tears and Sissy smacking her thighs, until Bufty had to dash to the bathroom, and they could hear her laughing from down the hall, which set them off again.

"Whew, sorry, Sidhal. We're not always like this," said Marlon.

"Yeah, we're usually much worse," said Rita, pressing her lips together to stop herself smiling.

"I am sorry for not coming back sooner, Mum," said Stevie. "For not telling you. It felt right to come back now, with Nana's birthday, and I had this feeling like I needed to see Irene, and I figured you couldn't all be mad at me at Christmas . . ."

"Come here, babe."

Stevie hugged Jayne and lay with her head in her mother's lap.

"Adam Lay Ybounden and Gagged!" roared Bufty, returning from the bathroom.

"We've moved on, Mum," said Judy. "You missed the boat."

"Fair dues," said Rita, "that was decent. Bravo, Mum." She almost added "Carol of the Balls" but stopped herself.

"I had a think about it on the loo just now," said Bufty, "and my opinion is, I'm proud as punch. A published author! Who cares if you're writing smut? As Rita said, it's honest work. We Gordon women have been making the world turn in its grave since time immemorial, s'pose there's no point stopping now."

"That's right, Nana. And you wouldn't believe how cushy this honest work is," said Stevie. "My Ministry payout was none too shabby, and Heather only charged me board, so I've saved a bit of money—not tons, but it's a start—and I want to buy a house for you one day, Mum. Anywhere you want."

Jayne's teardrops fell onto Stevie's forehead.

"Too much, Floss. You can't do that."

"Don't be daft, you deserve to be looked after. Everyone's looked after me all my life. Maybe I could stay up this way for a bit myself . . ."

"That's lovely, Floss," said Bufty.

"It's a fabulous idea," said Marlon. "But you'd better make a move. Prices are skyrocketing, and it's all because the affluent folks have worked out we're not *that* far from Auckland. Not nearly far enough if you ask me— sorry, Sissy. Those hideous beach developments round here don't help either."

"You lot got your place easy enough, didn't you? When you took over the bar?" Stevie looked over at the twins.

"With our combined KiwiSavers," said Mahalia. "And Dad's business as leverage."

"And it's still in the middle of nowhere," added Diana. "No matter what the developers tell you."

Rita considered her savings. Enough to drift by on. But unimpressive. Even by middle-of-nowhere standards.

"Mind you, back in my day you saved every penny, lived on beans and bought what you could afford," said Judy. "Let's face it, the younger generation expects to go straight to Park Lane and won't settle for Old Kent Road."

"No, we don't," said Sissy. "Remember my first flat? It was so damp I got a kidney infection."

"Nooo, that was from all the bottom-shelf vodka you chugalugged," said Judy, pouring another measure of honey whiskey into her teacup. "God, this stuff goes down a treat, doesn't it, twins? Besides, it's all part of the experience! Me and Pete froze half to death in our first house."

"And how much did it cost?"

"$18,000. Don't forget inflation, though."

"Sure, Mum. And Old Kent Road now has a bunch of investors whacking parking buildings on every corner."

"Ours was $15,000," said Marlon, "and we thought we'd never repay it in a million years."

"Our house must've practically been free, by that logic," said Jayne. "How much was it, Mama?"

"Let me guess," said Sissy, "you got it for $25 and four jars of tomato relish. No, six."

"We should all guess," said Marlon. "Whoever's closest gets first dibs on Irene's will."

Bufty and Avery's eyes met across the room.

Judy faced her mother. "How much *did* our house cost? I can't believe I've never asked you before."

Bufty squirmed in her seat.

Rita tucked her thumbs inside her fists and squeezed tight. "I don't think this is necessary—"

"Well—you see—" said Bufty at the same time. "We didn't buy it. We sort of inherited it. Sort of."

"From your dad?" asked Judy. "Isn't he the reason we grew up on the smell of an oily rag?"

"No, the bank took that house . . ."

Avery stretched her arms overhead and leaned back, with a series of pops from her lower spine.

"I gave your mum and dad their house."

"What?" Judy's eyebrows burrowed in the centre of her forehead.

"I gave it to them," Avery repeated. "It was mine to give, and that's about all there is to it. My father died, he loved Bufty, she'd spent so much time living there, looking after him. I was away doing my theological training, and in those days you could still get a little house when you joined a church as the minister. It was an empty home. Bufty and Wally needed somewhere to live. It had space for a family, and it seemed like a good idea. Like the right thing to do. So that's what I did."

The girls chewed on this information like gristle at the end of a roast. Were they angry? And what were they angry about?

By this point, having imbibed precisely enough liquor to justify such outbursts, Judy chose to take umbrage.

"Why didn't we know this? You can't *give* someone a house, that's absurd! Was this—" and she turned to her mother again, slossing honey whiskey from her cup onto her hand. "Was this your way of buying Dad's silence, because you two were having a lesbian affair?" She licked the whiskey off her palm. "Is that it? Our childhood home, a den of lies? Don't think we didn't see what was going on!"

"Judy!" Marlon dropped Jayne's hair again. Jayne looked down, shrinking in on herself. Sidhal continued to observe the family as if watching a David Attenborough documentary.

"For Christ's sake," said Rita, "don't be wet. Mum and Dad were poor as church mice, it was generous."

"Oh, so you knew about this?" said Judy.

"I heard stuff."

Now Marlon and Jayne turned to Rita, disgruntled.

"What is this, some kind of lesbian solidarity," hissed Judy, "all of you, with your dirty little secrets? How did you find this out, Rita, you were *never around!* Flitting across the globe with Posh Spice over here, but who knew all this time—" She was unsure how to wrap this up without saying anything irrevocably hurtful. Not a priority for Judy, but Rita's pinched face halted her.

"There it is," said Rita. "Surprise! I'm a lesbian! And so is she!"

Sidhal waved.

"And I didn't hide it from you. Sometimes you find things out when you listen more than you talk! Jesus, get a grip, Judy. What next, banging on about 'the odour of mendacity' like Big Daddy Pollitt?"

"Stop yelling!" Jayne put her hands over her face.

"Oh, put a sock in it, Jayne." Judy's eyes were lit from within. Though livid, she loved the thrust and parry. "Mind you, I always thought I looked like Elizabeth Taylor," she couldn't help adding.

"Yeah, and wouldn't it be nice if you did." Rita, who didn't have the stomach for fighting, felt queasy.

"No, *you* shut up, Judy," said Jayne, startling everyone, including herself. "Maybe if you weren't such a bossy bitch, we'd be more inclined to tell you stuff!"

"Me? A bossy bitch? Don't get me wrong, but what does that make you? The flake of the century?"

"Better a flake than a bossy bitch! And you were jealous because you wanted to be a rebel, Judy the Beauty, but you were such a square, and you hated that I lost my virginity before you." Jayne's face grew scarlet as her words gathered wrathful steam.

"As if!" Judy thudded her teacup on the side table. "At least I wasn't a barefoot and pregnant unwed teenage mother when I lost my virginity!"

"At least they didn't start calling me Judy the Slut because I kept hooning through husbands!"

"Oh, that is *rich*. What, pray tell, is so slutty about getting *married*?"

"No, no, no." Rita widened her eyes at Marlon. It was going to happen, the locked door with a key turning in the latch, Stevie and Sissy and the twins leaning forward like audience members at a play—

"Well, you didn't let the grass grow under your feet, did you? Not when you cheated on—"

"*GIRLS!*" Marlon planted both feet squarely and pushed herself to standing. "Cut it out! We've already done this once before, in—"

"Christmas 2001," chorused Rita, Bufty, Avery and Jayne.

"Oh yeah," said Stevie. "That was neither merry, nor bright."

"—so knock it off. Remember why we're here. Who we're here for."

Marlon might have successfully shut down this quarrel had Bufty, now crying, not sabotaged any chance of peace and another cuppa by shutting her eyes, tilting her head back, and yelling, "YOUR FATHER WAS GAY!"

Judy paused, mouth open to yell at Jayne. Jayne let out a low whistle. Rita didn't move a muscle. Marlon fell to her seat, as though pushed by a gust of wind.

Stevie pulled a pack of Rothmans from her bag and lit a cigarette from the candles on the table.

"Oh, do me a favour. Irene let me smoke in here." She held up the carton to the still-silent room. "Anyone? Not top-shelf, but not as bad as Winnie Blues . . ."

"High days and holy days," said Avery, though she declined.

"Good to take the edge off, isn't it," replied Stevie. "Ashes to ashes, as it were." They might've been loitering outside a pub, clutching their handbags. Jayne, sniffling, tapped the table. Stevie passed her a cigarette, which she also lit from one of the candles.

"Sorry, Mama," said Jayne, ashing into an empty wine bottle. "You know how it is."

Judy cast her righteous gaze upon Bufty.

"So, *Mum*, let me get this straight—"

"Straight's not the operative word here, Judy," interrupted Rita.

Bufty laughed hysterically, and once you heard that brassy Bufty laugh you had to join in, and soon they were all wiping tears from their eyes, crossing their legs and almost falling off their chairs, while Rita sat in the middle, bewildered ringmaster of an unregulated circus.

"I'm sorry, Jayne," said Judy, reaching over to her sister. "I am a bossy bitch, aren't I."

"I'm sorry too," said Jayne, taking Judy's hand. "I am a flake."

"Judy the Slut doesn't even rhyme," said Stevie absently. "Why didn't they call you Judy the Floozy?"

"Judy the Hoochie would've had poetic scansion," commented Diana. Avery's eyes lit up. "Or Jezebel Judy, for alliteration."

"Judy Whore-don," suggested Mahalia.

"Now we're talking," said Diana.

"Oh, come on," said Judy.

"She does have a point," said Rita. "Linguistic-wise, I mean."

"Hang about." Judy turned again to Bufty. "Back the truck up just a second. Dad was *gay*? What do you mean? Is Baby Ree in on that little secret too?"

"Hey, don't look at me."

"Mum?"

Bufty felt as though she were driving over endless judder bars. Avery's face softened into a familiar look. *You've done the hardest part. One foot in front of the other.*

So she explained.

Spiteful rumours were circulating by the time Avery went away to St Swithin's.

Wally was no stranger to rumours. You grew up quick and married young, and he'd only done the first one. He and Bufty struck up an affectionate repartee at the factory; went to the flicks, shared sausage rolls in the tearoom. In the right company, given encouragement, Wally was the most charismatic person you'd ever know. It's funny how a person can seem one way until you see the reality hiding underneath.

One evening—*Calamity Jane*—Wally drove Bufty home from the cinema, listening to her chatter nineteen to the dozen about Doris Day. He pulled in to the beach, led her onto the sand and pointed up to his mother's house, where he still lived.

"I trust you, Bufty. Do you trust me?"

She did. He dropped onto one knee. How many times had she seen this play out on screen? And now, here, for her, a man with his trousers digging into the sand.

"What if we made a go of it?"

That's not quite how they say it in the movies.

"I've heard things about you. You love someone, don't you? Someone you can't marry? Is that right?" Bufty felt the sand melting beneath her feet.

"Well, maybe you've heard things about me. Maybe I've got someone too. Maybe we can help each other out."

Wally stood, brushing sand from his trousers.

He wanted children. He didn't like any other women. He could only be a confirmed bachelor for so long. He wouldn't stand in the way of her and her person, so long as she didn't mind turning a blind eye to him now and then. It wasn't the best, but maybe they could make each other's lives better. Two good friends.

It was as if Wally had pulled down the moon and shone its light right in Bufty's face.

They had a laugh, didn't they? He was handsome. Not

dour, violent or a drunk. She had no idea what to do about her feelings for Avery. This might just be—not *the* solution, but *a* solution.

"I . . . I'll think about it," she said, and an electric charge jolted her, from the naked honesty and from being perceived so wholly, and she kissed Wally more passionately than she'd kissed any man in her young life.

"I've thought about it," she said, their mouths still touching. "We should get married. But only if Avery's okay with it. That's . . . that's the person's name."

Wally drove her to St Swithin's the next day, and they spoke with Avery. Each person gave their blessing for their part in the relationship. Avery knew Bufty wanted children. Knew she couldn't offer her that existence. She warmed to Wally, understood his intentions. They could all be part of each other's lives on their terms, as best they could until the rest of the world caught up.

After the ceremony at the cemetery for Bill Manrose, Avery took Wally and Bufty aside.

"I want to give you both the house. You already live here, Bufty, it's your home. Our home. Let me give this to you. Say you bought it from the estate, say what you like, but it's yours, for your family."

And as Wally inched through his final days, he asked to see Avery.

"I haven't got much time left," he said. "When it comes, I want you to lead the funeral. Your way, in your church, with you in charge. And, Avery—I know you'll look after Bufty and the girls, but remember Mum, too. She won't be overjoyed about a church funeral, and maybe not about you and Bufty, but don't give up on her. She needs family, and you're family."

"So girls, if he'd asked me flat to marry him," said Bufty, "I'm sure I would've said yes because that's what you did. He didn't have to lay himself bare like that. It was dangerous, you know, and it would have been a different marriage altogether if he hadn't been brave and honest. He told me, 'Bufty, that's the biggest trick of all. When people look at us, they'll see themselves reflected back. And all the while, we're only reflecting each other. Our real selves. Right under their noses.' All told, I'm thankful we could be . . ." Bufty's eyes, squeezed shut, opened. "Honest."

Silence sagged across the room, like an old helium balloon.

"Damn, Mum," said Rita.

"So he was *bisexual*?" said Sissy.

"So did you love him, or was it a farce?" asked Judy, still on the offensive. "Did you even want us?" Marlon elbowed her again.

"So you were *polyamorous*?" said Sissy.

"You youngsters and your need for labels," said Bufty, pulling a clean handkerchief from her handbag. "We didn't know, and the names we did know you couldn't repeat in civilised company. We knew we could be ourselves with each other. I loved your father, he and Avery respected each other, and most importantly, everyone loved *me*." No one laughed, though Avery smiled at her.

"Did Irene know?" Judy pointed at the box of ashes as if she might join in with her own opinions. To be fair, only death could staunch the flow of Irene's pronouncements.

"If she did, she didn't say, and I didn't tell her the whole story. But after your father died, I did explain how we were all above board, so to speak. She took a bit to come around to Avery, but of course she did, Irene was special like that. I think she was more miffed she didn't predict it herself."

"Why didn't Dad tell her he was gay?"

"I don't know, Judy. It was illegal and monumentally taboo, and people kept themselves to themselves back then. Although people keep themselves to themselves these days too. Don't they, Rita?"

"That must've been really heavy for you, Mum," said Jayne.

"Yeah, I think the three of you were very brave," said Marlon.

"I agree," said Stevie.

The colour returned to Bufty's cheeks.

"It's good to shout and cry and get it all out in the open," piped up Sidhal. "*Molto italiano*."

"You're not even fucking Italian!" snapped Judy. She shrugged. "What? She isn't!"

"Fair dues," said Rita.

"But you're family now, and that's why I can talk to you like this. And girls, Sidhal's right, a little airing of grievances makes the world go round."

"*Giusto così*," said Sidhal, looking on edge for the first time that day.

"But, Mum, you know . . . you could've trusted us with the truth," said Marlon. "We love you, Avery, no question, but it was a bit wearying, being the subject of gossip. Some of my friends were *very* funny about it, and I know Irene's standing in the community kept us safe, kind of. But it was a lot, and we'd just lost Dad, and you acted like it was normal. It was unfair on us, Mum! Sorry, Avery, we love you to bits, but—"

"None taken, I promise," said Avery.

"Anyway, it doesn't matter. Bygones are bygones." Marlon preferred to defuse rather than provoke arguments.

"You didn't have to be so scandalised," said Bufty, "it was the 1970s, not Victorian times. I didn't think it bothered you all that much, you seemed to get on with it, and it was so hectic with Floss here being born and your father's funeral and Bev Murphy running over Marlene Dietrich . . . it all got away on me."

"You mean you buried your head in the sand, let's face it," said Judy.

"Leave it alone, Judy," said Rita.

"What if I did?" Bufty blotted her nose with the handkerchief. "None of you brought it up with me until today.

We could've had this fight at Avery's and my wedding, goodness knows we could've had it at Christmas 2001! So now who's burying their heads in the sand? None of you knows what we went through."

"Mum's not wrong," said Marlon. "People who busy themselves with just-getting-on-with-it never stop to talk. Do we?"

Judy, still skittish from all the truth-telling, and with the unearned confidence that comes from needing to point the finger before it can point back at oneself, wasn't done sparring.

"Mind you, what about you, Rita? Everything has to be on your terms too, and we have to take it. You disappear and we can't stop you. You never talk to us. You couldn't even tell us you had cancer! Or that you were gay!"

This pushed Rita over a line, tripping and falling. She stood up. "As if everything isn't always on *your* terms! And what would you have done if I'd told you? Used that time to cure cancer? So I disappear. So what? We all know what you did with Mish—"

"*Hey!*" Marlon raised her hand. "We did this already, at—"

"Christmas 2001."

"That's right, and once was enough. Leave it, you lot."

Rita sat on her hands. She'd shown too many cards. And not enough.

"Ah, look, girls," she said. "I'm sorry for going away for so long. Why d'you think I'm here now."

"You mean you're hanging out with us because you feel guilty?" Judy's voice cracked, the ghost of Christmas 2001 looming over her.

"Yeah, that's exactly it. No, dingus. Okay, there is guilt, guilt at missing so much, and I keep thinking about if Irene had died while I was away—or vice versa—" Rita swallowed a sob and covered her mouth with her hand. "Ugh, I guess I'm trying to make up for it, or something . . . while I'm still . . ."

"Oh, my baby." Bufty waddled over and drew Rita towards her in a hug. "You can go live your life. You don't have to be stuck here."

"I know," said Rita, her voice muffled by Bufty's bulk. "But I'm kind of backed onto a ledge. It is what it is. Sorry for having a go at you, Judy. And Mum, good on you for saying your piece."

"Thank you, and I'm sorry, too," said Bufty, releasing Rita. "I shouldn't have hidden it all from you, and it got bigger and scarier the more I hid it. But I hope you never doubted I loved you. You know I wanted you girls with all my heart, so did Wally."

A shadow darted over Bufty's eyes.

"Of course you loved us," said Jayne. "We're about the luckiest family in the world to have you and Dad *and* Avery."

"Of course, Mum," echoed Marlon. "We're here now, that's what matters."

She elbowed Judy.

"Yeah, yeah, I'm sorry too."

Around the room, muscles unlaced, shoulders softened, upper teeth parted from lower.

"What if you'd been born later when it was okay to be gay, would you still have married Dad?"

"Oh Judy, what if all your fingers turned into bananas, then what?"

"Who wants a nightcap?" asked Avery hastily.

"That's the bloody ticket," said Bufty.

☾

Avery swayed on the verandah, reciting lines of Emily Dickinson. The twins, next to her, passed one of Stevie's Rothmans back and forth. Bufty, on the couch, a pink towelling dressing gown straining over her white dress, watched Avery while humming 'Moonlight Swim' and occasionally beckoned for the twins' cigarette. A request that went unheeded. Stevie turned Irene's tarot cards over one by one on the table beside her ashes, taking time to regard each image. Jayne snored on the other side of the couch, curled around a cushion. Marlon, Judy and Sissy danced to the second Beatles CD, and Judy told them there were two kinds of people in this world: those who listen to the *Forrest Gump* soundtrack and call it a day, and those who were there in the 60s, and listen to real music, and don't need the *Forrest Gump* soundtrack because they've already got albums by The Doors and Aretha Franklin, thank you very much. "Y'know what I mean? There's me, and then there's the sort who think 'Baba O'Riley' is called 'Teenage Wasteland'," she slurred.

And Rita and Sidhal, at the kitchen table, avoided eye contact with less conviction than they had that morning.

Later still, Bufty rested her head on a pillow in Marlon's lap, her feet on Jayne's lap, and read Irene's will. It was brief and left everything to Bufty to divide up as she saw fit, which wasn't a huge surprise, but still required a little lie-down. Irene's Howard Morrison Quartet CD played quietly.

"You're the true keeper of Irene's stories now, Mama." Marlon ran a wooden comb from Irene's room through her mother's hair.

"Tell us a story about Irene," said Jayne. "What was she like when you first met her? Did she do you a tarot reading for your wedding?"

Bufty shut her eyes.

"She was barely older than Sweet. But such authority—such gravitas. I felt like a giggling schoolgirl next to her. Which I was, more or less. Irene was striking—I can see how she caught your grandfather's eye—and she taught me ever so many recipes, how to keep a house, all the domestic duties she'd had to grapple with alone, and without half the modern conveniences. Things my mother never taught me . . . And yes, she did a tarot reading before our wedding."

"What card did you get?" asked Marlon.

"Three of Pentacles. I'll never forget it as long as I live. It sounded so unromantic, but Irene said the three pentacles represented three people coming together in a perfect union, creating a strong foundation and sharing resources to achieve a goal. Doesn't that send a shiver up your spine? I wondered if she considered herself the third person—of course, I was thinking about Avery . . . but Irene was there too . . . I'd never experienced anything like it before, and I cried buckets, no word of a lie."

"Bugger me," said Judy, drinking tea from the same dove-grey cup that earlier held her whiskey.

"Christ, nothing gets past Irene, does it," said Stevie.

"Did she tell you girls about the American soldiers visiting when they were stationed here in the war? She'd feed them, and they'd have a song, and she'd tell them their fortune and send them on their way. The town got a milk bar for all the soldiers, it was fantastic. They built the hospital where your father died, you know. I mostly remember the blackout curtains and the air astir with fear and apprehension, but we had a soldier boy or two visit us, only when Dad wasn't home, mind you . . . You know, a lot of Yankee babies were born that way. I'm surprised none of them took up with Irene—well, maybe they did, she was private about all that."

The combination of truth and booze had emboldened Bufty.

"So why *did* you two break up then, Rita? Sidhal? Go on, it's too late to be coy now."

"It's tedious," said Rita. "Girl meets girl, *bla bla bla*."

"I can't imagine our Baby Ree running through an airport to stop someone getting on a plane," laughed Marlon. "Or saying 'Is it still raining? I hadn't noticed'."

"There was a bit of an airport chase moment," said Sidhal, "but I'm sure you're not interested."

Bufty's jaw fell open. "You mean to say, my own daughter ran through an airport and didn't tell me?"

"It wasn't like that," said Rita.

"She's right, I did the chasing," said Sidhal. "A classic tale: the bored trophy wife seeking a thrill, the catering assistant for another of my silly little parties—that one was potted trout, chicken Marbella and chocolate mousse. My husband paid her to teach me how to cook to keep me occupied, a powerful spark ignited and . . . we decided on a whim to run off to Italy."

"I couldn't afford a decision like that," interjected Rita. "She decided, I agreed."

"And that was blissful for a while, until came the inevitable falling back to earth with a bump when Rita here 'couldn't keep doing this anymore' and had to come home . . . so I tried to stop her at the airport . . ."

"Oh my god," gasped Bufty, wide awake again. "A spark ignited!" *Finally, the fun type of drama.*

"So you came home from Italy because you missed us?" asked Jayne.

"Who knows. It was a long time ago. A blur. Yes, probably." Such a long-ago blur, that only Rita and Bufty remembered the proximity of Erana Milner's death to Rita's return.

"That's one way to put it," said Sidhal.

"How did you afford it all?" asked Judy.

"My family is very rich."

Sidhal's candour impressed Judy. Wealthy people were usually cagey, saying "My father worked hard every day of his life", or "There were never any handouts in my family, believe me."

"And my husband's credit card took care of the rest. To save face, he said I was visiting my parents, and told me he wouldn't cut my spending off as long as I didn't tell anyone about what I'd done . . . what we'd done . . . and he was there to pick up the pieces, more than once . . ."

Judy, with her piranha's sense for vulnerability, noted the strain on Sidhal's and Rita's faces.

"Don't get me wrong, but is this whole family gay except for me? Is that what we're doing now? Gay is the new black?"

Rita smiled briefly at Judy for the distraction.

"Not me," said Marlon, "it's Glenn all the way. I don't have the energy to try a new lifestyle. But I was enthralled by my friends' older sisters growing up. If I was born now, I possibly *would* end up a lesbian, by mistake I imagine. It seems so much easier to end up that way these days, doesn't it?"

"It does take a bit of effort," said Rita. "You're not gonna trip and fall and turn into a lesbian."

"Although that's what happened to me," said Sidhal. "So don't relax just yet."

A little joke! Judy continued to be impressed by old Posh Spice.

"Nope," said Sissy, "I've got enough on my plate with being vegan."

"We're here," said Mahalia.

"We're queer," said Diana.

"I knew it," murmured Judy to Sissy. "Those ripped denims spoke for themselves."

"I'm going to remember what you said though, Mum," said Mahalia. "I could see you as a soft butch."

"Very soft," added Diana.

Stevie lit another cigarette. "London. The accents alone. And who *doesn't* look like a worthy target when you've had a little *wink wink*, *nudge nudge*, am I right?" She sniffed, with her index finger over one nostril. "Don't be provincial, Marlon, we've been over this."

"You'd think you'd never met a lesbian before, Judy," said Rita. "It's not that confusing. Mum's right here."

"Yes, but I've never met *you* as a lesbian before," said Judy. "Though in hindsight the signs were there. And let's face it, there's no one else round here swinging that way. I had a hunch Rowan Clackhearst might've been a friend of Dorothy after he stopped returning my calls, but he got married . . ."

"I got married," said Bufty. "Didn't stop me."

"Mind you, Rita, are you allowed to call yourself a lesbian if you sit at home and do nothing?"

"You're right, Judy, we're supposed to go out and earn Girl Guide badges for our deeds."

"I went on a date with a woman once," said Jayne, smiling dreamily. "Only I didn't know it was a date. I thought she was going to talk to me about her homemade candles over a chardonnay."

"Did anything happen?" asked Diana.

"Yeah. I bought three candles," said Jayne. Even Rita laughed.

"Now that you mention it, Mum," said Marlon. "Dad never went in for the rugby, did he?"

"No, and between these four walls I think he was quite glad I bore him all daughters, even though the blokes at the factory acted as though our lives were without for not having a son."

"Is it gayer to not like rugby, or to *really* like rugby," said Diana, rinsing out the honey whiskey bottle in the sink. "All those men in shorts jumping on each other . . ."

"Either way, rugby sucks," said Mahalia.

"True enough," said Bufty.

"Unless it's women's rugby, hey, Mum?" Judy winked at her mother, and Bufty felt her heart dance. If only Irene could witness all this.

"But he was good at carpentry," said Jayne. "That was masculine of him, wasn't it?"

"Jesus was a carpenter," said Avery.

"Yeah, and look where it got him," said Stevie.

"You sound just like Irene when you say that, Floss," said Bufty. "Doesn't she?"

☾

Out on the verandah, Rita and Sidhal swirled teacups of Beaujolais. The black of the sky and the black of the sea merged, delineated only by a gleaming thread on the horizon.

"So that's your family," said Sidhal, at last.

"Well, you know. We do what we do." Rita paused. "How is your mother? Is she keeping good health? Did you patch it up with her?"

"Sharp as a frost nail," said Sidhal. "And yes, we did. Mummy's so frightfully open-minded now, she's convinced we never had a cooling-off. There's none so embracing as the formerly intolerant! I'm staying with her for a while. She's slowing down a lot these days, so I'll be rather close, relatively speaking . . ."

"And Proudfoot? Is he still defying the laws of gravity?"

"Proudfoot died in 2010, and I haven't had the heart to replace him. Look, Rita . . ." Sidhal moved imperceptibly closer. "I'm sorry about the cancer. Profoundly . . . so bloody sorry. I'd been meaning to say something to you all day, I simply had no idea I'd arrive in the middle of all this clamour."

"I never said . . ."

"Yes, you did." Sidhal smiled. "That is, your mother did, while she was pretending to be you. Abysmally, I might add. It's hardly Rita-ish to speak so freely, *tra l'altro*, to cheerfully tell me you're single. I may have realised her ruse a trifle sooner than my performance this morning suggested."

"For Christ's sake, she's such a busybody." Rita pretended to bash her forehead onto the verandah railing. "Sorry about your horse."

"Thank you. Don't hold it against Bufty. I wanted to visit you, regardless of whether I'd known you had cancer . . . or that you were single."

Rita tilted her head to look up at Sidhal. "So that's why you're here?"

"Which one?"

"Pick one." Rita couldn't stop fidgeting, changing position. Sidhal stood still as the sky.

"I just thought, maybe, you might need a friend. Do you?"

"I mean . . ." Two dimples threatened to puncture Rita's cheeks. "Do *you* need a friend?"

"Maybe I do, Rita, maybe I do." She touched Rita's glass pendant. "You've still got this."

"It's pretty."

"You never liked pretty things."

"I liked you." Only by the slight forehead twitch could Sidhal tell that Rita had surprised herself. "Walked into that one, didn't I."

"Wouldn't be the first time," said Sidhal.

Through the window, Rita's family draped themselves across the lounge in their various states of drunkenness, disarray, life and death. Like crayons left in the sun to melt. Maybe she wanted to be here. With them. On purpose.

Bufty pulled open the verandah door.

"Hullooo, Avery's boiled the jug, anyone for another cuppa? What's going on out here, then?"

"Oh, this and that," said Rita. Her hand grazed Sidhal's elbow. Something percolated and fizzed in her solar plexus. "C'mon you, let's go inside."

At 3am, a sense of propriety finally getting a look-in, they unrolled mattresses, disgorged pillows and blankets from nylon storage bags, lingered over toothbrushes and glasses cases, let conversations fade to black, a dreamlike tranquillity revealed from the parting clouds of the evening.

"Rita should stay here," Bufty murmured. "Rita and Floss."

"What's that, Mama?" said Marlon.

"Oh—I don't know what came over me, but—it appeared in my head, right this second. Like Irene was talking to me. It'll always be her house, but according to her it's mine now, and I think Rita and Stevie should move in here if they want. For as long as they want. And now I am *ready*-ready for bed."

Rita and Stevie glanced at each other.

"Bed sounds like a good idea, Mater," said Rita.

☾

"I'd offer you the bed, Sidhal, but Judy here snores like a drunken sailor," said Marlon, rubbing her eyes. "You're much safer out on the couch, trust me."

"Oh, c'mon!" Judy thwacked Marlon's backside with her dressing-gown belt.

"You're the one who said she was family . . ."

Bufty leaned against the doorway of the pink room. "I wish Irene could've seen us all today, I think she'd be proud. And honestly, imagine if we'd been in a church all morning. It wouldn't have been the same. This is the way to go."

"That's Irene," said Rita. "Always right, even when she's dead."

"Goodnight, my girls," said Bufty. "Now you need to think about what marvellous things you'll say about me at my funeral."

"Mum, you can't say that and walk off," said Jayne.

"Yeah, she'll have nightmares," said Judy.

Bufty pulled her robe across her chest and wriggled her shoulders. "My girls. All here at last."

"Y'know," said Judy, after Bufty turned out the light, "some of the best parties I've ever been to were funeral after-match functions. But there's always someone missing . . ."

"Irene knew that I liked opera," said Rita. She could just make out Irene's forget-me-nots hand-painted on the wall from the moonlight peering in through the window. The rest were smudged into the shadows blanketing her sisters. But she knew they were still there. The flowers, and her sisters. "See. I tell people stuff sometimes."

In the last soft breaths of that night, Rita dreamed. First of analogue sounds—water bouncing off stones, grass straining upwards, kānuka splintered by wedged iron. A woman in a black dress plunged her axe into the hunk of wood. Her tired face, her dark eyes, were Irene's—no—Whetū's—then Rita's face, just for a moment—smiling, wrinkles crushing into a wide beam like a lemon clutched in a fist, releasing its bright resin and oil, the tiredness falling away, and Rita was on the porch of a wooden shack, and she sank into the golden pool of the woman's arms, resting her head on the woman's chest.

"It's cool," said a silvery voice that sounded like Jayne's. "We're all here dreaming." Rita felt a calm bordering on bliss, the sun on her forehead, her ancestors' arms around her, the axe in her fist, tūrangawaewae warm beneath her feet.

Chapter Twenty-Five

In a later era when students suckled from water bottles on their desks like they contained mother's milk, when the importance of hydration was better studied and children's needs were considered with slightly more assiduity, Bufty and Avery might never have crossed paths in any meaningful way, might never have appeared to each other like Glinda the Good Witch descending from her bubble: at first a stranger, then all you could think about. As it happened, one midsummer afternoon when the air dripped like treacle from a measuring spoon and the sun stuck to you like a boiled sweet melted in your pocket, a parched and groggy fifteen-year-old Bufty overheated and fainted in class. The teacher, seeing Avery had finished her tasks, instructed her to walk Bufty home and put her to bed.

They made it ten yards from the school when Bufty said she would surely faint again.

Without a word, Avery hoisted Bufty up onto her hip, in the way you'd hold a child or willing cat—Bufty's head on

Avery's chest, clammy hands sopping into her shirt collar, the school shrinking in the distance, only able to croak directions to her house.

Avery, quite used to not being spoken to by anyone her age, silently put her to bed with a damp cloth and a mug of the coolest, most delicious water Bufty had ever tasted, and she waited while Bufty dozed. At 6PM Jock barged in and Avery scattered, but she haunted Bufty's thoughts, the tall gallant girl with far-apart eyes glowing like ruby slippers, and those strong hands against Bufty's legs, carrying her home.

The next day, Saturday, Bufty rose early and rode her bicycle out to the village to post a thank-you note in Avery's mailbox. She found Avery reading on the grass underneath a peach tree, a salt-and-pepper dog asleep beside her. Avery beckoned her over. Bufty didn't leave till Sunday evening.

Bufty's buoyant popularity shielded Avery for a time, and their devotion was not unheard of for girls raised on *What Katy Did at School.* And, of course, they slept in the same bed. It was more unusual to have a bed to yourself in those days.

"What do you want to do when you leave school?" asked Bufty one afternoon on Avery's verandah, resting her magazine on her stomach. "Goodness, I can see right up your nose! Here, help me up." Bufty kicked her legs back and rocked forward to sitting, while Avery pushed her shoulders. Giggling, Bufty rearranged her skirt to cover her knees.

"I'd like to do something worthy and clever," said Avery, gazing beyond the peach tree, each leaf an emerald swipe from a paintbrush. "Write a splendid book of poetry or come up with a new idea to philosophise about. I don't mind if fame eludes me while I'm living, so long as I'm celebrated after I'm gone, with the scholars of the future puzzling over my words." She glanced across at Bufty. "What about you? Given it any thought?"

"*Well.*"

Naturally, Bufty had this all planned out.

"First, I'll have lots of children close in age, so they'll be the dearest friends and never be lonely. I'll get that out of the way so I can still be young and have my looks when I pursue an acting career. What I'll do is, see, I'll move to New York City and take up a job in a lavish department store, working the perfume counter or amongst the mink coats, and I'll wait to be discovered by an agent buying gifts for his mistress. But I won't *just* wait, see—when I'm not at work, I'll scour the papers and audition, but if the agent sweeps past and takes a shine, I can let him have all the credit for discovering me. If no agent comes past, then I've got my auditions. Either way, I'll be a star of the stage, and parlay that into Hollywood fame, and befriend all the big names, and wear gowns designed by Orry-Kelly."

"And what of your band of children? Will they raise themselves?"

"Oh gosh, I didn't think of that. My poor little babies, I love them so much and I've abandoned them already! I'll have to work extra hard at being a famous actress so I can give them all the comforts and fineries they want." Bufty's face grew red as her voice rose. "Why am I so worried about this when it's imaginary?"

"Perhaps your husband could take care of them?"

"Oh yes, him! He'll be there too, I suppose. He won't want all that drudge, but since this is the realm of fantasy, I'll make him do it."

"Do you have anyone in mind?" Avery traced a figure eight on the blue-painted wood. "Kip Andrews? I think the only reason he hasn't left school is that he won't get to sit and look at you all day . . ."

"Kip the Kipper? I'd sooner die! No, my husband will be a first-rate dancer like Gene Kelly, not like all the galumphing boys around here, and he'll be suave like Cary Grant, and tall and noble like Jimmy Stewart, and ever so witty like James Cagney, and he'll have lovely expressive brows like Victor Mature, and a certain roguish *something* like Burt Lancaster has, you know, the way his eyes are—so—your eyes are a bit like his, aren't they? And he should have a refined accent like David Niven, or yours, or—or like the way Lauren Bacall talks, but if she were a man. I do wish my voice sounded like hers, I think everything in my life would fall into place if I could talk like her. But my voice is up here—" and Bufty waved her hands by her head "—all tinkly. But of course, I'll hire an acting coach to sort that out, and she'll be strict, but she'll turn me into a dazzling young thespian, ready for the screen."

"Not to trample over the realm of fantasy," said Avery, "but will you ever find the man who fits those criteria? He sounds too far-fetched."

"Gosh, I wish your father was younger, he's about the finest man I can think of. I should press him into a sheet of Mrs Kimpton's precious carbon paper and marry his twin. Then your actual father could carry on living his life without the burden of being married to some snip of a girl who giggles too loud and has no fortune or name to offer a man. Your little carbon-copy father couldn't afford choosiness, being made of paper, so he'd be content to settle. But he'd still be your father, of sorts, and then you and I could be together always."

Filling empty space with prattle was no hardship for Bufty, but something in Avery's blazing eyes prompted her to forge ahead.

"What about your husband, Avery? A roguish knave? A timid lad who's good to his mother? An insurance salesman who only eats boiled beef?" Bufty dissolved into giggles.

Avery laughed with her. "I don't want to have children—it's a monstrous thing to say, but I just *don't*—and I doubt any man could please me, nor could I please any man. They'd want me to stay at home darning their woollens while they go out and have all the fun. There'd be no time for reading, or learning, or thinking erudite thoughts."

“True enough,” nodded Bufty. “Did I ever tell you about when we were in primmers—before you came along—and Kip Andrews whispered in my ear in assembly that he was going to marry me as soon as we turned fifteen? It was so horribly impudent. Every morning when we lined up for class, I heard his loathsome whispered words and felt all bilious. And his father’s no better! Do you remember when I took you to the hunt ball? Mr Kip Andrews Senior sidled up to me and said, ‘If it isn’t young Miss Bufty Williams, you look like someone ought to sandwich you between two pink wafer biscuits.’ The impertinence, couldn’t you just die?”

When Avery’s mother Ruby fell ill, Mr Manrose had moved his family from Yorkshire to New Zealand, to live with his widowed mother in the warm house with fruit trees and clean fresh country air where he grew up.

This stability soured into sorrow when pneumonia took Bill’s mother and Ruby the following August, in a winter noted in almanacs and end-of-year records for its arctic frostiness. Avery stayed away from school till the new year and was too shell-shocked to make friends. And then, Bufty fainted.

On Bufty’s seventeenth birthday, she and Avery saw *Son of Paleface* at the picture theatre. They split a pink lamington in the tearoom afterwards, bristling with more energy than usual, like a kettle about to whistle, and they came home and played Whist, scarcely paying attention to who was winning, and then, with the lights out, their lips grazed for one tentative second, and one further, unambiguous second, and it made more sense to Bufty than any boy who’d crossed that threshold, more than anything she’d ever made sense of. And so their lips met again, in the same bed they’d shared so many times.

It’s possible, when Bufty rode home on her bike, head buzzing in the morning sun, she might have stayed there and never spoken or hinted by glance or wink or nudge that the kiss happened—and it’s possible her going back to Avery’s had nothing to do with her father, sloshed at 9AM, who’d forgotten her birthday, yelling at her for always spending time with that ugly tomboy bitch instead of her own flesh and blood, and throwing a plate at the wall, only missing her head because he saw two of her. But the fact is, Bufty packed a bag and cycled back to Avery's in the rain, and they stared at each other, neither knowing it but both asking: where can we go? Where is safe? Where can we be?

And they ran, ran to the beach, where the rain pierced the waves like crewel needles falling on crumpled silk, and the tide charged like a mongrel dog with teeth bared, and they reached a secluded inlet, jumping over a thin stream threading the shore, and behind the rocks they fell, fell onto the sand and onto each other.

There were hands—tangling—in rain-sodden hair—and their mouths met with honest intention—and Bufty thought *this must be what it's like to welcome your soldier home from the war* and every poem Avery knew crashed about her brain all at once and yet she couldn't identify a single line and she'd gladly forego reading another word for the rest of her life if it meant this kiss didn't have to end.

Their mouths parted for breath, and they lay back in the sand, gasping, laughing, clothes awry, hands touching so lightly, as intimate as lips meeting.

They realised they weren't alone when they heard the dog barking.

Hetty Uprichard only saw them lying there holding hands, but their hair was caked with sand, Bufty's dress was all rucked up, and an unearthly look danced in their eyes. She knew Bufty Williams needed taking down a peg or two. And this was awfully screwy.

"Hullo, Hetty," said Bufty, easing her dress over her thighs and affecting a light-hearted tone. As though they'd bumped into each other in the courtyard at school, as though Hetty wanted to borrow a pencil.

"Hallo, Bufty. Hallo, *Avery*." Hetty hooked her finger under the dog's collar. "Soot here ran off, and I had to chase after him and got caught in the rain. I can't fathom why anyone would be outside right now."

"No, indeed," said Bufty, patting her head to loosen the sand caught in her hair. "We were quite caught by the rain ourselves and hoped to seek shelter here—but the rain got us first, and we had a fit of the giggles. It was all a bit silly, really."

"Very silly," said Hetty. She smiled, supercilious, ominous. "I won't detain you. See you in school, I'm sure."

"Yes—goodbye Hetty, lovely to see you, of course. You too, Soot, good boy."

Neither Hetty nor her dog returned the sentiment.

Avery got to her feet, dusted the sand from her arms and led Bufty towards the terrifying, forbidden water, and Avery crouched, so Bufty followed, and Avery washed the sand from Bufty's hair. The tide gushed in around them and retreated with as much haste, in and out, in and out.

They walked back to Avery's house in silence and did not start shaking until they got in the door.

Bufty sobbed, but no tears came, only a grotesque, shuddering wail.

"Oh, I feel so unwell, so unwell," she moaned, clutching herself. "We've sinned, I know it, we've succumbed . . . succumbed! What if my father finds out, what if they send me away to Kingseat and electrocute me?"

Avery's muscular arms swaddled Bufty. Her hair smelled of salt water and sweat. Avery inhaled deeply, while she could.

"Listen to me. Listen. I'm going away. Up to a school in Auckland. I'm training to be an Anglican minister. You'll be better off here without me around raising suspicions. We'll pretend this never happened, and everyone will get on with it, even Hetty, I promise."

"I don't *want* to be better off without you," said Bufty, hardly understanding what she was saying. This was growing worse by the second.

"But you might be."

"They'll never let a girl become a minister. Surely not."

"They already have."

It was true. Not because of any cultural post-war shift in gender roles, with women mucking in to take on the men's jobs, but a small clerical error. When Avery arrived at St Swithin's, suitcase in hand, fees paid in advance, the Very Reverend Avery Moss twigged that he'd taken one pivotal detail for granted while leafing through applications. Embarrassed, the school let her stay in a modest room away from the other novitiates under the proviso that she kept it quiet. They waited for the young lady to capsize from the rigours and solitude of training. Unfortunately, Avery was at home in solitude, could out-quote a bishop chapter and verse, and, worst of all, had all the fortitude and reverence one would hope for in a reverend.

"We can't do anything about this right now. Maybe once we're grown women the world will change. And the wait won't be such a trial if we keep busy. Easy enough for you. Not so for me."

Bufty didn't like this proposal at all.

"I hate you. You're leaving me."

"You don't. And I'm not. I never will. I never could. 'Extinguish my eyes, I'll go on seeing you. Seal my ears, I'll go on hearing you. And without feet I can make my way to you, without a mouth I can swear your name.' And pay Hetty Uprichard no mind. You're worth a million of her. She'll never fit through the eye of a needle."

After a bittersweet Christmas, Avery left for St Swithin's. Her heart remained behind, wet and heavy, in Bufty's hands.

Instead of telling Avery that this idea was poppycock and she didn't know her own mind and should learn typing and get married, Bill Manrose listened to his daughter and gave his blessing to her vocation. Besides, no one could advise Avery Manrose with any conviction to try and catch a husband.

Even so, opinions abounded. Old Bunratty said he heard Avery was entering a convent, but she didn't *look* Catholic to him. Mrs Sally Uprichard, poisonous as her daughter, said she heard Avery had become unmanageable and 'peculiar' and was being sent to a reform school in Masterton. Kip Andrews said he'd heard Avery was training to be a reverend, and that was taken as hearsay and gossip as much as the other talk.

Bufty left school soon after. She'd only stayed on this long because she was part of the choir, the student newsletter and the speech and drama club. With Avery gone, these activities dulled and rusted, and Hetty's ignorant insinuations ensured that the other girls in her year kept Bufty at arm's length.

When it rains it floods. Bufty's father died, leaving her little more than the half-jar of mustard in the larder and the coins in his pocket. Though his absence was permanent and Avery's fixed-term, the latter made her feel harrowingly alone, the former addled and very tired.

But you got on with it.

Bufty and Wally married at Irene's house, with a wedding breakfast made by Bufty and Irene. Avery did not attend. Bufty's new life started now. The night before the wedding, Avery posted a note to Bufty.

The Buddhists say the only way to escape suffering is to escape desire. I shall be happy to suffer for you. You're going to have a good life, dearest Bufty.

As a gift to his bride's vanity, Wally paid for a photo to appear in the local paper with the headline, 'A Pretty Wedding'. Imagine finding someone who understands you, in a village like this. Not once, but twice?

"You must be a father, and I must be a mother," Bufty said to Wally. "We can't go at it with half of ourselves." Judy's birth swept away all doubt.

After her official sanctification, the diocese sent Avery to rural Canterbury, hoping the folks there wouldn't mind, or even notice, that she was a lady reverend. Notice they did, and after five years of battling, Avery was sent back home, where at least people had a head start on how abnormal she was. And while the villagers kept the original rumours on ice for Avery's return, it stood to reason that nothing untoward could happen between a married woman and a sanctified minister.

Wally encouraged Avery and Bufty's friendship. Though he would spend time away from the family for reasons Bufty didn't press him on, Avery and Bufty kept their relationship cordial for the duration of the marriage. It felt appropriate, though no known rules or precedents existed for the path they fumbled down in the dark.

"Damn the lot of them," said Avery, a month after Wally's funeral. "We're grown women. We've lived life hidden and cloistered, and it's time to face it untethered and raw."

Avery made it sound exhilarating, but Bufty wasn't so sure she had it in her to be untethered.

"Now—look, I mean—" Bufty hopped from one foot to the other.

"What is it?"

"Do you even want all this? Taking on four children? I don't expect you to remember it, but you told me once you never wanted children, to be tied down when you could be out in the world thinking great thoughts—"

Avery flinched. "I remember every conversation we've ever had, Bufty. I don't want to bear children of my own, but I love the girls, and I'm honoured to be part of their lives. Why, I'd cut off my right ear if it would help them."

"Let's not go that far." Bufty smoothed Avery's hair behind her ears. "They are picturesque specimens. And the girls are practically grown-ups themselves now."

Avery's cheeks reddened. "I think my father was so glad when I was born that I didn't have The Manrose Ears, he could forgive any trespasses, including being a whopping great lesbian."

"Oh, I live in fear every day that my ears will suddenly stick out like my father's did . . . wait, did Mr Manrose *know*?

About you being . . . a . . ." The word *lesbian* still shocked Bufty, surely couldn't belong to her.

"To be fair, you couldn't miss it," said Avery, "he never addressed it directly, but he slipped me a few books."

"What, blue novels! Never!"

"No, proper literary stuff, Gertrude Stein, Djuna Barnes. We're not so strange after all, people have been doing this long before we did. I know it's not simple, but . . ."

"It's not simple at all! Even if we could get married, we're not the same denomination, you're Anglican, I'm—well, I never was anything, Dad was too drunk, and Mum just didn't care enough to take me and Sweet to church. Anyway, how can I believe in a god who makes life so difficult? A god who says we can't get married and love each other? How can you believe in such a god, Avery?"

"*That* version of God has nothing for me, Buf. I believe in a God who is absolute, whose creation was always ever thus, and he created us, didn't he? We're his responsibility now."

Avery had an idea. They couldn't get married, but Avery could baptise Bufty, and that act could unite them in a small way, a ceremony in place of another ceremony, symbolising their unwavering faithfulness to each other, their faith in each other—in faith itself. Bufty, for whom God represented an inconstant, paternal metaphor rather than having any bearing on her soul, took more convincing.

"If we can't be married, at least we can both be Anglicans," reasoned Avery. "I won't make you do Bible study homework. It'll be our secret, and it's like sticking it to the so-called God in whose name people call our love forbidden. A funny kind of rebellion. That God can't stop me baptising you any more than he can stop me loving you."

Bufty hesitated.

"We'll do it at the beach. It'll be *very* dramatic."

Bufty was in.

And so once more Avery led Bufty to the beach, this time from the car park banked in by the entrance, on an aquamarine Sunday morning before the pearly mists lifted from the roads, no match at all for the artillery of sea spray they met at the shore. And Bufty wore a long white dress, and Avery rolled up her slacks and walked into the terrifying water, and held out her hand, and Bufty walked towards her, fearless, and they spoke words of commitment, and Bufty said "You won't let me drown?" and Avery said "I'll always catch you," and she commanded "Get on your knees," and Bufty dropped down into the water, and Avery fell with her, and tipped Bufty backwards, supporting her head and back with her big hands, and the water rushed around Bufty's ears, and her white dress churned with the water, and Avery brought Bufty back up and traced a cross of salt water on her forehead, and their breath intermingled with the wind, until the wind and God himself could no longer find a path between their faces.

And in a daze they withdrew to the cliffs, behind where the rock jutted out, and fell to their knees again, and first it was mouths—then hands—then—everything all at once, and with a snap of clarity Bufty no longer cared if parts of her bounced, or stuck out, or sweated, or whether her hair was becoming, and she found herself on top of Avery, and as their bodies ground together she said "You're beautiful," and she knew it to be true, and Avery knew it too, and they knew, also, it didn't matter a jot, they were beautiful, and beautiful together, and knowing was more exquisite than any god could conceive of, and Avery recited St Augustine to Bufty: "Now I pant for thee. I tasted, and now I hunger and thirst. Thou didst touch me, and I burned for thy peace."

And Bufty looked up at the sky with wild eyes, and it looked back at her with mercy.

☾

The morning after Irene's homecoming proved an Olympic ranking table of who could hold their booze. The hardened twins took restorative shots of Fernet-Branca from their box of liquor. Marlon, lousy with hangover, spreadeagled on the couch under a damp cloth.

Avery got on with making breakfast. She sliced button mushrooms, heated olive oil, watched the mushrooms hit the pan with a hiss, cracked eggs into a small bowl and whisked them with a fork, nudged them into golden curds with a flat-edged wooden spoon, fried vegan sausages next to the mushrooms, rinsed spinach from the garden with a pinch of salt, chopped the mossy leaves and let them shrink in the pan, brushed bread with olive oil and grilled it alongside dozens of hash browns till burnished, lined up two coffee plungers, filled Irene's teapot with mint from the garden and Bufty's mother's teapot with Bell teabags. Through the witchcraft of hospitality and innovation, Avery fed the forty thousand that morning.

"I haven't felt this indisposed since Dilys Glossop's twenty-first," said Marlon.

"Maybe I will stay here," said Stevie, leaning over the verandah, the water gyrating below, "maybe I can read tarot, too. It looked like a doddle when Irene did it. At the least, I can write heaps. Even paint again. Not much grist for the mill to be had round these parts, erotic-wise, but that water inspires me."

"Maybe," said Rita, spooning sugar into her dove-grey teacup.

"Sit down, Avery, you should eat and let us take care of the graft," said Marlon. "You've been at it like a gumdigger's dog all morning."

"I'm fine, you stay put, Marlon."

Marlon was relieved but had suspected Avery would demur. She would've leapt to action had Avery required help, though. That's what you did.

"Mind you," said Judy, too off-colour to lift a finger but still enough of a trencherwoman to put away four hash browns, "this is delectable, Avery."

"Judy, as Layman Pang said, 'What I do every day is nothing special, I simply stumble around'."

"These mushrooms are divine, I'll tell Layman Pang that much for free."

"You're a brick, Avery," said Sidhal, at the kitchen table with Rita. Her skin glowed like she'd just been to a beauty parlour. "I am well and truly knackered, but this cooked breakfast is a balm."

Everyone turned to look at her. It was still surprising to have a newcomer in their midst. Even Marlon lifted one corner of her facecloth to make sure she was still there.

"I wonder if Dad had a . . . y'know," said Judy, nodding towards Avery. "Did he ever tell you, Mater?"

"He didn't, bub," said Bufty, circling the room, collecting empty plates. "He had his story, I had mine, and we didn't press each other for details. It's like watching the telly and not seeing the show on the other channel. You know it's there, but you don't know what you missed."

Sissy came into the room, rubbing her wet hair with a stiff green bath towel.

"Right. I'm just going to say it: I've been eating fish. Sometimes. Sushi, salmon . . . a prawn. I couldn't stop thinking about it, so I did it." Sissy covered her face with the towel. "Go on, get your licks in, I've been insufferable. But life's short, right? And it was driving me wild, all the restaurants in Auckland . . ."

Between their hangovers and the previous night's revelations, the family met this confession with apathy, like ducks in a pond who have been fed too much bread by local children to be lured in by further crumbs.

"Well?" said Sissy.

"Life was pretty short for that prawn you ate," said Rita.

"What does your boyfriend think of all this?" asked Bufty.

"I don't care, he's so boring. I'm breaking up with him soon, but I want to see what he gets me for Christmas first. And I'm still vegan, mind you! Except for the fish."

"That's my girl, alright," said Judy.

"I'm winding you up, Siss," said Rita. "Do what makes you happy."

Jayne rolled over on the mattress in front of the couch and tented her fingers under her chin. "How did you and Avery *really* meet, Mama?"

Bufty smiled at Avery. "It's like I've told you, we were good friends, that's all. We used to come to this beach together. Back when you wouldn't be afraid to walk a fair distance to where you wanted to be. We were there, and now we're here."

"Now we're here," echoed Avery.

"Don't tell me it's a story for the next funeral," said Stevie, touching the box of Irene's ashes. "My nerves won't cope."

"Oh!" Bufty, scraping scraps and napkins into a black rubbish bag, froze. "The animals will be wanting breakfast, too, won't they?"

"I'll call Glenn," said Marlon. "He can drop round to feed them. Widgeon and Smoo will probably be at the front door waiting, like this." She put her hands on her hips and tapped her feet, then pointed to her wristwatch.

There was no question of anyone leaving.

Chapter Twenty-Six

Rita counted the dead. Traced their names inside her head.

The orange hospital chair dug into her back. Everything dug into her back, one way or another. At least this was only the present. Nothing deeper. Not a metaphor. She turned the page of her magazine and pointed to a woman reclining on a puffy forest-green couch.

"Bags that couch," she said. "Looks comfier than this set-up."

"An iron maiden would be more comfy than these chairs." Stevie, next to her, pointed at the woman's wine bottle. "Bags the plonk."

Jayne came into the waiting room, the guitar under her arm. Taking the seat on the other side of Rita, she plucked the guitar strings, creating a gentle veil of sound, fading the hospital's clinical beeping into the background. While Jayne strummed, Marlon parted her long hair into three even sections and braided them together. Sitting on the folded blanket on the floor by Rita's feet, the twins pointed at their magazine, each knowing implicitly they would always share any winnings, hypothetical or real. Avery appeared, holding a stack of paper cups and a large blue thermos. Bufty and Judy settled opposite Rita, Judy with her head on her mother's shoulder as they leafed through another magazine, reading it in earnest and making pronouncements and judgements on the years-old gossip. Avery unscrewed her thermos lid and poured cups of coffee, handing them from person to person. She offered coffee to the other people waiting: an older man with his arm in a sling, a mother bouncing a toddler on her knee. Bufty gave her coffee to Judy to hold and took Irene's green container from a tote bag. She removed the lid and passed the container around.

"Have I missed it?" Sissy, car keys jingling, plonked down beside Judy.

"Yeah," said Rita. "I jumped out of a cake."

"How are you, bub? You okay?" Bufty reached across to Rita.

"You can't ask her that, Mum," said Judy. Not because it was inappropriate, but because Rita would say something stupid.

"I'm closer to death than when I was last in this room," said Rita. "But so are all of you."

Jayne played a familiar chord on her guitar. Bufty's eyes lit up, and she joined Jayne's singing. Then Marlon. Judy, looking up from her magazine, sang as well, and so did the twins, Avery, Stevie and Sissy, their voices weaving together.

"*Could we start again, please?*"

Rita shut her eyes. But she wasn't embarrassed. She knew they were performing the apostle Peter's lines with exaggerated chest-clutching and eyes rolled to heaven. Rita's hand dropped to her side. No longer pointing at things she wanted in the magazine. Stevie's hand found hers, and their fingers laced together. Someone's hand stroked her head, another hand rested on her shoulder.

“Are we taking requests? How about ‘The Wayward Wind’ next,” said someone. Maybe Marlon. Or Judy. Their voices sounded so similar.

Rita opened her eyes and began to sing.

Acknowledgements

The road to *Hoods Landing* was a strange mix of deliberateness and coincidence, long-gaming the former and hoping for ancestral hands to tug on the latter. But it couldn't have happened in any other way, and so, there are many to thank.

Damien Levi, Āporo Press. Aside from creating community, coolness and rock pools of creative opportunity in Tāmaki Makaurau, your discerning eye and calm confidence amongst the chaotic mahi and business-as-usual insomnia have provided both commiseration and motivation. I'm so proud and honoured to be Āporo's first novel—and vice versa—and will never forget that phone call when you confirmed it. Thank you.

Ruby Leonard—sometimes I wish we were still back in those Schrödinger's cat days of editing rounds. You made the process a pleasure and the book better, and thank you for rolling with the eleventh-hour great-great-great-grandmother dream apparition to whom I couldn't say no.

Team Whitireia—Liam Robertson, Anna Morete, Oscar Smit, Erin Cutts, Brodie Joyce, Rhia de Jong—*Hoods Landing* wouldn't exist, like this, without this publishing programme. I hope more Aotearoa novels get to experience your guidance, enthusiasm and dinkuses. Thank you for the valuable editing back-and-forth and for holding my choices up to the light, and I hope one day to correctly quote a song lyric.

Mikayla Strahorn—thank you for your design vision and composure, for bringing *Hoods Landing* to life and for allowing Janna and Susie to become truly immortal.

Ngā mihi nui, James George—my supervisor at AUT in 2022, where an earlier version of this novel took shape. I'm glad I got even a glimpse of your vast knowledge, and your immediate understanding of my intention made me feel creatively and spiritually at ease. Any future writers would be lucky to have your input on their work. I freely admit that I joined the Master's programme out of WINZ-fuelled financial panic, but this novel and I met you at the exact right time.

Every tarot card mentioned in this novel was pulled by my dear friend Kim Laurenson. I committed to letting the story follow the cards chosen—and each one was unfathomably perfect. On the subject of my friends, you make me lucky, and I hope I can lend you some luck in return. Kim—I would trust you to perform open-heart surgery on me. Kate McLeod—from Māhuhu-ki-te-rangi to Mighty Mighty, loving each other is our inheritance. Charlotte Whitelaw—we should have been friends as kids, I'm glad we are now. Laughing with you feels like home. Ange Tran Van Sang—for your coolness and erudition across a long time and distance. Jen Eatson—for your honesty, for your understanding and for always being right. Cindy Walter—thank you for driving to Waiuku to be my new friend on that hot day. Your creativity and energy remain inspiring. Thank you all for providing so many forms of support and encouragement on the long journey to this moment.

To my 'Shot, Sappho' writing group, to whom this novel is but one of several children. Imagine finding an Algonquin Round Table of wit, stunning work, dreamy poetry picnics, mutual creative fuel, activism, support, literary commotion and real friendship right here in Auckland. Grace Shelley, Hebe Kearney, Holly-Blue Bercu, Anuja Mitra, Gemma Henderson, Zephyr Zhang, Divyaa Kumar, Elliot McKenzie, Tate Fountain and Cindy Walter, thank you.

To Aotearoa creatives, from whom there is so much to learn. I'd like to especially, though not exclusively, thank: Pip Adam—for showing generosity to writers before they think they deserve it. essa may ranapiri, for your wairua-affirming kindness. Michael Giacon, for your warm welcome. Izzy Robinson, for always making spaces more interesting and for including me in them. Ashleigh Young—I don't think I'd be writing this at this time without you seeing something in 'ACTIVITIES'. To everyone I've been lucky enough to swirl around a stage or a page with, and to all who have published my writing—including *bad apple*, *Overcom*, *The Spinoff* (thanks, Sam Brooks), *The Toast* and *Pūhia*.

To Renée, Ronald Hugh Morrieson, David Lynch, Robert Altman, Chantal Akerman and Carson McCullers. You're elsewhere now, but it's a privilege to have influences and to be influenced by you still.

To long-time readers for their patience and process-trusting. From those who have been with me since the early days of hungryandfrozen.com, through my cookbook and many reincarnation cycles, to all who saw early glimpses of this and other work, and kept me buoyant via Patreon.

Avani Nandakumar. Everything is fun and bearable and filled with bright happiness and possibilities with you, including the experience of bringing this novel to life. Even when I was wilfully sleepless and objectively annoying. I love you.

Whānau. I am lucky to come from hearty and creative and hilarious people, and I couldn't have written this without being from you and from here. Pourewa, Zelda—you were our beginning. Mum said it's sometimes like the ancestors are playing hide-and-seek and want us to do the work to find them. Someday we'll find your beginnings. To my mum, Kay, and my dad, Mark—thank you can't encompass any of it, but I mean it so much. At the very least, I first tried to write a novel somewhere around 1994. Thank you for never implying that I couldn't. To my brother, Julian—for taking my first official novelist portrait, for driving me home to find the photo of the dogs, for listening, and for letting me live, jobless, on your couch for too long. I'm glad you're you. To my Nana Elaine and Grandma Zelda, whose distinct voices speak to me still. To stroppy aunties, laconic uncles, rad cousins, Naysmiths, Vincents, Lawrences, Rosieurs, Bultes, harmonising on 'Happy Birthday', food on trestle tables lined with butcher paper, "got enough chairs, got too many guests", the cats, the dogs, the way the light fell when we brought Nana home, the chime of the grandfather clock, the taste of the tap water, the bubbling tar-seal, the cackling laughter, the words that became songs, the songs that became words. Thank you.

Special Thanks

Aj Fata, Alasdair Keating, Alexis McCullough, Always Becominging, Amber Easby, Amber Grafton, Angelique Tran Van Sang, Anna Jackson, Anna Rankin, Anna Varghese, Annette Russell, Anuja Mitra, Ash Davida Jane, Avani N, Brooke Soulsby, Cadence Galt, Carin Smeaton, Charlotte Whitelaw, Chris Tse, Danyel Holder, Dorian Wilson, Emma Barnes, Essa Ranapiri, Faith Wilson, Fiona MacLean, Francis Cooke, Grace Shelley, Grace Sinclair, Hana Chatani, Hana Pera Aoake, Hannah Jamieson, Hannah Tang, Hannah Terry-Whyte, Harold Coutts, Hayley Perfect, Helen Rickerby, Helena Mayer, Hinemoana Baker, Ineka Vogels, Jackal Wilde, Jane Arthur, Jane Groufsky, Jasmine Taylor, Jeremy Hansen, Jilly Taipua, Jo Eaton, John Plunket, Josiah Morgan, Josie Shapiro, Julie Zhu, Kōtuku Nuttall, Karen Hu, Kate McLeod, Katy-May Reed, Kendra Cox, kī anthony, Kim Laurenson, Laura Vincent, Leah Jing, Lisa Helm, Luca Tuavao Walton, Maddi Rowe, Malory Campbell, Manuia Heinrich, Matariki Williams, Matthew Whiteman, Melanie Hamilton, Melissa Oliver, Michael Fincham, Mika Reilly, Mitch Marks, Moira Clunie, Nathan Joe, Nia Vavao, Niamh Hollis-Locke, Nicole Anastasi, Nik Dirga, Nuanzhi Zheng, Pelenakeke Brown, Petra Jane, Rachel O'Neill, Rebecca Hawkes, Rochelle Kloc, Rosabel Tan, Rose Lu, Sally Greer, Samuel Walsh, Sarah Jane Barnett, Sarah-Rose Burke, Saraid de Silva, Sherry Zhang, Sloane Hong, Sophie McBride, Sophie van Waardenberg, Stacey Smith, Stacey Teague, Tim Wagg, Virginia Ferris, Zephyr Zhang.

WHEN WE CEASE TO UNDERSTAND THE WORLD

THE MANIAC

BENJAMÍN LABATUT

NO PLACE TO LAY ONE'S HEAD

FRANÇOISE FRENKEL

FORBIDDEN NOTEBOOK

ALBA DE CÉSPEDES

COLLECTED WORKS: A NOVEL

LYDIA SANDGREN

MY MEN

VICTORIA KIELLAND

AS RICH AS THE KING

ABIGAIL ASSOR

LAND OF SNOW AND ASHES

PETRA RAUTIAINEN

LUCKY BREAKS

YEVGENIA BELORUSETS

THE WOLF HUNT

AYELET GUNDAR-GOSHEN

MISS ICELAND

AUDUR AVA ÓLAFSDÓTTIR

MIRROR, SHOULDER, SIGNAL

DORTHE NORS

THE WONDERS

ELENA MEDEL

GROWN UPS

MARIE AUBERT

LEARNING TO TALK TO PLANTS
MARTA ORRIOLS

THE RABBIT BACK LITERATURE SOCIETY
PASI ILMARI JÄÄSKELÄINEN

BINOCULAR VISION
EDITH PEARLMAN

MY BROTHER
KARIN SMIRNOFF

ISLAND
SIRI RANVA HJELM JACOBSEN

ARTURO'S ISLAND
ELSA MORANTE

PYRE
PERUMAL MURUGAN

RED DOG
WILLEM ANKER

AN UNTOUCHED HOUSE
WILLEM FREDERIK HERMANS

WILL
JEROEN OLYSLAEGERS

MY CAT YUGOSLAVIA
PAJTIM STATOVCI

BEAUTY IS A WOUND
EKA KURNIAWAN

BONITA AVENUE
PETER BUWALDA

IN THE BEGINNING WAS THE SEA
TOMÁS GONZÁLEZ